Through Many Fires

Strengthen What Remains

By Kyle Pratt

Through Many Fires
Camden Cascade Publishing

CamdenCascade.com

Copyright © 2013 Kyle Pratt

Fifth Edition

ISBN: 0615808387

All Rights Reserved

Cover design and cover art by Micah Hansen

Editor Barbara Blakey

Dedication

Many authors say that their spouse is their biggest fan. My wife Lorraine most certainly is mine. This book would not exist without her support, ideas and constant encouragement.

I would also like to thank my friends and fellow writers, Joyce Scott, Robert Hansen, Barbara Blakey and Carolyn Bickel. You have all taught me so much about the craft of writing.

Prologue

T*hose who were murdered cry out for justice.* Senator Stevens scanned the pages of the terrorism legislation. *They will soon have it.* He was pleased with the progress of the bill, but he could not let up now. Sliding by a portly colleague, he maneuvered toward the senator from Oregon, "Do I have your support, Dave?"

"Sure, you do."

"Thanks." Stevens stepped away.

"What's the rush?"

"I need to bend the ears of a few senior members before the president speaks."

"Okay," he grinned. "Always on the job, eh?"

"Always," he said with his gaze fixed on the National Security Advisor. As Stevens neared he gripped the man's arm and asked, "Did he do it, Jake? Did the president include my proposal in his final draft?"

"Yes but," Jake lowered his voice to a whisper, "how many will support the president this late in his second term?"

"I know he's a lame duck, but we need to go on the offensive again. This bill provides a comprehensive approach to terrorism."

Jake shrugged. "You don't need to sell me. We need support from Congress."

"Okay." Stevens slapped the man on the back. "Thanks for taking it to the president. I *will* get the support you need."

He scanned the House chamber for another colleague when applause thundered. Turning toward the rostrum, he sighed.

The president stood behind the lectern, cleared his throat and smiled broadly. Stevens glanced at his watch. *Nine o'clock. I wish I had more time.* He waved to another senator, moved quickly to his seat and leaned back as the president began to speak. A departing aide casually opened a door to the house chamber.

*   *   *

One thousand yards away a nondescript van pulled into an alley and stopped. The driver leaned forward and muttered a prayer.

White light, as intense as the surface of the sun, seared the retinas of Senator Stevens. Before blindness registered on his brain, superheated air scorched his lungs. The chair splintered as scorching wind threw his body through the wood and upholstery. His skin blistered, boiled and dissolved.

Chapter one

W alking toward the door with his co-workers, Caden Westmore sneaked a look at his watch. *8:55.* Feeling a hand rest on his shoulder he turned.

The Chief-of-Staff thrust his free hand forward. "Well, how does it feel to be Chief Foreign Policy Advisor?"

"I'm sure you knew Stevens would promote me days ago," Caden said as they shook hands, "but I only found out a few hours ago." He shrugged. "I've hardly had time for it to sink in."

They continued to talk as they stepped outside. The January wind tingled against Caden's face and the icy air reached deep into his lungs. The winter sun had long since gone down; he could see his breath in the glow of the restaurant window.

Buttoning his suit jacket, he said goodbye. A gentle snow fell, tickling his exposed hands and face, as he ambled up the street towards his car. He glanced at his watch. *Two minutes till nine.* The dinner had ended at just the right time. Congress would be assembled and waiting on the president. He turned the corner and picked up his pace, eager to get to his car and listen to the address on the radio.

Caden smiled as a woman with flowing blond hair walked past. Images of Becky came to mind. He wished she was with him in D.C. *I should call and tell her about my promotion.* He retrieved his phone and tapped her name. At the sound of her soft southern accent he smiled "Hello beautiful."

The night flashed as bright as a desert noon. Light penetrated his suit and warmed his back like a hot summer day. He squinted then closed his eyes tight. Even with eyelids firmly shut, a blood red glow filled his vision. He flung his arm across his face. The phone squealed. He jerked it away. Then there was silence. Tentatively he opened his eyes as all the world seemed to wait—but for what?

"Becky? Becky?" He glanced down. The phone seemed to be off. He pushed the button, but it did not turn on. He dropped it into his pocket. *What happened?*

The crackling of a rifle shot ricocheted around him. But unlike a rifle shot the sound did not fade, it grew and echoed. He turned left and right trying to see where it came from when a boom like none he had ever heard reverberated through him. He stumbled, regained his footing and wiped his eyes only to have wind slap him several steps back. Dust hung in the air. Car alarms and people screamed. Caden's eyes darted left and right. Dozens stood like him, confused statues. Never-ending rolling thunder filled the night as debris, carried by a strong wind, buffeted him.

Several feet away a woman screamed. Caden followed her terrified gaze. His heart pounded. As if the gates of hell had been thrown open, out from the very bowels a satanic belch of fire and light raced towards the heavens. Lightning crackled across the sky in a dozen directions as he watched in disbelief. A boiling mushroom cloud formed in the southern night sky.

A cacophony of horns sounded as the normally quiet suburban street filled with panicked people all going away from the cloud. Repeatedly jostled and shoved he wondered where the crowd came from.

Screams grabbed his attention. At the street corner the blond woman from moments ago was knocked to the ground by the frightened crowd. Others trampled her in a panic. He tried to help her, but the throng was like a riptide going in the wrong direction. Caden struggled to stay on his feet as he was shoved and spun around. The surge of the mob carried him away. Looking back over his shoulder, he saw only the growing torrent of people and cloud.

Caden thanked God the horde moved towards his car. As the flow of people brought him near, he pushed and shoved his way to the vehicle. He jumped into the driver's seat, slammed his foot on the gas pedal and turned the key. The car sputtered and died. *God, help me!* He realized he still had the gas pedal to the floor. *Calm down. Calm down.* He took his foot off the gas and turned the key. The car coughed and shook, then started. Caden let out a sigh, pulled away from the curb and joined the fleeing masses.

Traffic was already heavy as a plan formed in his mind. He would go to his apartment and get everything he could. *And then what?* Just get away from the blast. But to where? *Becky!* He would go to Becky in Atlanta. Caden wondered if she was safe. Had Atlanta been attacked? Would it be attacked? He tried his phone again. It turned on, but when he tried Becky's number nothing happened. *What about Mom and Dad, Peter or Lisa?* He was sure they were okay—for now. He speed dialed his parents, then his brother, then his sister, but there was only silence. Looking at the phone in frustration he noticed there was still no signal. He threw the phone on the seat beside him.

The roads were jammed. Every stoplight and streetlight was out. Escape from the firestorm was painstakingly slow. It was like some horrible nightmare where he tried to run, but couldn't. He could walk faster than his car moved. Usually the drive from the restaurant to his apartment in Bethesda was a mere ten minutes, but tonight, it was the longest half-hour of his life. When he finally pulled up to his building he was relieved that, at least on this night, there was plenty of parking in front.

As he ran into the lobby the darkness slowed him.

"Mr. Westmore, what happened?" The woman shined a flashlight in his direction. "The explosion. The power is out."

The voice came out of a fog, familiar but distant and detached. *Yes, of course, the power is out.* He continued across the lobby.

She grabbed him by the arms. Even with such feeble light he saw the terror that filled her eyes. "What happened?"

He recognized her—the building manager. "Nuclear explosion. Get away from here." He raced across the lobby and felt his way down the hall and up the stairs.

In his apartment, he snatched a flashlight, grabbed the camping gear from the closet and threw it next to the door. Dragging a duffle bag from his army days behind him, he hurried to the bedroom. There he yanked open drawers and poured the contents into the sack. Anything that landed on the floor stayed there. He pulled the drawer from the nightstand and spilled it on the bed. Then he grabbed the cash, ten old silver dollars and the .38. Both were gifts from his father when he moved to the big city. *Thanks Dad, I might need the gun.* His dad had always said keep a Bug Out Bag prepared and handy, but Caden thought it was unnecessary and a bit paranoid, so he never did. Now he was throwing one together with a mushroom cloud growing in the distance.

He flung open the cabinet doors in the kitchen and shook his head. *What a miserable collection of food.* He dropped a jar of cheese dip, a box of cereal, a can of olives and several similar items into the bag.

The faucet only gurgled as Caden twisted the knob to fill a canteen. He cursed. In the refrigerator, he found a pitcher with water. He poured it into a thermos. He emptied a liter soda bottle into the sink, then hurried to the bathroom. He took the lid off the back of the toilet, dropped it to the ground with a thud, and plunged the canteen and then the soda bottle into the water tank. *Becky would be horror-struck to see this, but the water is clean. Becky!* Twisting the caps on his water supply, he trotted to the living room and grabbed the phone. No dial tone. He tapped the receiver. Silence.

Clutching the duffle bag, Caden headed for the door. *Can opener.* He ran into the kitchen and grabbed it and a random assortment of flatware.

Lugging his belongings, he abandoned the apartment, thrust everything into his car and joined the slow exodus.

Traffic was worse than rush hour. Honks sounded and brakes screeched in a continuous assault on the ears. Caden didn't merge onto the beltway—he pushed; his car acquiring dents and scrapes in the process. When finally in the stream of traffic he saw several cars headed towards the blast. *Who would be so foolish? Who would head into the city?* He bit his lip. *People with family downtown.* He sighed. *God help them.*

A motorcycle cut in front of him. Caden pressed his horn, but the rider, slicing between cars, was already yards ahead. Another cyclist roared past so close that he could have reached out and grabbed him. He checked his speedometer, five miles per hour. *At least the bikers are getting away.* Glancing at his gas gauge he sighed with relief. *Three quarters full.*

Caden looked left into the storm. Flames licked the sky in a swirling, spinning, demonic dance. Every cloud glowed with the reflected light of hell. *Even if the firemen can get to the inferno the water mains are shattered, the pumps have no power. The city will burn for days. Maybe weeks.* He turned on the radio. Mellow jazz filled the car from the satellite receiver.

"Music?" *Where's this broadcast from?* He shook his head. *Not Washington D.C.*

Cars swerved in front of him. Ahead, a sign barely readable in the dark, announced the exit for highway 267. Accompanied by soft jazz he maneuvered to the exit.

Glancing in the review mirror, Caden saw fire consuming the dying city.

Dying! How much radiation have I been exposed to? Snow dotted his windshield. *Could it be fallout?* He wondered if his escape was short lived. Would he soon die anyway? The blast seemed close but he had been in Silver Springs. *Surely the explosion must have been over downtown, the Whitehouse or Congress.*

Congress! Like a punch to his stomach he realized Senator Stevens, his boss, was in the Capitol for the State of the Union Address. *Oh my God, if I'm right they're all dead, the president, every senator and every representative.* Memories of the people he worked with flashed through his mind. *Dead. Everyone was at the Capitol, the justices of the Supreme Court, the Joint Chiefs of Staff. All dead.* Scott and Rachel had stayed behind at the office. *Dead.*

Caden weaved his car from one side of the road to the other like a drunk as he avoided wrecks. One moment he sped up, the next he slammed on his brakes. *Are we at war? Who did this to us?* A driver cut in front of him. *Have other cities been hit?* Brakes squealed. The car in front fishtailed. Caden swerved. Behind him cars piled into one another.

With traffic stopped, he leaned on the steering wheel, catching his breath. He looked down at the radio. *Maybe, just maybe I can get something on it now.* He switched his receiver over to the AM band and pressed search. After several moments it locked on a station.

A voice struggling to sound calm filled the car. "...fighters from D.C. and surrounding cities are attempting to get control of the firestorm as survivors flee the metro area..." The signal faded.

Ahead he heard metal crunch and scrape and looked up from where he had rested his head on the wheel. A tow truck pulled the wreck to the side of the road. He wondered how the truck had gotten to the scene. As soon as there was space, cars began squeezing past. He followed.

"...fallout spreading downwind towards..."

He cursed the radio as it fluctuated between static and inaudible. He considered trying to find a more reliable station, but was afraid he might lose his only source of news.

"...blast centered over the capital mall..."

His stomach churned. Cold sweat ran down his forehead. "So it is true they're all dead." Bile rose in his throat and he wondered if the churning, sweating and nausea was radiation sickness. *No, not this soon.* The symptoms were most likely shock.

"…fires raging…loss of power throughout the metro…"

Even if this radio station was fading in and out there was hope of a good signal later.

"…life is in imminent danger do not use the telephone or call 911…"

That thought brought him back to his cell phone. He grabbed it and the display showed one bar. *Yes!* He had a signal. But no dial tone. Despite a momentary feeling of guilt, he phoned anyway. Nothing happened. He tried again and again. Looking at the car ahead he could see the driver with a phone to his ear and realized that perhaps a million people were doing exactly what he was doing. The whole system had been destroyed, damaged or was hopelessly overloaded.

He thought of Mom and Dad, back in Washington state. They must be worried sick about him. He tried their number anyway and heard only silence.

He dropped the phone on the passenger seat as a familiar sound cut through the static of the radio. He had often heard the sine wave attention signal as he grew up, but it had always been a test. This was no test. The Emergency Alert System had been activated.

"The Secretary of the Army, Benjamin Oates, has ordered the activation of the Emergency Alert System to advise citizens in the nuclear disaster zone…"

"Secretary of the Army…." The announcer continued but Caden did not hear. It took a presidential order to activate the EAS. *If the secretary of the Army did it…* His mind recoiled from the truth. *All of them—The whole cabinet…they're dead.*

Caden drove on into the night.

In the early morning darkness, he passed a sign welcoming him to West Virginia and, only as he went by, realized it was lit. *Electricity!* He looked at his gas gauge. It danced on the "E". *Please God, an open gas station.*

A mile ahead, sitting at nothing more than a wide spot in the road, was an all night gas station and market. Six of the eight pumps were busy even at this early hour. Caden pulled into an empty spot and was pleasantly surprised that his debit card worked. While the tank filled he retrieved the five-gallon can from his trunk. He smiled remembering all the times Dad had told him to always have jumper cables, basic tools and a gas can in the car. After filling them both with every drop of gas they could hold, he pulled up to the store to buy other supplies.

As he entered, the clerk looked at him with a wary eye then, apparently deciding he was okay, returned to watching the television.

Caden desperately wanted to join the clerk, but first he had to get provisions.

"...was detonated at ground level and was small by modern standards, estimated at less than 20 kilotons. These factors also limited the electromagnetic pulse to the immediate vicinity."

Seeing cases of bottled water on the shelf, he picked up a couple of bottles. *Water is more critical than food.* The words from his army training hung in his mind. He grabbed a case.

"FEMA has set up a command center at Andrews Air Force Base. Other relief and medical centers are being established outside of the red zone."

Sandwiches caught his eye. Three would do.

"No reliable estimate of casualties is available but all area hospitals have been inundated. The most severely injured are being moved to hospitals up and down the coast from Boston to Richmond and Atlanta."

At the mention of Becky's hometown, Caden glanced at the television.

"Now we turn to Steve in the weather center."

He was surprised that they would give a weather report at such a time. Who would want to know about the temperature now? Within moments his eyes were fixed on the screen with intense interest. They were showing wind direction from the blast and fallout patterns. The breeze last night had been blowing off shore, taking the radiation out to sea, almost directly away from where he had been in Silver Springs and Bethesda. Caden felt a huge burden lift from him. He would live.

The weatherman was still on camera, but he just stood staring ahead. As Caden watched a look of horror spread across his face. The image shifted to a man sitting behind a desk, his face strangely tight.

"We are receiving reports that there has been an attack on Los Angeles. I repeat. We have unconfirmed reports of a nuclear blast, just moments ago, in the Los Angeles metropolitan area."

Chapter Two

Certain that food and gas would soon be in short supply, Caden reassessed his needs. It took three trips from the market to carry five cases of bottled water, three gas cans and a Styrofoam cooler full of food covered with ice to his car. He opened the back door and pushed the food and water in.

While he filled the gas cans he tried again to call Becky and his parents, then cursed his lack of success. Looking up in frustration, he saw the first hint of morning color in the sky. He glanced at his watch. Dawn was less than an hour away. He loaded the gas into the trunk as cars began arriving. A van parked at the last available pump. A woman, her hair disheveled as if she just awoke, jumped from the vehicle and ran into the market while a stubble-faced man filled the tank and retrieved cans from the car.

Pulling away from the pumps, Caden noticed a pay phone at the side of the store. It was worth a try.

His heart skipped when he heard the ring. When someone picked up the receiver he shouted. "Becky? Is that you?"

"Caden? Caden! I was afraid you might be…Where are you?"

He delighted in hearing her speak. In conversation with friends, she spoke slower than most, with a soft accent that betrayed her southern birth, but now that was all gone.

"Where are you," she repeated. "I've been trying to call you—your apartment, even your office."

Quickly, he told her how close he had been to the Washington attack and that he was coming. "I'd really like it if you left Atlanta."

"I can't. Not right now."

"This is not the time to be in a city."

"The technicians are setting up an auxiliary studio at the affiliate in Birmingham, but until they finish, well, these attacks are the biggest news story ever. The network wants everyone covering it."

Caden used every persuasive weapon available to convince her to leave, logic, love and finally guilt. "Is your career more important than me, than your life?"

"What are the chances of more bombs? And even if there are more, New York or Chicago are more likely targets than Atlanta."

Realizing that she would not leave he said, "I'll try to call you tonight, but if there is another attack, will you leave?"

There was a pause. "We'll talk when you get here."

After he hung up, he tried calling his family but didn't get through. He cursed. *I should have asked Becky to call them.*

The majority of traffic would use the freeways, so Caden avoided them, sticking to the secondary roads. Gradually, the morning sun painted the sky with pink and gold. He turned on the satellite radio and scanned the stations. Fewer than half were operating. There was some music, but all the news and talk channels spoke of nothing but the attacks.

"This just in, Secretary of Homeland Security, Michael Durant, has assumed the duties of the President."

Durant! That egotistical....

"As we reported earlier, Secretary Durant was involved in a traffic accident yesterday on his way into Washington D.C.

for the State of the Union Address. He was taken to a hospital in Baltimore where he is recovering.

He's last in line of succession. All the others—they must be dead.

As if to confirm Caden's realization the announcer went on, "More senior officials in the line of succession are assumed to have died in the attack on Washington."

"President Michael Durant." *God help us. That political hack has exceeded his level of incompetence.*

The sun peeked over a nearby hill as he entered a small town. When Caden stopped at a red light, a rotund, middle-aged man in a dark suit and tie, walked across the street in front of him. He watched as the man walked to an electronics shop, unlocked the door and entered. Caden pulled into the parking lot.

The bell on the door jingled as he entered the store. The big man stood behind the counter, his jacket straining against his bulk.

"You're my first customer today."

"I suspect you'll be busy."

The man nodded grimly and unbuttoned his jacket.

"I'm looking for a shortwave radio with weather and the AM band."

He hung the jacket behind the counter. "I think I have exactly what you want right here," he pulled one from the shelf. "Four shortwave bands, weather, AM and FM and you can charge it by winding this crank or," he popped up the top, "with this solar panel." He set the radio on the counter. "These features may come in handy."

Caden agreed.

"Why are you interested in the weather band?"

"For information on wind direction and fallout and the NOAA frequencies carry emergency alert information."

"Oh." The man took another of the radios from the shelf and set it behind the counter. "Anything else you need?"

"Any MURS radios?"

"No, sorry, we don't get much call for them."

Caden knew it was unlikely. "How about a couple of General Mobile transceivers?"

"GMRS? Sure." The clerk took four off a nearby shelf. "These are the best model that I carry."

Caden watched as he again set the extras behind the counter.

Looking up, the big man smiled, "I'll probably sell out today and I want some for my family."

"Do you have cell phones? Mine doesn't seem to be working well since…."

"Were you close to D.C.?"

"Yes," he nodded. "Too close really."

"The Electromagnetic Pulse probably fried or at least damaged your phone. I can hook you up with a new one."

Caden had heard something about EMP years before. Now he wished he had paid more attention.

He put his new phone in his pants pocket, but left everything else in the bag as he walked from the shop. Back at his vehicle, he set the new things down on the floor in front of the passenger seat just as two cars raced by him. He watched the vehicles stop at a nearby grocery store. Already dozens of cars were out in front. *It's going to be a very busy shopping day*. As he drove by, a clerk put up a handwritten sign that read, "No out of town checks."

Caden continued south on the state highway out of town. Traffic had been heavy, but as the sun rose towards its zenith, the northbound volume appeared less. Still, cars full of adults, children, dogs, cats and suitcases zoomed past in the opposite lane. There were mini-vans and SUVs filled with boxes, their luggage racks full and pulling trailers. He marveled at the number of RVs heading north in the dead of winter. He rubbed his eyes and yawned. *Where are they all going?*

A man walking north with a gas can prompted Caden to look down at his dashboard. His tank was three quarters full and he was going sixty. *Speeding for the first time since the attack.*

Starting into a turn, he looked up. Smoke and fire billowed just ahead. He slammed on the brakes. Caden gripped the wheel as the car slid.

Mere inches from the edge of the flame, his vehicle stopped. He could feel the heat. Caden looked over his shoulder and backed away and off to the side a safe distance. Cars continued past using the shoulder to slip by the accident one-by-one. *That's why northbound traffic seemed lighter.*

He yanked the door open and jumped from the car. The smell of burning oil, gas and flesh thrust memories from dark corners of his mind, but with it came instinct and training. He pushed the memories aside and assessed the situation. There were no bodies or injured on the pavement. A pickup truck was engulfed in flame. In it he saw one body, blackened and burned beyond hope of life. *Were there any passengers?* Flames swirled around the truck. They had either fled or were dead. *But this is at least a two car accident.* He climbed up the slope to view the other car. From this vantage point he surveyed the accident. Apparently, a northbound SUV had passed in the curve and hit the pickup. The front of the SUV was also on fire. If anyone was in the back of that car they were dead from heat and smoke. But there was a third car, a two-door compact. Flames were just feet away but it was not on fire— yet.

Cars slipped by going north and south using the wide shoulder. Occasionally, one stopped. He could see some people trying to use their cell phones. He doubted if they were able to contact emergency services.

A car stopped. The driver yelled, "Are there any injured?"

He looked over the scene once again. He shook his head and mumbled, "All dead." Then louder, "I don't think there is anything we can do."

The man nodded and then drove on.

Caden wanted to continue his journey, but hesitated. It felt wrong to leave so quickly. He reached into his pocket for his new cell phone. He would at least attempt to report the accident.

Something moved in the third car. He stepped forward struggling to peer through the smoke. A woman struggled to sit up in the vehicle. She held her head.

"Are you okay?" Caden took tentative steps down the slope, into the smoke and heat.

She was an older, gray-haired, woman. She looked at him with dazed eyes.

"I'll be right there."

She opened the car door and fell hard to the pavement.

Instinctively he dialed 911 and was surprised when he got through. He described the situation as he reached the woman. Quickly he pulled her upwind out of the smoke and heat.

"What is your location?"

"Where am I?" He looked around in panic. Several cars stopped, but no one was close enough to ask. A rusted pickup truck heading north pulled into the southbound lane and stopped. A large lumberjack of a man stepped out.

Still holding the phone to his ear, Caden shouted, "Where are we?"

"Just north of Beckley on Highway 19," the big man said.

Caden repeated the words then cushioned the woman's head.

"Is she alive?"

Moving his fingers along the side of her neck he said, "She was a bit ago." Caden found a weak pulse. A black and blue lump marked her forehead and blood matted the right side of her head where she hit the pavement. *She's going to have an awful headache.*

The big man got a blanket from his truck and covered the woman.

"Thanks." Caden said.

The man nodded. He looked at the cars going past. "They're all afraid. Running as fast as they can to somewhere…anywhere." He looked Caden in the eye. "I've seen this fear…." His eyes seemed to look far away. "Iraq, Afghanistan. I never thought I'd see it in America."

The wail of a siren came on the breeze. Normally, Caden tensed at the sound, but not today. Now it was the sound of comfort.

Paramedics arrived followed closely by a fire engine. Within seconds, the injured woman was being treated.

Yes, they were treating her and that was good, but it was more than that. *We are not islands in a storm, each separately enduring whatever is thrown in our direction. We are still citizens bound together by ethics and laws. We help each other.*

Caden walked a few feet up the slope, away from the madness of the road, and dropped to the ground in the shade of tree. Leaning his head against the trunk, he suddenly felt exhausted. He yawned and watched with heavy eyes as the medics loaded the woman into the van and whisked her away. He gazed at the flow of traffic north. *But how many cars passed without helping?*

The big man folded his blanket, nodded to Caden and resumed his trip north.

Well, some of us help each other.

Caden retrieved the liter soda bottle, still filled with water from his apartment toilet tank and splashed it liberally on his face.

Only as he resumed his journey south did he think of the nearly thirty gallons of gasoline he carried in the car and the inferno that might have been. He shuddered and drove onward with more care. Traffic thinned as the day waned. Caden passed numerous stations with signs out front reading, "No Gas." The sun was a yellow smudge on the horizon as he approached the Georgia border. Rounding a corner, bright lights nearly blinded him and he slowed to a crawl. A soldier stepped forward, his hand held out signaling Caden to stop.

Caden rolled down his window as the man came alongside.

"We've set up a roadblock here. This county is now under martial law and a dusk to dawn curfew."

Caden's confusion must have been apparent.

"It's a precaution against looting and lawlessness."

Gradually his eyes adjusted to the spotlights. He saw a Georgia State Patrol and county sheriff car in the shadows. He glanced at the soldier's insignia and name badge, Lieutenant Turner. Caden looked at the road ahead. Two Stryker vehicles with their 50 caliber guns pointed in his direction sat in the center of the road.

Lieutenant Turner gestured. "You can sleep in the parking lot of the Border Market."

Caden looked back over his shoulder.

"And frankly sir, you look like you need some sleep."

He rubbed his face and stifled a yawn. "Is there any way I can get to Atlanta tonight?"

The officer shook his head. "No, not tonight." He pointed again to the parking lot. "Get some rest. The road might be open in the morning."

Caden drove into the parking lot that had become a makeshift community of more than fifty cars, vans and trucks. Several families cooked food over camp stoves. Dozens watched a television set up outside of a camper. Large "No Gas" signs hung from orange tape that circled the gas pumps.

If I can buy food I should save what I have in the cooler. I'll check in a few minutes. He leaned back his head.

*   *   *

Caden bolted awake. His eyes shot from right to left. His heart raced and cold sweat covered his face. Two people walked casually by, silhouetted by streetlights. Had he been dreaming? Fading images of death and fire lingered in his mind.

He glanced at his watch. He had slept just over six hours. Stepping out of the car, he stretched and wiped his face with his sleeve. Before dawn, and continuing the final leg of his odyssey, there was his stomach to consider. He stretched again, locked the car, and walked to the convenience store.

"We're out of most everything," the clerk said as Caden entered, "and I'm only taking cash, no checks or credit." Caden nodded and the man's eyes quickly returned to a television that hung from the ceiling behind the counter. Five others leaned on the counter with him watching the news.

Caden walked down one nearly empty aisle and up another looking for anything he might need.

"Now back to the national news desk," a television reporter stated as he finished his story.

"Thank you for that report. Rebecca Thornton is here with us now. She has compiled the latest information on the terrorist group claiming responsibility for the attacks."

Caden's eyes snapped to the television at the sound of his fiancé's name.

"I told you they were terrorist attacks," an older man said.

As Caden walked toward the television, he studied the studio background trying to figure out if Becky was in Atlanta or Birmingham. *Could she have gotten to Birmingham during the night with roads so jammed? Could she have flown?* He shook his head in frustration, unable to decide.

"Can I get you anything?" the clerk asked.

"No, just watching the news."

"Where are you from," another asked.

"Washington DC."

"Were you there when the attack happened?"

Caden nodded.

"What was it like?"

Eyes fixed on him as he told the story of his escape from Washington.

"What are you doing here?"

"I'm on my way to Atlanta to pick up my fiancé." Caden pointed to the television."

"Her? She's your girlfriend?"

Caden nodded.

Around the counter, there was general approval of his choice.

Becky's voice continued in the background as those beside him discussed how long it would take Caden to get to Atlanta.

A potbellied, middle-aged man in an angler's vest said, "Under normal circumstances it would be just a couple of hours."

"But the traffic is nuts south of here," someone added.

The first man nodded. "Everyone is leaving the city."

"They're talking about making the freeway one-way out of the metro area."

With a slow, southern drawl an older man at the end of the counter said, "Have her meet you here."

Everyone agreed.

Static erupted from the television. Power failed. Darkness filled the air.

Chapter Three

The store clerk, his mouth agape, retrieved a portable radio from behind the counter. He turned the dial until he found a Georgia station.

Caden heard what he already feared, Atlanta had been attacked. He walked out of the store into the chilly night and drifted across the parking lot. Some families ran to their cars and hurried north, away from the blast.

She's dead.

No, perhaps she went to Birmingham.

So many have died. The ache in his heart ebbed and flowed between hope that Becky might be alive and despair that she and so many others were already dead.

He found himself on the edge of a group huddled around a radio. "The mushroom cloud is still climbing over Atlanta. Firestorms are raging throughout the metro…"

Caden walked away. He did not want to hear strangers announce the death of the one he loved. In a daze, he stumbled along the edge of the parking lot by the road. He hardly noticed the squeal of tires as he aimlessly continued onward. A horn blared. He was knocked hard to the pavement. A woman screamed. Gravel peppered the side of his face as the car sped away.

"Are you okay?" someone asked as he sat up.

He would be bruised, his face stung, but nothing seemed broken. He nodded. "Yes, I'm okay."

The small crowd dispersed as if nothing had happened. Caden walked to his car, slid down beside it, staring straight ahead. He wanted to be angry with himself for not driving faster, for not insisting she leave, for not saving her, but he was numb and the only emotion he seemed capable of was guilt. He sat there until the first rays of morning light glowed on the horizon. A woman carried a small television from a nearby RV. She placed it on a table as a man adjusted a satellite dish on the top of the vehicle. An image snapped on the screen as a crowd formed. Caden didn't want to watch, but the news was like a siren song that drew him in.

As the sun peeked higher, he learned that the bomb detonated downtown. One report mentioned the network headquarters building was gone and added, "It appears Rebecca Thornton was reporting live from the studio when the blast occurred. Here is her final report."

The voice, the face, were cold steel stabbing his heart. He turned and stumbled toward a gray leafless tree standing alone in a nearby field. Caden's eyes fixed on what must have been a mighty oak now broken and alone in the field. He stumbled toward the shell of the tree and collapsed against the hollow trunk.

He remembered the first time he saw Becky. He was just days out of the Army after a combat tour in the Middle East and had put off any serious relationships while in the service, but then he was willing to entertain the possibility. He had gone to the beach with friends. Becky, a fair-haired beauty with a soft southern accent, was the friend of a friend. She had intrigued him early on, but gave him scant attention. As he strolled on the water's edge their paths crossed and they talked. It was then he found out she couldn't swim. "Come on. I'll teach you." As they waded into deeper water, he placed his arm behind her. "Lean back. I'll show you how to float." As she did, he placed his other arm under her legs.

She smiled nervously. "Don't let go of me."

"Never." He wanted to pull her in tight against him and kiss her, but she had the air of a southern lady, and he didn't want to offend. He walked deeper into the surf as he told her how to hold her back and head. Suddenly he fell below the surface of the water. He had stepped off a ledge and was still sinking. Fish swam by as he looked up to see Becky flail in the ocean above him. He stroked and kicked with all his might as she sank into his arms. Holding her, he swam to the surface. She wrapped her arms tight around his neck.

"I'm so sorry," he said as they surfaced.

She gasped for air.

"Hold on to my waist, I'll take you to shore."

As they came up on the beach, he explained about the ledge and apologized again, but he was sure that was the end of the relationship. Later that day she playfully accused him of trying to drown her, but her smile told him all he needed to know. That night they kissed.

Caden leaned hard against the broken tree. The trunk creaked as his body heaved in tears. Memories were all he would ever have. She was dead.

The sun crept higher in the sky. Caden hadn't noticed until now the cars leaving the nearby parking lot. He knew he should check the wind direction and fallout pattern from the Atlanta blast but he couldn't find the will to act. Repeatedly he cursed his slowness in coming to her, his unwillingness to order her out of the city, his inability to save her. He told himself a thousand things he should have done, a thousand things that might have saved her. Those opportunities were lost to him now.

Footfalls crunched the stubble of the field. Caden looked up enough to see well-polished boots. Slowly his eyes crept up the camouflage uniform.

"I am sorry to hear about your loss." It was Lieutenant Turner.

Caden nodded.

Turner sat against the tree in the shade of the trunk. For several minutes, he said nothing.

"My wife and son were visiting family in Alexandria, Virginia." He turned his head and looked at Caden. "Do you know where that is?"

"Yes, I lived in Bethesda."

Turner sighed. "It's been a rough couple of days." He took a sip from his canteen. "You want a drink?"

Caden's throat was parched. "Thank you." Not knowing how much water the Lieutenant had, he took a single mouthful.

"I'm busy all day with my men, but there is always some part of me that is worried about my wife and son. Sometimes when I see a child or a woman, just for a moment, I wonder, 'is that my family?'" He glanced back at the checkpoint. "When the supply truck came this morning, I hoped it brought mail." He let out a deep breath. "I pray they're safe."

"You have hope."

The Lieutenant nodded. "Yes, I do. I pray they are out there somewhere…safe. Perhaps they're with my parents in Richmond." He looked slowly from side to side as if searching for something. "Do you have anyone, a mother, father…."

The words stunned Caden. "Yes." In his grief he had forgotten his parents, his brother and sister. How could he forget them?

"They need you now."

Caden knew those words were true. His mother would be heartbroken with worry about him.

A commotion spread across the parking lot. Turner stood as one of his men trotted up to them.

"Lieutenant, the civilians say the fallout from the Atlanta blast is heading this way."

Turner held out his hand to Caden.

He grasped it and with the Sergeant's help, stood. "I've got satellite and shortwave radios in my car."

The three walked briskly to the parking lot. Caden unlocked the door of his vehicle, clicked on the radio and set it to search. It didn't take long to find a strong signal.

"...law. Winds are out of the south bringing the fallout over northern Georgia. FEMA is advising residents to shelter-in-place and non-residents or refugees to evacuate the area."

Caden slumped in the seat. He had held a vague, irrational hope of heading south to see Atlanta and find Becky. He stared up at the sky. Clouds slid slowly north. Following behind those clouds was the slow death of fallout. South was no longer an option.

A soldier ran up holding a sheet of paper. A frown grew on Turner's face as he read.

Chapter Four

Caden sat in the car while Turner read. The tears for Becky were invisible now, the grief hid within. The pain he felt tore at him, but Turner had reminded him that he had family. It made him feel immature, even a bit ridiculous, but if tears came again; let them come with his arms around his mother.

Turner handed the paper back to the soldier. "Tell the men to saddle up. We're leaving ASAP."

"Where to?" Caden asked. "Richmond?" He knew that was unlikely, but he hoped his new friend might be heading home.

He shook his head. "Not even Virginia. The orders are to take my men to Fort Rucker in Alabama and help set up a refugee camp." Though the Lieutenant was about his age, he looked at Caden with a fatherly concern. "Which way will you be going?"

"West. I've got family out that way."

"Follow us to Rucker. It'll be safer and maybe even faster."

*   *   *

For the first couple of hours, Caden made good time as he followed the army convoy, but as the day wore on, more military vehicles joined the procession, civilian traffic increased and progress slowed. He was sure the line of army green trucks and jeeps stretched over a mile long.

The GMRS and CB radios on the seat beside him crackled with pleas for gas, assistance with repairs, news and rumors. Thousands biked or walked along the side of the road, rough looking individuals and entire families dragging suitcases and carrying more. He felt guilty riding alone in his car.

A young woman barely out of high school, by the look of her, carried a small baby along the road. As he passed, their eyes met. Should he offer her a ride? If he stopped, the convoy would move on. Would he be separated from them? Would he be overwhelmed by the desperate people along the road? A bend in the road hid her from sight.

He drove on wondering what kind of world the baby would inherit. Visions of cities burnt and desolate filled his mind, gray ash lying like a blanket of snow across a cold and lifeless land. A land poisoned by radioactive fallout. He remembered reading somewhere that cockroaches could withstand high levels of radiation. *Because of the foolishness of man the cockroach shall inherit the Earth.* He shuddered at the thought of a world full of cockroaches, but otherwise sterile.

An hour later, the young woman and her baby were out of sight and probably several miles behind him but there were many children and babies along the sides of the road. Would they live? How many had already died? Images of the friends he had lost in the last 48 hours flashed through his mind. The mental list of casualties always began and ended with memories of Becky.

He remembered the last time they went out to dinner. Becky liked French cuisine, but he was more of a meat and potatoes kind of guy, so that night they compromised on Italian. The restaurant had been a good choice, small and quiet, with excellent food cooked by an Italian family. They had planned to go back. Tears welled in his eyes. They would never go back.

Brakes squealed. Caden turned his head toward the sound of crumpling metal. One car careened off another, up the shoulder of the road, scattering pedestrians in all directions. Except for the two cars that collided no one stopped. Like a river disturbed by two stones, the westward flow quickly resumed. Caden resolved to focus on driving.

Tones came across one of his radios. A tense voice carried over the airwaves. "10 55, 10-33, west on highway 59, milepost 83."

Caden tried to remember the 10 codes. He looked in the rearview mirror. Nothing was obviously amiss behind him. Returning his attention ahead he spotted a milepost that read '81.' The highway followed the contour of a hill, limiting his view ahead.

From behind, horns blasted. Metal crunched. In his mirror he saw pedestrians scurry like bees from a hive. *Fear. That is what is causing this.* People were frightened, fleeing wildfires and, he glanced at the gray sky, the unseen poison of radiation. The winds were still out of the south. Good for him, death for others.

Smoke flowed into the air from the far side of a nearby hill. Cresting the knoll Caden saw a burning pickup truck, smashed against a tree. He stared at the scene as the convoy continued down the slope. Pedestrians darted in close to the flames. *Why would they do that?* Then he noticed a crumpled small car that had been hidden by fire and smoke.

The convoy halted. Caden stepped from his vehicle when he saw Lieutenant Turner walking back toward the accident.

"There's a woman under the car," someone yelled.

Turner shouted to his men and ran toward the burning vehicle. Caden followed. The car sat to the right of a growing inferno. He gagged on the smoke and fumes. Soldiers knelt behind the wreck and pushed up. It lifted. Caden could only see one limp arm. He grabbed it and pulled. She was still trapped. "Higher, lift higher."

Turner and the other soldiers grunted and pushed.

Caden's face felt dry and hot as the flames licked closer.

More soldiers joined the effort.

"The fire is moving this way. Pull her out." Turner shouted.

Caden reached under the car, grabbed both arms, and pulled. The body moved. He stumbled back, regained his footing and pulled her clear. Others took and moved the bleeding woman clear of the flames.

Caden stumbled back several feet and sat on the ground trying to catch his breath. The woman was covered with dirt and blood, both separate and mixed together. It was hard to tell her age, but she was young. A growing pool of blood surrounded her. The medic was also young, a corporal no older than twenty by the look of him. After checking for a pulse he worked frantically on the injured woman bandaging and taping her wounds.

Lieutenant Turner called to a soldier checking out the burning car. "Anyone alive?"

"No. Gas cans exploded on impact. Two people, both toast."

Caden turned away from the fire and blood. Off to the left a lump of pastel blue blankets caught his eye. Drawn toward them he stood, walked over and pulled back the top cover. "There's a baby here!" He drew back the remaining layer revealing a blue shirt emblazoned with "Future Quarterback," across the front.

The medic continued to work on the woman. "Is it hurt?"

Caden couldn't see any blood. The babies eyes were red and puffy, he had been crying, but wasn't now. "No."

The medic called to one of the soldiers, "Come here. Press here—hard!"

Caden cradled the baby in his arms his eyes fixed on the woman, her blouse now dark with blood. He wondered if she had thrown the baby out of the way of the car in a desperate attempt to save it. That thought brought him comfort. "Is she going to make it?"

The medic didn't answer, but began CPR. Then he stopped and sat back on the gray gravel. He looked up at Caden and the baby. "I couldn't stop the bleeding," he sighed. "She's dead."

The other soldier, his hands crimson, walked away.

The medic looked even younger now. His eyes glazed. Caden wondered if this was his first taste of death. He stood holding the baby. "You did what you could."

Turner walked up and stood by his medic. "She died?"

The young man nodded.

Turner knelt beside him. "Did you do everything you knew how to do?"

"Yes, sir."

"Then you did all that any of us could for her." He held out his hand and helped the medic stand.

Turner, walking toward the convoy, called down the line, "Platoon sergeants, gas up as needed, but get it done quickly."

As soldiers trotted to the fuel truck with cans, Caden raced to catch up with Turner. "What do I do with the baby?"

"We haven't been able to contact local police or paramedics." The lieutenant stared at the body of the mother now covered by an army blanket. "Take the kid to Fort Rucker. We'll be there by morning."

"Me?"

The medic walked up, his hands still red with the woman's blood. "Here, you might need this." He handed Caden the woman's wallet and a pastel blue diaper bag.

Caden looked down at the baby. *I'm not a father, and I don't want to be.*

A newer model red Lexus pulled up within inches of Lieutenant Turner and Caden. A man jumped out leaving a woman and three children inside. "You in charge here?"

Turner nodded.

"I see you're refueling. I need gas."

"Military vehicles use diesel and we don't have any to spare."

Knowing this was not quite true, Caden stared at the Lieutenant with his best poker face.

"I can see a fuel truck up there," the man gestured along the convoy, "you've got plenty."

"What part of the word diesel is giving you trouble?"

Off to the side Caden saw another man running toward them holding a gas can.

Turner started to walk away when a pickup pulled onto the gravel in front of him. Two bearded men stepped from the vehicle. The driver approached Turner, crunching the stones beneath his boots. The other stayed very close to the truck.

"I need gas," the driver stated.

Caden noticed the man who stayed close to the car held a rifle at his side.

Turner held up his hand to the driver. "The convoy uses diesel and we don't have extra."

Looking down at the baby in his arms, Caden knew the situation could turn ugly any second. While Turner continued talking with the civilians Caden walked back to the car, laid the baby and the diaper bag on the seat and discretely slid his pistol in his jacket pocket. As he walked back, he noticed a sergeant positioning men along the flanks of the civilians with just a nod or a raised eyebrow.

One of the bearded men asked, "You wouldn't mind if we just checked to see what kind of fuel you have, now would you?" He lifted the rifle and set it on the hood.

"If you try, I *will* kill you."

"This is America you can't just shoot us."

"This is martial law. I can." He unsnapped his holster. "And I will."

Clutching the pistol in his pocket, Caden's eyes darted from Turner to those wanting gas. Turner would not relent and give them fuel, Caden was sure of that. He prayed the men would back down and leave. The only sound he heard for several moments was his heart beating in his ears.

The man with the gas can cursed and walked on.

Caden took a breath.

The driver of the Lexus spat on the ground and drove away. The bearded man grabbed his gun and threw it in his truck.

As that vehicle pulled away, a soft rain fell. Turner looked at Caden, "We do have some regular gas. Have you got enough?"

"Yeah, Thanks, I'm fine."

Caden opened the car door and the baby wailed. With a frustrated sigh he turned on the portable radio and scanned the NOAA weather frequencies. Over the cries of the baby he listened.

"…rain is out of the south and free of fallout…"

Winds out of the south were safe now that they were west of Atlanta. Once again he had been lucky, or blessed. He struggled to safely strap the baby in. He had no car seat so he tried wrapping blankets around the child and the seatbelt.

He turned on his car radio. "…other news, Homeland Security, working with the Nuclear Regulatory Commission and the International Atomic Energy Agency has identified the plutonium used in the bombs as from a North Korean reactor. The New York Times reports that President Durant is meeting with senior military advisors. Repeating our weather news the rain is out of the south…"

He sat back in his seat, finally satisfied that he had done his best to secure the child for the trip. The raindrops that gently tapped against the windshield were just water—no fallout. He and the baby would live another day, but America was dying one body blow at a time and perhaps tonight, like a wounded warrior, she would lash out at those who had hurt her.

Caden pulled the pistol from his pocket and set it on the floor behind him. He turned on the windshield wipers. While he waited for the convoy to move on he looked through the wallet. There was over a hundred dollars in cash. "Well, young man, you have a college fund." The Driver's license had an Atlanta address. He flipped past it to a photo of the baby. There was writing on the back. He looked over at the baby, "So little guy, your name is Adam."

*   *   *

Floodlights illuminated the predawn darkness as he approached the main gate of Fort Rucker. Even at this early hour people streamed in. Guards stopped Caden moments after the convoy passed through the gate. They ordered him to park his vehicle in the sprawling civilian camp. He looked at Adam, sleeping peacefully in the passenger seat, and decided not to protest. He would get a couple hours sleep, turn the child over to the proper authorities and be on his way to Washington state in the afternoon.

As Caden drove across the main compound, he passed dozens of tents and several buildings being remodeled. Floodlights bathed them and, even at this hour, workers climbed scaffolding and dashed about like so many ants. Ambulances pushed through the crowded street toward the hospital ahead. As Caden continued along, several helicopters, with red crosses emblazoned on the side, landed in a nearby parking lot and off-loaded patients.

Caden parked near a small grove of trees at the edge of the base, away from most of the other refugees. Looking in the baby bag he found formula and disposable diapers. "Even during the madness and chaos your mother was trying to care for you." He sighed. "I guess that is all any of us can do—try." He fed and changed Adam. When the baby was wrapped in blankets and resting comfortably beside him Caden leaned his seat back as far as it would go and covered himself with a blanket. "Goodnight Adam." He shut his eyes.

The baby cried.

*　　　*　　　*

Caden yawned as he climbed the stairs of the base hospital. Every muscle in his body ached. But then, yesterday in the convenience store parking lot, he had been hit by a car and for the last three days he had slept in one. He looked at Adam cradled in his arms and with a tired grin said, "And you didn't let me sleep much at all."

Reaching the top step, he stared out a window in frustration. Acres of what had been green grass along one side of the runway was now a vast sea of tents, trailers, cars, vans, people and mud sprinkled with tiny patches of green. The congestion, mud and filth, brought back memories of camps in Iraq and Kosovo.

The lights flickered and went out as Caden pushed open the door. His gut tightened.

The room took on a dark, oppressive aura. Windows along one wall provided the only light for the large, open ward. Patients were packed into every available space on beds, cots, gurneys and mattresses on the floor.

Hardly breathing, he weaved his way across the room toward a doctor. His stomach churned with irrational fear.

The lights snapped back on. Caden took a deep breath. For over a year after his return from Iraq he flinched at the sound of a gunshot and his stomach knotted. How long, he wondered, would lights blinking out cause that same reaction.

As Caden approached, the doctor glanced up from a badly burned woman and demanded, "What?"

He quickly explained.

Bent over his patient, the doctor asked, "Is the baby sick?"

"No." Caden tried not to stare at the woman lying between them.

"Injured?"

"No."

He straightened up, rubbed his back and while writing notes on a clipboard asked, "What do you want me to do?"

"Take him."

He rubbed his face and eyes and for the first time looked at Caden. "I've got over six hundred patients sick, injured or dying. Right now I'm not doing well-baby care."

"Where's the child welfare office?"

The doctor shook his head.

*   *   *

Disposable diapers were impossible to find, but a friendly nurse gave Caden four cloth ones and a half-dozen safety pins. Back at his car, Caden looked at the material, looked at the pins and then at Adam. "So do you know how to do this?"

Adam, bundled in blankets and lying on the grass, giggled.

"Well, at least you're not crying—yet." From the trunk of his car he pulled out a camp lantern and stove. He lit the lantern and hung it from a tree on the passenger side of the car. A yellow glow pushed back on the darkness. He had no table so he set the stove on the ground near the lamp and warmed some stew. As he bent over the stove, he caught a glimpse of a slender figure dart, at the edge of the camp light. He moved so his back was to the car. He held up a can. "You like stew?" he asked the baby.

Adam cried softly.

"I really don't care for it either." In the shadows to his right leaves rustled. Caden's heart raced, his senses on full alert. He knew the knot in his stomach was unreasonable, but such gut reactions had served him well in combat.

The child wailed.

Caden needed quiet so he could figure out who was moving in the darkness and why, but the child gave him none. He walked back to the car and casually slipped his hunting knife in his waistband. "Now little guy calm down," *Where's my pistol?* He remembered. It was behind the driver's seat. He would either have to climb into the car from where he was on the passenger side or move to the dark side of the vehicle. *No, I'm just being paranoid.* Still, he sat facing where he had last heard the crackle of leaves and seen movement. He rocked the baby with one hand. "Now, now, everything will be alright."

Adam's wail softened to a whimper.

From behind, Caden heard the pump of a shotgun.

Chapter Five

How did they get behind me? He had last heard someone move through the leaves and branches to his right, but the pump of the shotgun came from behind.

"Turn around.   Keep your hands where we can see them."

Caden complied.   Two men with stubble-covered faces stood before him wearing dirty, hunting camouflage and ball caps.   The one on Caden's left was about as tall as him, the other shorter.   Both had beer bellies.   They looked like good-old-boys in the bad sense of the phrase.   One held a twelve gauge and the other a 270 hunting rifle with a scope.

His every muscle taut, and in a voice more confident than he felt, he asked, "What do you want?"

"Most everything you got, except the kid." They both laughed. "Move away from the car and get on the ground."

Caden was certain that if he obeyed he would never get up. He didn't know what he would do, but he was sure he could do nothing on the ground. "No. Take what you want, but I'm standing."

"Like hell you are!" The man with the 270 moved forward to Caden's right.

Caden's options were few. The baby was to his back, the car to his left and the crooks to his front and right.

"How about we just kill your kid?" Mister 270 pointed his rifle at the whimpering baby.

A gunshot tore through the camp.

Combat training kicked in. Caden jumped to his left, toward the robber with the shotgun. In one smooth motion, he pulled the knife from his waistband and plunged it into the man's chest.

The man gasped. Disbelief etched his dying face.

Caden grabbed him intending to use his dead body as a shield, but there was no need. The other robber was on the ground in a growing pool of blood. Adam wailed, but he could see no injury.

Caden dropped the body he held.

At light's edge stood a young woman with long dark hair. In her outstretched hands she held a pistol.

Caden knelt and pulled his knife from the body, uncertain of the girl's intentions. Slowly he stood. His eyes were fixed on her, but her eyes, like her pistol, were fixed on the body that lay between them. "Ah—thank you," he said.

She did not move.

"Are you alright?" He inched forward hand outstretched. "Give me the gun. Okay?"

Her eyes flashed wild and she jumped back pointing the pistol at Caden's chest.

"Okay, okay, keep it," he said stepping back, "but don't aim it right at me."

Very slowly she lowered it.

He stepped back. "My name is Caden."

She nodded. Then moments later whispered, "Maria. My, my name is Maria." She looked at the whimpering child on the ground. "They would have killed the baby." Her eyes were full of fear as she looked at Caden. "They would have killed you."

"Yes." He set the bloody knife back on the dead man. "Thank you for saving my life."

He considered what to do next. He felt they were justified in killing the two robbers, but still they had taken two lives. Someone had to be notified. He retrieved his cell phone from the car and was relieved to hear a dial tone. He knew only one phone number on base and called Lieutenant Turner.

While they waited he tried to find out more about Maria, but most of her responses were either yes or no. Within minutes, a jeep and a van arrived. Turner walked up to Caden as a tall officer spoke with Maria. As the man escorted Maria toward the van, Caden glimpsed the gold oak leaf insignia of a major. Caden started to follow.

"Please stay here, sir," said one MP. "The Major would like to interview the young lady first."

Caden leaned against his car and watched while the MP examined the area and took photographs.

"What do you know about this girl?" Turner asked as he joined Caden at the car.

"Her name is Maria and she's a good shot."

Turner chuckled. "Well, that's two excellent things to know about a woman. Let me see what I can find out."

Caden watched his friend walk toward the van. There his eyes shifted to Maria. She took Adam into her arms and leaned against the vehicle. She was out of earshot, but a tall man asked her questions. Her head cast down, she appeared to be focused on the baby. She wasn't talking much, but her long black hair gently swayed as she nodded or shook her head. She looked younger than him, perhaps early-to-mid-twenties. Even in a faded denim jacket and worn jeans, she was pleasant on the eyes. He recalled she had the merest hint of a southern drawl. Despite her accent it was clear her roots were south of the border.

Turner stood quietly to one side of Maria while the tall officer continued the interview. It seemed the MPs were more interested in Maria than him.

A medic came and examined the two bodies then double timed off to the group around the van.

Maria's head was cast down, but she did seem to be answering a few more of the major's questions. After a minute of staring at her and trying to figure out what she was saying, she seemed to pause and shudder. Turner called and someone came with a jacket. Caden shivered. *Is it cold or are we both going into shock?* He had no answer, but he pulled a coat from the car and, returning to the hood, put it on.

After what seemed like hours, Turner and the major walked over to Caden.

Turner introduced the senior officer who quickly asked. "Where were you when you first saw the two men?"

Caden moved to the spot.

"Tell me what happened,"

Caden looked back at Maria as she sat in the police van holding Adam. She had saved his life. He wanted to help her if he could. He thought about telling a version of the story where he shot one man and knifed the other. "Ah...." he sputtered as he determined how to spin his yarn.

Turner coughed, pointed to the bodies and asked, "Are these the men who killed Maria's parents?"

The Major gave Turner a harsh glance. "Yes. These are the suspects," he said flatly.

The news hit Caden like a fist as he stared at the two bodies. That was why the Major had been so interested in her, why they had questioned her first and for so long. *These guys murdered Maria's parents.* While the men hunted Caden, she hunted them. Caden knew the two men would have killed him, but now the realization hit him with new force. He owed her his life. Emphasizing how she had saved him, he told the major what had happened.

"Lieutenant Turner tells me you were with Special Forces."

Caden nodded.

The major looked down at the man Caden had killed and bit his lip. After several moments, a slight smile came to his face. "We'll need the pistol and the knife." He looked Caden in the eye. "I won't ask if you have any other weapons."

"Thank you."

Four medics arrived with stretchers and body bags. The major nodded to them. Turning back to Caden he said, "Normally, we would jail both of you until the investigation was complete, but these times aren't normal." He sighed. "And considering all the chaos and crime right now, I've got better things to do than lock you two up and I don't have a facility for the kid." He looked slowly around the campsite. "Look, I believe both of you." Glancing at the medics as they hauled the bodies away, he shook his head adding, "And they needed killing." The Major stared at Caden. "We have to investigate. Can I trust you to stay on base until this matter is cleared up?"

"Yes, sir." Caden frowned. Now it would be days or perhaps even weeks before he could continue his journey home.

After everyone left, Maria sat near the campfire, cradling Adam in her arms. Caden walked up to her.

She pulled the baby in against her chest.

"Do you have a campsite, a place to sleep?"

She shook her head.

Caden slid down against his car. "I have blankets and a sleeping bag. You can stay here if you like."

She nodded. "Thanks."

Caden fixed his gaze on the young woman. She rocked Adam back and forth while staring at the fire. He expected tears from her, but there were none. Had the tears for her parents already come and gone or were they yet to flow?

He remembered the first person he had killed up close. When the fight was over and the squad back at base camp, he trembled. Tears welled in his eyes, but he wasn't sure why.

He wasn't sad. He was a soldier and had done his duty. He held his emotions in check that night for fear of what his comrades would say, but the face, the eyes, of the man he killed still haunted his memory.

Caden sighed and stared at the ground for several moments, then looked across at Maria and the baby. She held Adam close but gently with experienced ease. Anyone might mistake them for mother and child. Thoughts turned to his own mother and father. He should call home. He imagined how the conversation would go. *Hi Mom. How are you doing? Good. And the rest of the family? That's good news. Where am I? Fort Rucker in Alabama. Yes, I was on my way home, but now I've got to wait for a few days. Why? Well I was just interviewed by the military police because I killed a man. Calm down, no, I'm fine. You see Maria.... Who's Maria? We met a couple of hours ago—at the robbery. She shot one guy, because he was going to hurt Adam, and that gave me the chance to knife the other one. Who's Adam? Oh, he's the baby....* Maybe it would be better to call home later.

Caden looked to the lights of the main camp. He had chosen this isolated spot to be away from people and that had nearly cost him his life. He looked to his right at the dark patch of blood stained earth. He was certain the old nightmares would return that night. If they stayed neither of them would get much sleep. "Maria, we should move."

*   *   *

Caden sat under the canopy Maria had created to shade Adam. Somehow, in the three days they had been there she had acquired a variety of rope, string, a tarp and two wooden poles necessary to build it. They had both done well to get this far. *I guess I'm a survivor.* He pondered the thought for a moment and concluded that he was right. He had skills and he used them to find solutions that allowed him to live.

Maria had gone with Adam to the market area. He found it pleasant to lean against the car in the shade of the awning while reading a three-day-old edition of the "Montgomery Advertiser." The day after the shooting, the radio briefly reported the capture of terrorists with a nuclear bomb in New York City, but the article in the paper gave a detailed account of the cooperation between the FBI and Homeland Security. *At last a victory.* But the delight he felt at the news was squelched when he read a nuclear bomb had exploded four days ago near the naval base in San Diego. *Five cities, hit by nuclear bombs. All those people dead or dying.* He shuddered and tried to put the horror from his mind and wondered why no action had been taken against North Korea. They had provided the uranium used in two of the bombs.

He flipped the page and was surprised to see an interview with Senator Cole of Montana. *He's alive?* Skimming the article he learned the senator remained out west with his wife for the birth of the third child. Caden grinned. *That is going to be one spoiled kid.*

A glance at his watch reminded him of the appointment with the military police. *Hopefully I can resume the drive home tomorrow morning.* He looked about at the tightly-packed campsites. *How will I get my car out of here?* Out of the corner of his eye he saw Maria approach with Adam. Caden was about to put down the paper when Maria stopped and talked with Debbie Miller in the next campsite. The Millers were nice people and he hoped they would survive, but he wondered. Maria, on the other, was a survivor in her own way. *Perhaps that is why I'm so attracted to her.* He set down the paper as Maria strolled up to the car.

"Did you find any formula?"

"No," she sat on the hood of the car, "but Debbie gave me a can of milk."

"That's nice," he said still focused on the article. "What did people do before formula?"

She laughed.

Caden looked at Maria as a smile beamed from her face. He thought about what he had asked and his face flushed. "Okay, stupid question, but what do we do?"

She held up the can. "Give Adam some canned milk I guess. You can still buy the fresh stuff at the market, but...."

Caden was surprised. "Really, paper money will still get you things?"

"Yes, but it's all really expensive."

Caden stepped from under the canopy, folded the paper, and dropped it on the car seat. He reached into his pocket and grabbed one of the silver dollars he had taken from his apartment. Flipping it in the air he said, "Let's go get Adam some fresh milk. Save the can for later."

Looking at the coin Maria asked, "What's that?"

"My dad would say it's real money."

As they walked toward the market she said, "I met someone from Washington state."

"Oh?"

"He said his boss was Governor Monroe."

His mouth dropped open. "Monroe?"

Maria nodded nonchalantly. "Do you know him?"

"We've met." he smiled as his mind raced. "He's governor of Washington state —and the leading candidate for president."

"Really?" Her eyebrows rose. "The guy, David Weston, said that the governor wanted to get to Olympia as soon as possible. Isn't Seattle the capital of Washington?"

Lost in his own thoughts, Caden hardly heard what she said. He had worked as an aide to a senator and had military experience. Monroe might be in need of a man with his talents. He looked across the vast refugee camp. He would have to find David Weston— today. *He's my ticket to a new job and a trip home.*

Chapter Six

The barrack's door protested with a loud squeak as Caden yanked it open and hurried out of the cold rain. Movement caught his eye when he was halfway across the lobby. Turning his head he saw a man, seated alone in the corner, staring down at a sheet of paper. The man wiped away tears. Beside him on the floor were the tatters of a quickly opened envelope.

Bad news. So much pain and suffering these days.

As the man raised his head from the letter, Caden recognized him. *Turner!* Remembering their discussion days ago about family, Caden's gut twisted into a knot. Turner had been hoping for a letter and now he had it, but this must be news his friend did not want to hear. Immediately his mind jumped to the worst possible scenario—his friend's family had not survived the Washington blast.

He paused, unsure of what to say. "I was coming to see you, ah…" Caden looked at the door, "Should I go?"

"No." He wiped the tears from his cheeks, stood with eyes fixed on the letter.

Caden glanced at the door once again. He wanted to go, but felt he should stay. "Is there anything I can do?"

"It's okay, really."

Caden was certain Turner's wife and children were dead. "I'm sorry."

"You don't understand." A smile spread across his face. "My family, they're alive."

Caden shouted with joy and grabbed his friend in a bear hug. They stumbled backward as tears ran down the cheeks of both.

After several minutes of smiles, laughter and talk, the two men made their way up the stairs toward Turner's barracks room.

"You actually got a letter?" Caden rubbed his chin. "The more I think about the post office still functioning the stranger it sounds."

Turner grinned as he unlocked the door of his room. "Neither rain, nor snow, nor nuclear bombs." He chuckled at his own joke. "Susie, my wife, sent it the day after the attack on Washington. It must have followed my unit as we moved."

"Have you talked to your family?" He stepped into the small room, and looked for a phone, but did not see one. He pulled his cell phone from a pocket. "Use this."

Turner gestured toward a chair. "It won't work."

Caden shot him a quizzical look as he sat down.

"Have you been able to call your family?"

"No, but you might be...."

Turner shook his head. "President Durant issued an executive order placing phone and Internet system under military control. Long distance communication is limited to government business."

"Why?"

"To keep them available for the good guys and keep any remaining terrorists from communicating."

"Won't they just send letters?"

Turner shrugged. "Maybe, but that's slower and I suspect letters are being monitored also. Actually, a computer nerd in my squad said you could still use the Internet if you know the IP address for a site."

Caden recalled how his father had the IP address for a prepper blog site taped to his laptop. *But I don't know any IP addresses so I guess the Internet and the phones are unavailable for now.* He shook his head. *The government controlling and probably monitoring the calls and letters of citizens —what is the country becoming?* He pushed the thought out of his mind. "I came to offer you an assignment." He glanced about the room. Folded clothes were scattered about.

"Oh?" Turner sat beside his duffle bag.

"I'm trying to get a flight back to Washington state for Governor Monroe...."

"The presidential candidate?"

Caden nodded. "I met with David Weston, his Chief of Staff, late yesterday. He offered me a job as military liaison, if I could arrange the flight."

Turner smiled approvingly.

"And considering all the chaos, I wanted some additional security until we meet up with the Washington Guard." He held up some documents. "The base commander has already approved my plans."

Turner shook his head as he folded a shirt. "I don't know if I can help you."

Caden gestured at the neatly stacked uniforms beside a duffle bag. "Are you deploying again?"

"Rucker is being turned over to the Alabama National Guard. All regular army personnel here are being deployed west."

"West?" Caden thought for a moment. "Washington is west."

Turner shrugged. "Okay. The transfer was supposed to be confidential, but word has already leaked."

He grinned. "Well, If you're going west anyway do you have a problem with it being JBLM or Fairchild?"

Turner shook his head.

"Good." He started to say goodbye, but asked, "Do you know why you're being sent west?"

"You know that North Korea supplied material for the bombs?"

Caden nodded.

"We may be headed to Korea but," Turner shrugged, "ours is not to question why…." He continued packing.

Caden made small talk for a few moments then said, "I hope you are able to talk to your family soon."

"Thanks. I would really like to before we ship out to Korea or wherever."

Caden agreed and departed.

The rain stopped as he walked from the barracks. The clouds were thinning and the day felt brighter and warmer. The world might be falling apart, but at least he was rebuilding his life. His pace was quick as he walked down the street. As he entered the flight operations building a C-130 roared down the runway.

"Washington state?" The officer stared at the computer screen. "Yes, we have two planes tonight headed for Fairchild. One is full of cargo, the other full of soldiers." He shook his head. "Sorry, no space."

"Come on, I need a seat for a governor. This man may be the next president."

"When Monroe is president he can bump military cargo and get on the plane."

"Is space that tight?"

The officer nodded. "I might be able to get him onboard a flight, but not his entourage."

Frustration grew in Caden's gut. Governor Monroe would arrive tonight and if he was to get this job, and get home, he would need to prove his usefulness, but as of yet he had no flight and therefore no security detail either. Caden shuddered at the thought of reporting failure and then asking for a job. He tried to think of all the larger bases in the region.

"Northwest," the man mumbled as he stared at the screen. "Only Fairchild today, but…. What about Joint Base Lewis-McChord?" He said looking up. "That's in western Washington."

Caden nodded. He knew JBLM well. "How many flights are going there?"

"Oh, we have three flights tomorrow to that base."

Caden's brow shot up. "Three?"

"How many spots would you need on the plane?"

Caden thought quickly, the governor, his wife, David Weston and himself. Weston had also mentioned two Secret Service agents were with the governor. "Six and a security detail of maybe four more."

"Ten people?" He bit his lip as he scanned the computer screen. "Maybe…yes, I think I can do that, but I'll need an okay from the commanding officer."

Caden smiled as he slid the general's order across the counter.

*　　　*　　　*

Late in the afternoon Caden walked from the military police office. He unfolded his to-do list. Before the MPs had cleared him to leave, they had taken every piece of identification he had and entered it into a database. Finally, they approved him for travel and issued a red, white and blue ID badge.

"Don't lose this," one said sternly. "This is your Homeland Security ID. You will need it to cross state lines, get through checkpoints and onto any federal installation."

Caden slipped it in his pocket.

Running down his list he checked off, "Get approval from the MPs to leave." Now only 'Brief David Weston on progress,' remained on his list. Caden ambled along the road that followed the flight line. Several planes were being fueled. Dozens of military personnel with assorted trucks and tankers busied themselves about the hangers and aircraft. *All regular army personnel sent west?* A large formation of troops marching toward the flight line caught his attention. *Multiple flights to JBLM and Fairchild tomorrow. What's going on?* The image of the boiling mushroom cloud over Washington and the firestorm filled his mind. *Wars and rumors of wars.* He shuddered at the thought. *The war has already begun—and we're losing.*

Briskly he proceeded toward the refugee center. After talking with Weston he would share his good news with Maria. He approached a large asphalt lot that had been used for military formations, but the refugees had converted it into a bazaar. As he reached the edge of the market, the sun hung low in the sky casting long shadows amidst the rows of improvised stalls covered with tarps and canvas. His eyes darted from stall to stall as he walked through the market. There seemed to be some of everything there, car parts, camping supplies, computers, dishes, books and magazines. It was possible to buy food from local farms, but the price was high. Ahead was a stand with apples. He would buy one and share it with Maria over dinner that night.

As he walked away from the booth, apple in hand, he saw Maria approach with Adam on her hip. The two seemed to be attached these last few days. He waved and Maria smiled.

As she neared, her eyes seemed to twinkle in anticipation. "Did you get the job?"

"I think so." He told her that Weston had eagerly asked for his help and how he had arranged a flight to Joint Base Lewis-McChord.

"Where's that?"

"Just south of Seattle," he said with a broad grin. "So, I am out of here."

She frowned. "When do you leave?"

Caden looked toward the airfield with a smile. "Tomorrow."

"So you're leaving Adam and me behind?"

His head snapped around and he looked into her eyes. "I...ah, Adam? And you? You want to go? I hadn't thought...."

"I agree." She turned on her heels and walked briskly away.

Caden stood for a moment reviewing what had just happened. He was hurt by her anger. Admittedly he had forgotten about Adam in the excitement of the day. Perhaps subconsciously he had expected Maria to care for him. Everyone in the camp assumed she was his mother. *And me the father?* He pushed that out of his mind. *Did she say anything about wanting to go with me to Washington? No! But then has she had the chance to ask? No.*

He grunted and walked slowly along as people passed him on all sides. *They would only complicate the trip. I'm not even sure I have this job.*

Someone bumped into him. "Excuse me."

Caden didn't look up or reply. *I can't ask the governor to help strangers.* He walked in the direction she had gone, trying to decide whether to talk to her. *I don't owe her anything.* He winced. *Yes, I do.* She had saved his life and that was a debt he was honor-bound to repay. Shuffling along, his eyes fixed on the ground, he realized he had been thinking only of himself. Her company was pleasant and he wanted to share with her all he had accomplished during the day, but now he felt alone and his triumph was diminished. *It might be nice to have someone to talk to, if she wanted to come along.* Even Adam was growing on him.

From behind Caden heard a familiar voice call him.

"Were you able to make the arrangements?" David asked.

Caden briefed him on his successful day.

"That's great."

Caden smiled, but his heart was not in it.

"Come back to my camp. I've got some news stories I want you to see. I figure with your military and intel experience you might have some insights into what is going on."

Caden wanted to find Maria, talk with her, change flight arrangements so she could come with him, but he felt obliged to go with David.

As the last orange glow in the western sky faded, a C5 cargo plane lumbered along the tarmac. David led him away from the refugee camp toward the base administration buildings at the far end of the installation.

Dozens of men with shovels and two backhoes dug a trench several hundred yards long across their path.

"They're dividing this place into a secure military section and a refugee camp." David pulled a badge from his pocket and clipped it to his shirt as they crossed a makeshift bridge over the trench. "In a few days civilians will need a Homeland Security ID to get on this part of the base."

Caden glanced at the badge. It was the same type he had been issued earlier in the day.

Moments later, they walked around to the back of the administration building. "This is my new car," David said as he approached a silver Ford SUV.

Admiring the spotless car, Caden nodded.

David opened the side door. "I bought the car the day after the first attack."

Caden thought for a moment. "You flew here with Governor Monroe and after the attacks needed a way home."

David smiled. "Pretty close." He pulled out two folding chairs and motioned for Caden to sit down while he shuffled through folders on the car seat. "The Governor and I flew to Tallahassee to meet with Governor Hagen. Florida is a critical swing state. But that night...the night of the DC attack, I was meeting with campaign workers in Pensacola. I immediately contacted Monroe. We had a meeting scheduled the next day in Atlanta. He decided we should all meet there, but...well...you know what happened."

Memories of Becky on the television at that awful moment shot through his mind. Caden frowned and nodded.

With a weak grin on his face he said, "I paid for the car with a credit card."

"I don't envy your payments."

David was still for a moment. His eyes stared into the distance. "Will I ever make a payment?"

Caden shrugged and felt strangely cold.

Weston sighed and pulled a folder from the floor of the car. "Here is what I wanted you to look at." He handed it to Caden and sat beside him. "It's clippings and photocopies from newspapers mostly. Anything I thought might lend some insight into what or why this is happening."

Caden opened the folder. Several reports near the top of the stack he had already read. Setting those aside he came to an article from the Miami Herald.

A group claiming to represent the terrorists has stated the city of Detroit will be granted another twenty-four hour reprieve due to the large Muslim communities in the vicinity. This is the second announced reprieve for the largely evacuated Metropolitan area. Authorities continue to hunt for nuclear material and have intensified efforts to locate terrorists as the last residents leave the area.

Caden set the report beside him. *Interesting, but not insightful.* He picked up the next clipping.

Iran has introduced a resolution to the
United Nations Security Council authorizing the
Peoples Republic of China to enter North Korea,
occupy all nuclear facilities and dismantle
them. The North Korean government has stated
that, if the resolution is adopted, they will
allow the troops to cross their border and take
control of the facilities.

He paused and then reread the article. *I understand why the North Koreans might cooperate with the Chinese, but why would Iran care?* He rubbed his chin. *Why would China risk this kind of intervention to help us?* He thought for almost a minute while David wrote in a notebook. Finally Caden lifted his head and declared, "North Korea, Iran and China are working together on the attacks...." He paused. "And something more, I suspect."

"What?"

"I don't know, but they have a plan that is advantageous to each of them."

Two soldiers walked casually around the building, rifles slung over their shoulders. They looked at David, his badge still pinned on his shirt, smiled and nodded. They looked at Caden and stopped. "Does your friend have an ID?"

Caden fumbled in his pocket, retrieved the badge and clipped it to his shirt.

The sentries walked on.

*   *   *

Moonlight bathed the night before Caden returned to his camp. Maria and Adam were gone. With a growing sense of loss he looked about, wondering what to do when he saw the Miller's youngest daughter emerge from the shadows.

"Have you seen Maria?" he asked.

Debbie Miller stepped into the light and rested a hand on her daughter's shoulder. "I've been praying you would come."

"Can you help me find her? Do you know where she is?"

"I've been talking with her, but…." She sighed. "Maria is struggling with a lot of things right now. So many of her loved ones have died and now she feels abandoned by you…." Sadness enveloped her face. "And by God." Suddenly her eyes became stern and her voice harsh. "If you're leaving tomorrow morning perhaps it is better if you just go away."

This woman sounds like my mother. "I admit I was thinking only of myself. I don't want to leave without her, but we don't have much time."

Debbie eyes locked on Caden. "Do you care for her?"

Caden took a deep breath. Everything was happening so fast; cities burning, Becky dying and now his struggle to get home. In the midst of all of this, Adam and Maria had come into his life. *Do I care for her? She saved my life, of course I care for both her and Adam.* He exhaled slowly and nodded. "Yes, I do."

Minutes later, he stood before Maria as she sat leaning against a car with Adam asleep on her lap.

"I'm sorry," he started, "I owe you…."

"You don't owe me anything." Her voice tinged with anger.

"Yes I do, but it never occurred to me that you might want to leave with me."

Maria tipped up her head and stared at him. A cold, haughty, laugh escaped her lips. "Do you think I want to stay here—in this mud hole?" Her voice grew louder. "How cold do you think I am?" She looked at Adam as her words fell to a whisper. "My parents were murdered here."

Words stumbled from his mouth as Caden attempted in vain to reply.

"Fly off with the governor. Adam and I will do fine."
She looked at him with fire in her eyes. "I didn't kill that man
to save your life. I did it for myself—for my father, my mother
and for Adam." She gestured wildly toward the airfield.
"Leave!"

Caden started to speak, but changed his mind and walked
into the darkness.

Chapter Seven

Caden lugged two duffle bags from the terminal and dropped them on the tarmac near the plane. The loadmaster and two airmen pushed crates up the ramp at the rear of the Air Force C-130.

He hardly noticed the activity. *Nine days ago.* A mere nine days had passed since Caden walked happily down that Washington D.C. street thinking everything was right with the world. So much had gone wrong in a week and a half. Mentally he kicked himself for making things worse. He should have been quicker getting to Becky. He should have insisted she leave Atlanta. He should have found a way around the roadblock and not fallen asleep in the convenience store parking lot.

While the emotional part of him wallowed in guilt, reason told him that he had done all he could to save Becky. Yes, he could be a thoughtless jerk, but he had tried desperately to reach her.

He looked up and down the empty tarmac. *My thoughtlessness hurt Maria.* He sighed deeply. So many people he cared about had been hurt or killed and the memories of the dead pressed down on him. *God, just get me through this day.*

A door opened at the terminal, interrupting his bleak memories. A soldier stepped onto the runway followed closely by a Secret Service agent. As he watched, another soldier and David Weston exited the terminal. Next a silver-haired man in an expensive, but creased, business suit appeared—Governor Monroe. Caden had attended several conferences with Senator Stevens that the Governor had also attended, but had never been formally introduced. Monroe looked back at the door as a lady, about the age of the governor emerged. Caden assumed she was Monroe's wife. David talked to both of them as another soldier appeared with the second Secret Service agent. The group of passengers, now complete, moved as one toward the aircraft.

As the Governor approached Caden said, "We should be ready to leave in twenty minutes."

"Thank you." The Governor's eyes scanned the length of the plane. "You're Mr. Westmore?"

"Yes, sir."

"You did a good job arranging this flight."

Caden was about to thank him when the lady he'd noticed moments before linked her arm in Monroe's and asked. "Who is this, Daniel?"

He smiled gently, and touched her hand. "Oh forgive me." The Governor introduced his wife Celeste.

She shook his hand, "Where are you from?"

"I'm from Washington, Ma'am."

"Oh? D.C. or Evergreen?"

Caden smiled, "The Evergreen state, Ma'am. I grew up in Hansen, a small town southeast of Olympia in the mountains. I still have family there."

She grinned. "I do believe I've visited your town. Isn't there a ski resort nearby?"

"Yes," Caden nodded. "That and tourism are the only real industries since the collapse of the logging business."

The Governor chuckled and held up his hand. "That was another administration."

Small talk continued for several minutes until the loadmaster announced, "You can board now."

Caden grabbed his duffle bags and walked up the access ramp with the others. He dropped the load near the front and exited the plane. His eyes drifted back toward the refugee camp and then to his watch. Slowly he stepped up the ramp jingling the keys in his pocket. *I should have done something with my car.* He looked up and down the runway, then walked to the top of the ramp. Again, he paused and was about to board, when he heard a vehicle race down the tarmac. Turning he saw a jeep screech to a halt near the bottom of the ramp.

A soldier quickly exited the jeep with a duffle bag and full kit and jogged into the plane. Turner and Maria sat in the back talking. Caden wanted to rush up to Maria and hurry her onboard, but he paused as Turner continued to talk to her. The surrounding noise drowned out their voices. Maria stared down at Adam as she bounced him softly on her knee. The driver glanced over to Caden with a bored expression. Turner stepped from the jeep and with his kit walked toward Caden and the plane.

"I got her this far," Turner said as he ambled up.

Caden looked at Maria, sitting in the back of the jeep. He wondered what he could say to her. He thanked Turner then asked him, "What took you so long?"

Turner's right brow shot up. "She wouldn't come! Said she wasn't going anywhere and didn't want to talk to you."

Caden's heart sank. He had only minutes to convince her to go with him.

Turner groaned. "And when she finally did get in the jeep she didn't have one of those Homeland Security IDs." He shook his head. "If I didn't know the guard on duty she wouldn't be here now." Turner put his hand on Caden's shoulder. "She's quite the spitfire," then he continued onto the plane.

As Caden walked toward Maria he wondered what Turner had said to get her this far.

Maria sat stiff and unmoving, like a statue.

As Caden approached he tried to look her in the eye, but her eyes moved only to the baby.

"Will you look at me?"

Neither her eyes nor her lips moved.

The turbines whined as the pilot brought the engines to life. *Great, now it will be even more difficult to talk.* "We don't have much time…." It was almost a shout.

"I've lost everything. All I have is time."

"I'm sorry you…."

"Don't feel sorry for me," she yelled over the roar of the engines.

Caden shook his head. "That is not what I meant." In a voice both calmer and steadier than he felt he said, "I respect you too much to feel sorry for you."

She glanced at him with just the slightest hint of a smile, but her eyes quickly returned to Adam.

"I am sorry. I'm sorry that I was thoughtless, but I do want you to come because…." He tried to find words, but he couldn't. He wished he merely said he wanted her to come and left it there, but he hadn't. He had started to say something more, and now he didn't know what that was. He wanted her to come because she had saved his life. He wanted her to come because she was resourceful and he enjoyed her company, but for some reason he didn't wanted to say more than that. "…because I miss your big brown eyes and I want you with me."

Finally she met his gaze. "If you want me to come, I want to go with you."

"I want you to come." He looked at Adam. "I want you both to come." Caden held out his hand for her.

A smile lit her face. She dropped the baby bag into his hand, and walked to the plane.

Caden grinned and reached into the jeep to grab her duffle bag. One bag over each shoulder he followed her onto the plane.

Cargo filled the center of the aircraft, except for the most forward part. Even in this front section, smaller crates were strapped down in the center, but he could at least see over it. Bunched together at the front, everyone sat along the windowless fuselage.

Looking at the cargo and the simple web seats Maria said, "I've flown economy before, but this...."

Caden smiled, "Welcome to Air Mobility Command. No movie, no peanuts and no drinks." He bent down to help Maria strap Adam in a seat. "For entertainment you can watch the pilot fly the plane." They both looked toward the cockpit; no door or wall separated it from the aft part of the aircraft.

Maria continued to look forward as Caden's eyes drifted back to her face. When she turned and their eyes met, his face flushed. He sat down next to her. As the plane rolled down the runway, Caden turned to her. "The other day you mentioned brothers and sisters are any...ah, still...."

Slowly she shook her head. "They were all in Atlanta."

The aircraft lifted off.

Maria smiled, but her face was filled with sadness. "Mom and Dad had come to get me. I was in my senior year at the University of North Florida in Jacksonville.

Caden heard the landing gear retracting and then the thud and clunk that told him they were up and locked.

"Grandma and Grandpa were driving my brothers and sisters to the lake house we have in southern Georgia." A tear ran down Maria's cheek. "We were all going to stay there." She paused, put her hand to her lips and took a deep breath. "Dad was talking to them on his cell phone. Grandpa was still in the heart of the city on I-75 when it happened."

Caden squeezed her hand. "I'm sorry. I lost someone in Atlanta too."

She wiped the tear from her face. "I thought you had."

"Really? Why?"

"From the look on your face every time someone mentions the city." She paused. "Did you love her?"

"Yes. Yes I did."

The pilot announced they were at cruising altitude, and if they needed to move around they could. David Weston walked back. The plane bounced a bit, and he grabbed a cargo strap to steady himself. He first glanced at Maria then fixed his eyes on Caden. "The Governor would like to talk to you."

Caden realized he was still holding Maria's hand, but did not pull it back. "I'll be right there."

Weston walked away.

Caden frowned. "I am sorry about…well, everything."

"I know," she said with a nod.

He felt the keys in his pocket press against his leg. "I should have given my car to the Millers."

"I did."

"What?"

"I gave them the spare key you gave me and told them if I didn't come back, the car and everything in it was theirs."

They both laughed.

"Go on," she took her hand away, "don't keep the boss waiting."

As Caden walked aft, the Governor retrieved a briefcase from under his seat and stood. He motioned for Caden to follow him, and together they moved toward the rear of the plane.

"David gives you high marks for logic and analysis and I've come to trust his opinion." The governor sat near the rear of the plane and Caden took a seat leaving one between them.

The Governor opened his briefcase. "I've asked my staff back in Olympia to start a special background investigation on you, but considering the current chaos, who knows when that will be completed." He pulled out a folder marked SECRET in bold red letters. "I know you were Military Legislative Assistant for Senator Stevens." Setting the folder on the briefcase he paused. "I spoke with him several times regarding foreign policy. He appeared very knowledgeable."

"Yes, he was smart, well read and," Caden smiled, "he had a good staff."

The Governor grinned. "I'm sure he did." His eyes drifted away and the smile left his face. "He seemed like a good man."

Caden nodded. "He was."

Monroe took a deep breath, then exhaled. "So many have died." He shook his head slowly. "You were also in Special Forces. Both those jobs require a clearance."

"Yes."

"Thankfully both NSA and CIA headquarters have survived and the intelligence community is functioning. Homeland Security stopped the terrorists in New York and Detroit."

The last news Caden had was that no bomb had gone off in Detroit, but he hadn't heard that the city had been secured. "The terrorists in Detroit—they've been caught?"

The Governor nodded and handed the folder to Caden. "I'd like you to look at some intelligence and give me your analysis."

Caden carefully read the stack of news stories, handwritten notes and classified documents. Many of the newspaper articles were ones David had already shown him, or he had read earlier, but he was vigilant to review the details.

Finally, he glanced at his watch, put down the last sheet, and looked at the Governor. "No terrorist organization has the money or expertise to assemble and transport these nuclear bombs." He looked the Governor in the eye. "This kind of attack takes money, a large covert network, and extensive planning. This is state sponsored terrorism, but it is bigger than North Korea or Iran."

"Who?"

The plane shuddered and Caden grabbed the seat webbing. "Like I said to David yesterday, I'm certain North Korea, China, Iran and maybe someone else are all working together.   We know that North Korea supplied the plutonium." He paused. "I can't prove it, but my guess is that North Korea is a pawn of China. This isn't the end game, this is mid-game maneuvering." Caden paused then asked, "Are we repositioning troops in prelude to an attack on North Korea?"

"I don't know.   Iran sponsored a Security Council declaration that allows United Nations inspectors, along with the Chinese army and technicians, into the North to dismantle all nuclear installations."

"I read that it had been introduced." Caden thought for a moment. "Did it pass?"

The governor shrugged. "Last I heard it was before the Security Council."

"I believe it will pass—the Chinese won't veto it."

The Governor's eyebrow shot up. "Why would China use North Korea and then help us?"

"They're not helping us. They're covering their tracks."

Reflecting on his words Caden was certain he sounded like a conspiracy nut, but he couldn't put all the parts together. He rubbed his chin. "I need more information about what China and Iran are doing right now. Do you have current intel?"

"Yes, back in Olympia."

"Then can we resume this when we get there?"

Putting the folder away the Governor nodded. "Certainly."

Back in his seat beside Maria, Caden did what he always did on flights; he slept. Only when the pilot announced they were on approach to JBLM did he awaken.

"How do you sleep in these web seats?" Maria asked.

"Years of practice," he said stretching sore muscles. "I'm glad you are here."

"I knew you were a good man even before we met."

"Huh?"

"I was watching the day the two guys tried to rob you."

"What has that got to do with staying with me or…"

"You were trying to figure out how to change diapers."

Caden smiled. "Yeah, so?"

"Bad men don't change diapers."

He laughed.

"Then, later that night, when you told me Adam wasn't your son, that his mother had died in an accident and you were caring for him—only a good man would do that."

Caden smiled and gently squeezed her hand.

"I'm glad you wanted me to come."

Maria held on to his hand, looked at him and smiled.

His feelings for Maria grew stronger by the day, but it angered him. *Becky was alive a week ago.*

White light shot from the cockpit momentarily filling the plane.

"What was that?" Maria asked.

The plane lurched to the right, then abruptly to the left.

Luggage, blankets and boxes flew about.

Someone screamed.

Alarms blared.

Adam wailed.

Maria grabbed the straps that held Adam.

Caden tightened Maria's belt.

The plane rolled to the side.

Caden hurtled across the fuselage.

Chapter Eight

There was a vague awareness of self. Images of fire, mushroom clouds, scarlet blood and black death stormed through the mind and then melted into pools of oblivion. An indeterminate time later a sweet voice flowed into the void. The words gave comfort, but like voices heard in the distance the mind could not grasp the meaning. The mind cried out to reach the gentle sound without knowing how or why.

Gradually images of a family mixed with dreams of Maria and a toddler named Adam. Once again he heard her and strove to comprehend. When the melody of her voice stopped, he fought against the darkness to reach her.

His head ached, like someone pressing hard against the side of his skull. As if for the first time he became aware that his eyes were closed. A constant beeping annoyed him. *Someone turn it off.*

Slowly he opened his eyes. Plain white sheets were pulled neatly up to his chest. Wires ran from various places on his body to a monitor that continued to beep and irritate him. Metal railings lined either side of the bed. A simple nightstand was beside him and a gray metal chair stood near a door. In the corner sat a cot with a rumpled blanket.

Gently he rubbed his bandaged head. Shifting slightly he looked out the window. The sun was not visible from his position, but the sky was clear blue and light flowed into the room. *Where am I? A plane, I was on a plane. What happened?*

The door creaked.

"You're awake!" With a huge smile on her face Maria zipped into the room. "Nurse," she stopped and turned toward the open door, "he's awake." She came closer with Adam in her arms and the nurse was right behind.

"How do you feel?" Maria asked.

"Okay, I guess. How long have I been out?"

"Almost two days," The nurse checked the monitor. Gesturing toward Maria with her pen, she continued. "Your wife and son have been here around the clock."

"Huh?"

Continuing to write she made a slight gesture with her head. "They both slept in that cot for the last two nights."

Maria quickly smiled and bounced Adam on her hip. "We both wanted to be here when Daddy woke up."

Wife? He reached up and felt the bump on his head. *Do I have amnesia?* He was reasonably sure he didn't. *What's she doing?* He looked at Maria. Her face was flushed and wore a forced grin. He decided to play along—for now. "Oh, that's nice." His eyes shifted between Maria and the nurse. "What happened?" They had been on approach to JBLM. Alarms had gone off. "We crashed." It was both a statement and a question.

Maria shook her head, then seemed to change her mind. "Well, almost. You strapped me in as the plane rolled on its side." She told him how he was thrown across the plane, hit his head and then, bleeding from the wound, tumbled about as the pilot righted the craft and made a hard, but successful, landing.

The nurse hung the chart on the bed. "I've got to notify the doctor." She hurried from the room leaving the door ajar.

Caden could see that Maria and Adam were fine, but he asked, "Was anyone else hurt?"

Maria nodded. "Yes. The pilot has two cracked ribs, the Governor's wife dislocated her arm, there were lots of bruises and some cuts, but you got the worst of the injuries."

Caden sighed with relief. There had been so much death these last few days. He didn't want to mourn anyone else. "I want to see..."

"Everyone else has already been discharged. The Governor and his staff have gone to Olympia and Turner and his men flew to Fairchild. I'm sure they enjoyed getting on a plane so soon after that landing. I don't think I'll ever step on a plane again."

He reached up and felt the bandages and his sore head. "What caused the plane to crash or land hard or whatever?"

"Seattle."

His head pounded again. "Seattle caused our plane to crash?" Then he understood. "Seattle is gone?"

"Yes, well, part of it. The bomb was on a boat in...what do they call all that water?"

"Puget Sound?"

"Yes. The terrorists were out on Puget Sound and the authorities found out about them. Their boat must not have been in position when they detonated it. The wave from the blast caused a lot of damage to the port area, there were fires and radiation but fortunately the damage was less than in other cities."

"Oh." He looked at the electronics beeping and blinking in the room.

She seemed to anticipate his question. "The plane was still a couple thousand feet in the air. You might remember, we saw a flash when it happened."

He shook his head.

She moved toward the door. "News reports say there was only limited damage in Tacoma, mostly in the port area, and people in Olympia didn't even see the flash or get hit by the pulse."

Checking along the rails he found the controller and inclined the head of the bed. He gently propped himself up and discovered, through pain, bruises on his legs and torso.

"I'm really glad you're okay," Maria shut the door. Again her face flushed. "Ah...I suppose you want to know why the nurse thinks we're married."

"I've got to admit I'm a bit curious about when that might have happened."

"When they brought you in, I came along." She grinned sheepishly. "I guess I was pretty frantic. They asked me to sign some papers and I realized they thought I was your wife. I didn't want them to wait while they sorted things out so I signed as Mrs. Maria Westmore."

He felt he should be annoyed by her deception, but all that emerged from him was a laugh.

"And besides as your wife they let me stay here." She looked about. "This room is warm, they have clean, running water and the food in the cafeteria is good."

He shook his head. "If hospital food is now considered good, then the world as we know it is finished." He rubbed his chin. "And David and the Governor? They think we're married?"

She nodded. "Did you ever say otherwise?"

He thought for a moment. "No," he said slowly, "but I'm a bit embarrassed."

"Why?" she said with irritation in her voice and eyes.

"When Lieutenant Turner escorted you to the plane at Fort Rucker, they must have thought we were having a serious marital quarrel."

She smiled enigmatically. "We were."

*   *   *

Caden flipped through the channels. New York had been spared and was once again the nation's capital, but of much more significance to him at that moment was that the city was the home of several news networks and they were all back on the air.

"Turn it down some, please."

Caden glanced at Maria.

She pointed to the baby sleeping on the cot. "It's going to wake Adam."

He pressed the volume button.

Someone knocked on the door.

Adam cried.

Maria sighed.

Caden looked at her, a portrait of exasperation and shrugged. "Come in."

Governor Monroe smiled as he stepped into the room. "I hear you're recovering well."

"Thankfully I have a hard head," he said, muting the television. "I thought you had gone to Olympia."

Maria took the crying baby from the room as Governor Monroe pulled up a chair and sat beside Caden's bed. "I did, but I wanted to see you before you were released and headed home. He made small talk for a minute and then said, "On the plane you spoke of North Korea and China working together."

Caden nodded.

"You also said that the Security Council resolution to allow Chinese technicians and troops into North Korea would pass."

"If my theory is right then yes, it should pass." Caden sat up more in the bed. "Did it?"

The governor nodded.

"Then I expect North Korea to attack the south very soon."

"Why?"

"That was the price North Korea extracted from China."

The governor moved his chair closer. "I've got to admit, I don't follow."

"China is behind all of this, but they need plausible deniability, so they tell the North Korean government to supply the fissionable material."

"But the North has sold nuclear technology before, why do you think China is behind these attacks?"

"The North has a reputation for selling to the highest bidder, but they're not stupid. They know if the material is used for attacks against us it'll be traced back to them and we would certainly retaliate."

"So why would they do it?"

"The North's economy is in a shambles." Caden gestured with his right hand for North Korea and his left for China. "They need the money that China would pay for their cooperation, but I'm sure they demanded two more things."

Monroe looked confused. "What?"

"First, the protection they get from this U.N. resolution."

"How does a Chinese invasion protect them?"

"It's not really an invasion. The Chinese are probably retrieving nuclear processing equipment they loaned to the North, but the Chinese can state to the world that they are there by request of the United Nations and assisting UN inspectors. However," Caden wagged his finger, "we can't attack the North without killing Chinese troops and U.N. inspectors who are there by authority of the United Nations."

The governor nodded. "I see."

"And since we can't attack North Korea without killing Chinese soldiers and U.N. personnel, the North is free to attack South Korea."

Monroe swore and rubbed his chin.

"It's really just an educated guess. I could be wrong about…."

He held up his hand. "No, no. I think you are right. North Korea has been cooperating with China and the United Nations, but they have been protesting alleged incursions by South Korea for the last two days."

"I haven't heard this on the news?"

Monroe looked Caden in the eye. "President Durant declared martial law in much of the country. News is being censored."

"The first amendment…."

The Governor shook his head. "Officially the 'Homeland Security Advisors' are there to keep the media from reporting anything helpful to terrorists, and I guess they do that, but nothing that puts Durant or what is left of the federal government in a bad light gets past them."

Caden shook his head. His country was dying in more ways than he had imagined.

Maria entered the room holding a sleeping Adam, and sat on the cot.

Monroe smiled at Maria as she sat down. "Durant is right to restore the federal government," he said turning back to Caden, "but not at the expense of liberty." He looked Caden firmly in the eye. "Things will change when I'm elected in November."

Caden nodded. "You've got my vote."

"Thank you." His faced relaxed into a smile. "However, there is another reason I'm here," the Governor said in a more upbeat tone, "I've got to get back to Olympia, but before I leave I wanted to ask you to join my advisory staff, if you're up to it."

Caden smiled. "This is a great opportunity—joining the team of the leading presidential candidate...."

"Actually, at the moment, I'm the only candidate."

Caden's mind raced for a moment and then recalled. The other candidate had been Senator Horton. He would have been at the joint session of Congress on the night of the bombing. "Oh, yes."

"Will you join me?"

Caden was unsure why, but he looked at Maria.

She shrugged.

"Yes, I would be proud to work for the next president."

"Great. I'm heading back to Olympia this afternoon. I talked with the nurse on duty. She tells me you should be released tomorrow. Meet me at my office in the capitol when you get there. I'll just keep you a little while and then you can head home and check on your family." They shook hands and then the governor stood, nodded to Maria, and left the room.

Caden turned and smiled at Maria. "It will be nice to get home." As he said it, he realized his home was not her home. "Well, when we get to my house...it'll be nice for you too." His face burned. "You'll like it...they'll like you."

"I know what you mean. I'm fine now. I'll be fine there too."

Again he smiled, grateful for her understanding heart. Slowly his eyes lifted to the still muted television. The caption at the bottom of the screen said, "Presidential Press Secretary." There behind the podium stood Rebecca Thornton—Becky.

Caden pushed buttons wildly attempting to turn on the sound.

"What's wrong?" Maria asked.

"Ah, nothing…"

Chapter Nine

C aden looked out the window. Rays of light shone through the trees at the edge of the hospital grounds. *The day has been bright, but now the sun is setting.* Returning his gaze to the television, he continued his fruitless flipping from one channel to the next. For several hours he had searched the networks for more video or information about Becky, but all he found was that one brief sound bite that told him she was alive. How had she escaped Atlanta? How had she become President Durant's press secretary? Why was she working for Durant? He had no answers, but he was determined to find them.

*   *   *

Maria told him that many of the soldiers from the base had deployed to provide security and assistance for a wave of refugees moving south, away from the Seattle destruction and contamination, but none of that made it into the news. All he had seen on TV was stories of the valiant Coast Guardsmen who pursued the terrorists and lost their lives in the blast. He was sure that medical facilities were overwhelmed and the doctor had more urgent tasks than to release him, but he was anxious to go.

The doctor finally appeared around ten the next morning. After examining Caden he said, "You have a concussion. Two weeks ago I would have kept you another day, but…well…you'll be fine."

He scribbled notes on the medical chart. "Get a copy of your record when you leave, and see a doctor when you get home."

Caden nodded.

Maria left Adam on the bed with Caden and returned moments later with a wheelchair.

"I don't need that," Caden said.

"It's a rule," the doctor mumbled. "Just till you're out the door."

If you're well enough to go home why do they make you use a wheelchair? Another one of life's great mysteries.

After the doctor departed, Caden said, "Let's get packed."

"I'm done."

"Okay, I'll get started."

It didn't take them long to pack his duffle bag. As they folded and locked the bag he asked, "Where's my gun?"

"Military police," She retrieved a slip of paper from her pocket. "They have it. The officer said you could get it when you leave."

Caden grumbled as he looked at the receipt for his gun. *I guess I wouldn't expect the Army to allow patients to keep guns in a hospital.* They would have to stop by the MP office as they left.

As soon as they were out the door Caden stood—and wobbled. *Okay, you do have a concussion.* He touched the edge of the wheelchair to steady himself. *Take things a bit slower.* He had planned to sling the duffle bag over his shoulder and march away from the hospital, but dizziness changed his mind. He dropped the bag on the sidewalk while Maria returned the chair to the hospital.

They walked slowly to the military police office adjacent to the front gate. Several dozen people packed the small lobby of the office when they arrived. Every chair was filled. After several minutes an older man waved Maria over.

"You must be tired carrying that baby," he said. "Take my seat."

"I couldn't."

He pointed to a young man near the head of the line. "That's my son. We won't be here that much longer."

"Thank you," she said, sitting down.

For more than an hour the line inched forward. Caden was hungry, but close to the front of the line when he felt a hand rest on his shoulder. Maria stood beside him. "You should have stayed seated."

"My butt is sore."

Caden nodded. His feet were sore.

Up ahead they heard, "I'm here to see my client."

The MP behind the counter said, "May I see your security badge?"

"Why? You know me."

"Orders," he said as if it were the millionth time. "That's all."

The man pulled out his badge.

Maria's eyes widened as she whispered. "I don't have one of those badges."

"Don't worry. It's my gun. They don't need to talk to you."

Five minutes later Caden was at the head of the line. Placing his badge and the receipt on the counter he explained they had his revolver.

The corporal nodded. "Are you heading directly off base?"

"Yes."

"I need either military or homeland identification and a concealed carry permit." He pulled out a form. "Fill this out while I get your weapon."

When the corporal returned Caden noticed the gun was unloaded. "Where's the bullets?"

"You don't really expect us to give you a gun *and* the bullets do you?" The corporal paused for just a moment. "Keep it concealed until you are out the gate and clear of the sentries. If they see the gun they will take it from you or worse."

The corporal looked past Caden. "Are you with this man?"

Maria nodded.

"May I see your badge?"

"Why?" Caden asked.

He sighed. "Orders, that's all."

"I don't have one."

"You can't be on the base without one."

"I was on the plane that landed during the attack on Seattle."

"Boarding an interstate flight requires a Homeland Security badge. Do you have a passport?"

She shook her head.

Concern crossed his face. "Maybe a driver's license?"

Maria smiled and quickly pulled it from her pocket.

His eyes remained fixed on the license. "I'm sorry this doesn't meet the requirements of the Real ID law. "Lieutenant, could you come here?"

While the two MPs talked, Caden's concern grew.

"Do you have any other identification?" the Lieutenant asked.

"No."

"Anyone on base without proper ID must be taken into custody." The Lieutenant looked at Maria and shrugged. "Orders. Sorry."

Mari's eyes begged Caden to find a solution. "You better take Adam."

Anger and adrenaline flowed. Caden's every muscle was taut. He wanted to punch the two soldiers in the room, but knew it would solve nothing. Reluctantly he took the now crying Adam into his arms.

*   *   *

Gray clouds darkened the sky as Caden stumbled into his barracks room late in the afternoon. Without turning on a light he laid Adam on a blanket. "Kid, you sure are heavy. How does Maria carry you around all day?" After caring for the child, Caden collapsed in a chair.

He reviewed the day. The one bright spot was that he was able to get this barracks room. Most soldiers were deployed.

He had to admit that the MPs had been polite—but firm. They had escorted them into the back and reviewed their story. Caden tried to phone Governor Monroe, but the phone's screen was black, the battery dead. The lieutenant let him use his, but Caden reached only a secretary at Monroe's office. Everyone he talked to informed him it was illegal to board an interstate flight, cross state lines or enter a government facility without some type of Real ID, preferably a Homeland Security badge or a passport. As far as the military police and the Office of Special Investigations were concerned she would remain in custody until it was determined how and why she had boarded the flight. Caden tried to get an appointment with the Base Commander, but he refused to see him. He had no idea how to help Maria.

Adam slept surrounded by bundles of blankets. Caden picked up a newspaper someone had left and attempted to read, but he just stared at the page. He tossed the paper aside and grabbed the TV remote and clicked from one news program to another. He zoomed past one station, then paused and tapped the controller back. *Lyon Chapfield.* He sneered as he remembered the many times they had spoken. *He's so far out in left field he's in the bleachers.*

He was about to move to another channel when Lyon's words caught his attention.

"Tonight in closing I feel I must speak out about the security policies of President Durant."

Here it comes, commentary from the lunatic left.

"I do not argue with the need to apprehend the terrorists who have murdered hundreds of thousands and destroyed eight major cities, but in the process of waging this war we have become a police state."

Caden focused on the screen. A few weeks ago he would have laughed at the idea of America being a police state, but with Maria in jail he found himself nodding in agreement.

"Homeland Security badges required for travel from state to state, long distance phone lines and Internet service seized and shutdown except for government use and now," Chapfield looked to his right, "government censors at the network…."

Caden heard pounding in the studio.

Chapfield's words were rushed. "All this in the name of security. Well, it was Benjamin Franklin who said, 'Those who would give up essential liberty to purchase a little temporary safety…,'" Chapfield looked to the side, "They…deserve…" Shouts came from off screen. The network logo appeared on the TV accompanied by soft music.

Caden finished the quote. "…deserve neither liberty nor safety." He stared at the screen as the music continued. His stomach knotted. Had doors been busted down? It sounded like it. Had the 'Homeland Security Advisors' taken Chapfield off the air, arrested him, for speaking his mind?

Caden turned off the sound, but kept on the television while he tried to absorb all that had happened both on the screen and in his life. The agony of the terrorist attacks had morphed America into something unrecognizable. His eyes were open but all he saw were visions of fire and death in the nation's capital, refugees trudging along the highways, Becky on the television followed by static. *There is a need for security, but censors busting down doors?*

He shook his head. Maria languished in jail because she didn't have proper travel documents, but she was not a terrorist; even Chapfield was not the enemy. *Do I agree with Lyon Chapfield?* His mind rebelled at the thought. After some deliberation he concluded they had a mutual agreement with Benjamin Franklin.

Caden's father would say that rights were God given; that government could not take them away but, in every practical sense, the government was taking away rights.

Caden had learned the habit of reading newspapers and watching the news from his father. Politics, current events, God and liberty were often topics of dinner table discussion— at least among Dad, Caden and his younger brother and sister. He smiled as he recalled the many times his mother asked, "Can't we talk about things normal families discuss at dinner?"

Since leaving home he had remained informed about politics and current events. Home. God. Liberty. These had been taken for granted and now seemed so distant, so elusive. "God help me. Help Maria."

Thoughts of Maria merged into thoughts of family. *I should phone my parents.* Once again he imagined how the conversation might go. Who's Maria? Why is she in jail? They think you're married? Who's Adam? But, he decided to call anyway. He flipped open his phone, and then remembered it was dead. He dug through his duffle bag, found the charger and dialed. The number rang and rang, but there was no answer. He swore and Adam stirred. Caden remembered the many times his dad had said, "if someone really wants to talk to me, they'll call back." *Dad, get an answering machine.* He looked through the phone address book for his brother or sister's number, but was embarrassed to conclude he had never entered them. They had always communicated online and now that was impossible.

He leaned back in his chair, eyes closed in frustration. When he opened them the network had returned to news. He turned on the sound and watched as a man he had never seen before introduced stories of FEMA work in refugee camps, government food distribution and how Homeland Security had apprehended five more terrorists. There was no mention of Lyon Chapfield or growing tension in Asia. Caden turned off the television and threw the remote aside.

His eyes drifted to the window as the sun dipped below the horizon. He continued to watch as inky blackness spread across the sky. Caden imagined demons, released by the bombs, pouring out from the gloom of the cities. As they raced across the land they spread terror and consumed all light and hope.

Like a drowning man, his thoughts reached toward Maria. Desperately he yearned for her to be with him, to lift him from the blackness. He was conflicted and confused that it was not Becky that he wanted by his side.

He called home again, but the ring this time was strange and no one answered. A long night stretched out before him. In a desperate attempt to push back the darkness he turned on the lamp beside him and there in a small pool of light he sat as the demons overtook the world and sleep slowly overtook him.

Loud knocking roused Caden from his chair. He stumbled toward the door as he wiped sleep from his eyes and then his mouth on his sleeve. Finding the knob he opened the door and squinted at the fresh-faced private who stood before him.

"Are you Caden Westmore?"

"Yes."

"General Collins would like to see you."

"Who?"

"The base commander."

"He would? Now? What time is it?"

"Eight thirty." The private looked Caden up and down, "In the morning."

"Give me a minute." He stumbled toward the bathroom. As he passed the still sleeping Adam an unpleasant aroma hit him. "Unless you want to change a diaper, I'll need a few more minutes."

*   *   *

His face washed and shaved, Caden hurried up the steps to the Administration building wearing his least creased clothes and with a more pleasant smelling Adam in his arms. Once inside the secretary had offered to look after the baby, but Caden felt Adam might be helpful in getting Maria released, after all a mother should be with her child.

As Caden entered the office he saw two men. A silver-haired general sat behind the desk. Ribbons on his uniform told of battles fought and won. A lieutenant, a few years younger than Caden, stood to the side of the desk. On his chest were a mere two ribbons. Caden looked squarely at the General. "Thank you for seeing me, sir."

The General nodded and gestured for Caden to sit. Looking at a file he said, "I hadn't planned on seeing you, Mr. Westmore. Frankly, I have more important things to do."

He bounced Adam on his knee. "Well, I appreciate you taking the time."

"You're here because we have a mutual friend."

"Oh?"

"Governor Monroe called me yesterday afternoon."

Caden was pleased his message had gotten through.

"The governor and I have known each other for some time. We talked for nearly an hour about the terrorist attacks, establishing refugee camps, emergency food distribution, coordination with FEMA and," he paused, "your wife."

A momentary urge to tell the General they weren't married was quickly suppressed.

The General picked up his coffee cup. "This morning I was still drinking my first cup when his chief-of-staff called me." He took a sip. "The only thing he wanted to discuss was getting your wife released."

Caden stifled a smile.

The General leaned back in his chair. "That's when I decided to get this sorted out early." He opened a file on his desk then gestured toward the lieutenant. "CID can't find a marriage certificate. Now, that doesn't surprise me considering all the cities that have been attacked, but something does confuse me." He looked Caden square in the eye. "The Lieutenant here tells me that just days ago you were working for Senator Stevens in Washington DC and that at about the same time the young lady we have in custody was a student at the University of North Florida."

Caden's heart pounded.

The general looked carefully at Adam and then at Caden. "And is this your child?" He leaned back in his chair, but his eyes remained fixed.

Blood pulsed in Caden's ears.

"Care to put all those pieces together for me, son?"

Chapter Ten

How many times had his mother told him, "If you tell a lie you have to tell more lies to cover it up?" He had forgotten her words for a time and now he was faced with a decision, either tell a whopper of a lie or come clean and face the consequences. Caden was not worried about his own situation. What could the General do? Tell the Lieutenant to cuff him and throw him in the stockade for lying about being married? The military had more important things to do right now. Maria was the one in jail, the one without proper documents. She might be labeled a security risk. Her freedom might well depend on what he did in the next few seconds.

The General stared with an emotionless gaze.

God help Maria. Caden took a deep breath and let it out slowly. He looked at the baby on his knee. "Adam's mother was a refugee. She was walking along an Alabama highway with thousands of others when she was hit by a car. We tried to save her, but she died. I found the baby near her body and have been taking care of him since."

No emotion crossed the General's face. "Go on."

"The first time I saw Maria was when she saved my life—and Adam's." He went on to explain about the robbers and that he later found out they had killed Maria's parents.

The general's eyes narrowed. "She tracked down and shot one of the killers who murdered her parents?"

Caden nodded.

A hint of a smile flashed across his face. "Go on."

"Maria…well, she developed a bond with Adam that night. She's as protective and attached as any mother. I think for the first few days she stayed with me because I had Adam. By the time I met up with Governor Monroe's staff everyone thought we were a family. It's my fault everybody assumed we were married. I should have said something, but…." Caden leaned back in the chair and sighed.

The General nodded. "My parents taught me that there are two kinds of lies, those of commission, where someone voices a lie, and of omission, where someone remains silent and allows others to believe something that is not true. You have managed to do both and in the process attempted to deceive me and my friend, Governor Monroe."

Caden felt like a child caught and scolded by a teacher. He wondered if, telling the truth, he had done the right thing for Maria.

General Collins looked through the pages of the file then at the Lieutenant. "Is that essentially the story she told you?"

"Yes sir, except she said it was her fault she had no identification and that people believed they were married."

The smile returned to the general's face, but this time it remained. "That's some woman you found. I wouldn't cross her." He stared at Caden for a moment. "You owe Governor Monroe an explanation."

"Yes, sir."

The general closed the folder. "Frankly your petty deception is a waste of my time. I don't care whether you are married or single or shacked up or whatever. I just need to know whether the people on my base are a threat to security or not—and I think she is not." He turned to the Lieutenant. "Release her and get them both off my base."

*   *   *

A cold, gray sky greeted Caden as he followed two military policemen to a jeep outside the building. He sat in the back with Adam as the soldiers drove to the barracks. Drizzle dotted the windshield. He stepped from the vehicle and shivered. Adam whimpered. In his room he pulled out a jacket for himself and wrapped the still whining infant in several blankets.

Caden dropped the duffle bags into the jeep and in moments was whisked out to a main road, past the Post Exchange and then by a closed gas station.

"Why is the gas station closed?"

"There hasn't been a delivery since the day before Seattle was hit," The driver said.

"Within minutes of that attack the line at the station stretched for over a mile," the other MP continued. "By the end of the day there wasn't any gas left."

As they approached the main gate, Caden remembered that he had been required to leave his pistol behind when Maria was arrested. He asked the driver to stop. "I need to get something from the MPs."

Grabbing his duffle bags from the back of the jeep Caden asked, "Will my...ah, Maria be brought here?"

The driver shrugged, "Maria? I was just told to get you to the main gate."

He nodded in understanding.

"Good luck," the driver said and drove off.

Caden soon stood in a long line in the lobby of the building. That gave him too much time to think. He was sure that General Collins would talk to Governor Monroe in the next few days. *I really want to talk to the Governor first and explain, try to explain, what's going on between Maria and me. What is going on between us?* There was no denying that his feelings for her were growing. He wasn't sure he wanted her to be his wife, but he didn't mind people thinking she was. He needed to slow down, think things through. *How do you take things easy and slow when the world is falling apart around you?* As he thought about it he decided that the best way to explain their relationship to the governor was the way he did with the general. *Tell the truth? Maybe it is just that simple.*

Mom and Dad always said the truth was simple. Mom and Dad! He pulled out his phone and punched in the number. All he received in return was a rapid busy signal. He tried several more times without success.

"The best time to try is late at night," a women behind him in line said. "The phone lines are usually busy during the day."

That seemed reasonable. The military and government probably had control of most circuits and the few available for civilian use were probably swamped during the day. He thanked her and slipped the phone back into his pocket.

The image of his former boss, Senator Stevens, floated through his mind. *Dead.* He thought of the party with his co-workers he had attended that night. *How many of them are dead?*

The bloody face and body of Adam's mother replaced those images and lingered momentarily until he recalled the image of his fiancée Becky on the television and the blackness that followed the Atlanta blast. *How had Becky survived? How had she become press secretary for Michael Durant? President Michael Durant.* The thought of her working for him made him cringe.

As the line moved slowly forward, Caden dragged his duffle bag beside him. Adam didn't weigh much, but after an hour in line he felt like a ton. *How did Maria hold him all day?* He imagined putting the well-bundled child on the floor and pushing him along with his foot, but quickly dismissed the notion.

Finally, an MP once again handed Caden his unloaded pistol. He placed the weapon in his jacket pocket and walked out of the office past two soldiers with M-4s.

Returning to his thoughts, he recognized that he was glad that Becky was alive, but he desperately hoped that Maria was waiting for him outside the gate. That realization made him feel guilty, but his pace along the sidewalk quickened. As he rounded the corner and headed toward the bus stop he was nearly running. Wiping drops of cool rain from his face he scanned the group waiting for the bus. Maria was not there.

Taking shelter under a nearby tree, Caden sat on his duffle bag, turned up his collar and re-bundled Adam in his blankets. Would Maria soon be there or had she already been there? *No, I went almost directly from the General's office to the gate. Maria would think to check the security building. She must be coming.* He looked around, but did not see her. He wondered if she blamed him for being arrested.

An old school bus, painted like a tie-dyed shirt, rumbled down the lane. With a bang the engine died and the bus rolled the last few feet to the stop. The side door opened and out jumped a man in bib-overalls and gray hair down to his mid-back tied in a ponytail. As he popped the hood, he called over his shoulder, "Be just a minute and we'll head on our way south folks."

Caden took a big whiff of the air. *Why does everything smell like french-fries?*

As the man worked on the engine, a woman in a long, flowery dress stepped out and hung a sign on the side of the bus. Soon she was collecting payment and allowing people onboard.

Caden remained seated as he read the sign. The trip could be paid for with canned food, various ammunition ranging from .22 caliber to shotgun shells, silver or cash. You could ride the bus for a silver quarter or sixty-five paper dollars. Caden rubbed his chin. *Either they are gouging riders or inflation is soaring.* He sighed. *With production across the country falling inflation is probably running unchecked.* At sixty-five dollars a person, cash seemed to be the most expensive, but what was the going price of silver?

In red letters across the bottom of the sign it red, "No checks or credit cards." His gaze returned to the bus itself. It appeared to have been painted with anything that was available at the moment. Colors ranged from red to green and black. In some places it was a single color while other parts were painted with flowers and trees. Noticing the cracked windshield and at least one bald tire, he was certain the bus would never pass a DOT inspection, but he was also sure no one was bothering with inspections now. Caden had ridden similar buses while overseas in the army, but had never seen such a thing in America.

"I've died and gone to Woodstock."

The voice came from behind him. In one swift motion he turned, saw it was Maria and shot to his feet.

Still in his arms Adam screamed.

Maria embraced them both.

"I was worried I wouldn't see you again," he said.

"I was worried too," she replied.

"I thought you might blame me for your arrest?"

Her face registered both compassion and amusement. "Why would I do that?" She looked at the bus. "Is the bus heading toward your home?"

"Yes," he nodded. "I have to stop in Olympia on the way and talk to Governor Monroe, but we should be home in a few hours."

"Good. I'm beginning to feel like a gypsy." She moved toward the bus and stopped. "Do we have $130?"

"No." Caden rummaged through his bag and pulled out a silver dollar. "I really didn't want to use a silver dollar for a bus ride but…well, we need the ride."

The driver climbed onboard and started the engine.

Caden again smelled french-fries as he and Maria boarded the bus and sat in the only space available, the bench seat right behind the driver. With a shudder, the vehicle pulled away from the curb.

As the bus entered a deserted freeway, Maria asked, "How far is it to Olympia?"

"Where you going in Olympia?" the driver asked over his shoulder.

"The capitol building," Caden replied.

"The capitol? That's surrounded by the military."

Maria sighed.

"It's about 18 miles," the driver continued as he weaved around two burned-out cars.

Holding on to the bar with one hand and the baby with the other Maria asked, "Are the regular buses not running?"

"You not from around here?"

"We recently flew into JBLM," Caden replied.

"Oh," he nodded. "Things started falling apart with the D.C. blast. Many people left Seattle, Tacoma and the suburbs for anywhere else, but most things continued to work until the Seattle blast. Then everyone who had stayed tried to leave— all at once." The driver turned almost sideways in his seat. "From what I hear, power and water are mostly down in Seattle and Tacoma and the only people left are police, the military, gangs and victims. Olympia is relatively okay, but stores are sold out of most everything. What is left is either rationed or in short supply. When the buses stopped running a couple of days ago we started using our old bus to make a little money. Notice how there are no cars on the freeway."

Caden nodded.

"No gas. Civilians can't buy it at any price."

"Where do you get the gas to run the bus?"

"You can modify a diesel engine to run on just about anything—even used cooking oil." With one hand on the wheel he turned almost completely around. A broad grin spread across his face. "Smell that french-fry aroma? That's what this is running on."

Maria cocked her head to the side. "french-fries?"

"No," he waved his free hand. "The vegetable oil used for cooking them."

Across the aisle sat the woman who collected the fares. In a nonchalant voice she said, "Curve up ahead, sweetheart."

He turned forward again, but continued to talk. "There are still a few restaurants operating in Olympia. They serve the military and political types mostly and get food from area farms. We get the vegetable oil from them after they're done with it, filter it and use it to run our bus."

Maria gripped the bar in front of her as the driver weaved around abandoned vehicles. "So the regular buses aren't running?" She asked again.

"Nope. They're barely keeping the lights on in this area."

There were places where cars and trucks were stalled, wrecked or abandoned but, the driver explained, the police and military kept the freeway passable. Caden had driven this freeway many times as a teen and while going to college and soon he recognized the Olympia area. Minutes later the bus pulled off the freeway and down empty streets. Soldiers or military vehicles were at many of the crossroads. Some shops were open, but most were boarded up or burned out. They turned off Capitol Way onto a side street and almost at once Capitol Lake was to their right along with Heritage Park, but it wasn't a park. It was a huge refugee camp. The capitol stood on top of a large hill before them.

"This is as close as I can get you," the driver said pointing to the building.

As they stepped off the bus Maria gripped Caden's arm. "That was one wild ride. I feel like I should kneel and kiss the ground."

Caden heard her, but his gaze was locked on the sea of tents, cars and people that filled what had once been a green, lakeside park.

As the bus pulled away the smell of french-fries was quickly replaced by the smell of human waste. In the distance police sirens wailed. Immediately to their left stood a huge tent with FEMA printed on the side. Before them, almost blocking their way, stood an uncountable number of tents, cars, RVs and campers. Smoke rose from hundreds of campfires. Along the edges of the camp were Humvees and soldiers.

Somehow he had expected conditions to get better as he got closer to home, but things weren't better. Lifting his gaze to his immediate destination, the capitol, he was filled with both dread and a feeling of destiny. Freedom, law and order were all holding on by a thread. The nation would either regroup, fight back against those that attacked it, or descend into tyranny or worse, chaos.

He turned to the woman by his side. *And what about Maria? What about Becky?* There too, he was at a crossroads. He needed answers and he knew where to get them. "Come on," he said pointing to the capitol, "that is where we need to go."

Chapter Eleven

Maria gazed at the capitol high on the hill. "How do we get up there?"

Military vehicles clogged the road. Caden decided to avoid it. "Follow me," he said and headed into the camp. He looked toward the capitol every few minutes to keep his bearing as they walked through the maze of tents and vehicles. "This is less organized, dirtier and colder than Fort Rucker."

Maria nodded and held the baby tight.

Brightly colored tents stood side-by-side along meandering paths of mud. The smell of damp, sweat and waste filled the air. In any wide spot along the way people huddled around a fire. Children clustered under blankets in the doorways of tents. After several minutes, Caden gave up avoiding muddy puddles and trudged right through them. Soon the lower half of his jeans were more brown than blue.

It took longer than thirty minutes to cross what had once been a park. At the far end they came to a ten foot high chain-link fence with rolled barbed wire on top.

Caden followed the fence to the bottom of the walkway. There was no gate.

"They're shutting these people in," Maria said with a hint of fear in her voice.

"They were building a fence around the camp at Rucker."

"There were gates. People moved in and out all the time."

"Perhaps they will here."

"This camp is more crowded and these people seem hungrier, more desperate." She shook her head. "I don't want to be inside when this fence is done."

Caden didn't want to be in the cold, muddy camp either. "Come on." Following the barrier, they moved back in the direction they had just come. It didn't take long to find troops erecting a new section of fence. Unsure if anyone would challenge them, Caden moved a few yards beyond the soldiers. They stepped across the invisible line and turned up the roadway. No attempt was made to stop them.

Maria looked back. "Why would they stay inside?"

"For the promise of food and," he said pointing to the soldiers, "perhaps security, and because they have no other place to go."

Maria turned and headed up the road toward the capitol.

Caden followed and within minutes they came to a Humvee and several soldiers at a roadblock. A private called out, "The capitol campus is closed. Return to the camp."

"Wait here," he said to Maria. Taking one step forward he said to the soldiers, "My name is Caden Westmore. Governor Monroe is expecting me."

The private stepped forward, locked eyes with Caden and slowly scanned down to his mud encrusted shoes and pants. "You're kidding, right?"

Caden showed his Homeland Security badge. "Call the duty officer and give him my name."

The private told him to wait and walked back to the other soldiers. A couple of minutes later the soldier returned along with a staff sergeant. "Normally the Governor's visitors drive up," the senior man said.

"It's been a long trip, staff sergeant. May I...we, go up now?"

"No, not yet." The man paused and looked hard at Caden.

He met his gaze.

"You been in the service?"

"Army. Seven years."

He nodded. "What was your rank?"

"I made captain before the last force reduction."

"Okay." A slight smile crossed the soldier's face. "A lot of people have tried to get past us over the last few days. Most are desperate, some are mad or scared, but you're not any of that—and you got my rank correct. Well sir, why don't you and your wife..."

"Friend."

"...come on up here and we'll get this sorted out."

It took a while to contact the governor's staff, but in less than an hour Caden, Maria and Adam were stepping from a jeep at the foot of the capitol.

Maria sighed, "I always seem to be looking up at this building. So many steps"

"Forty-two," Caden said with a smile. "Washington was the forty-second state in the union.

"I wish it had been the first."

"Let me take the baby."

She handed Adam to him. "Thanks."

As they reached the top of the steps, David Weston came out of the building holding a clipboard full of papers. He greeted them then turned to Caden. He said, "The Governor is in a meeting right now and would like you to join them." He looked Caden up and down and said, "Maybe after you clean up."

Caden handed the baby back to Maria and headed for a lavatory while David settled Maria in a nearby guest house.

Caden left his duffle bag just inside the door of the conference chamber. Governor Monroe sat at a long table that dominated the center of the room. Men and women in business attire and military uniforms sat all around it. Many more sat in chairs along the walls. Caden found an empty seat and then turned his attention to an army major briefing the group.

"That is correct the last fully successful attack was against San Diego over a week ago. Since then we have captured the Detroit bombers and were in pursuit of the Seattle bombers when they detonated their bomb. We believe the terrorist network involved in these attacks has been broken. FBI and DHS are pursuing the remaining perpetrators."

The governor nodded. "Can we get the people back home?"

"Well sir," a civilian said, "we, FEMA, are using the media to spread the word that it is safe to go home. A significant portion of Seattle and Tacoma residents are now in two main areas. In the north, beyond the restricted zone, there are several camps along the freeway. Going south, the camps again follow the freeway from Olympia toward Portland and also west toward Aberdeen.

"Using food, fuel and security as an inducement we are attempting to move these populations back to the clear areas of Seattle and Tacoma and surrounding communities. For those that can't go home, we are setting up two large refugee camps, one north of the metro area and the other to the south."

"There are hundreds of makeshift camps," another person said. "If you come in from the north you can see one just down the hill from here."

FEMA guy said, "We are fencing that area so no more people can get in…"

Maria was worried about getting out, but people want to get in!

"...and as fuel becomes available we will relocate them to the southern camp or return them home. However, we are hampered by logistics. Our most critical shortages are in food and fuel, but almost all supplies are at critical levels."

Again the governor nodded. "Unless we get the economy moving the people can't go home to their jobs, but unless the people go home to their jobs the economy can't get moving." He sighed. "How many Washington refineries are operating?"

"Only the Tacoma facility was damaged in the blast. The others are operating, but the pipeline was cut by the bomb. We have enough fuel to support military, police and fire operations and keep hospitals with power problems operating. No more. We just do not have the fuel to move hundreds of thousands of people back to their homes and even if we did they would starve after they arrived."

Someone asked, "Can we get aid from other countries?"

"The Durant administration tells us that some will be coming from Canada, Australia and South America, but not enough. Trade with Europe has halted and that, along with the collapse of several large banks, will likely send their economies into a downward spiral. The Japanese stock market has been closed for a week. Their economy is in depression.

The only economy strong enough to send significant aid is China and, we have been informed, they are demanding trade concessions and continued payment of our treasury and other debts to them in something other than dollars."

Briefings continued from each advisor or agency representative, but Caden's attention was drawn to a large map at the far end of the room. It displayed the Seattle metro area with a red oval enclosing the southern portion of the city, several suburbs and the international airport. This area was labeled, 'Blast Damage.' A slightly larger area outlined in blue line was labeled EMP. *At least the bomb was detonated at ground level. If it had been launched by even a short range rocket the electromagnetic pulse would have covered the entire metro area or more.*

A wavy orange line labeled, 'Fire Damage,' outlined a much larger area. An even larger black oval extended south into Tacoma and east toward the mountains was labeled, 'Fallout."

Waterborne disease, looting, burning, shortages of bandages and pharmaceuticals, brownouts and blackouts and it will all probably get worse. Caden slumped over in his chair as the weight of the troubled nation pressed down on him.

Suddenly people stood and moved toward the door. Roused from his thoughts Caden looked for Monroe and found him in a cluster of people still talking and listening. *I really want to explain to him about Maria, but how do I get a moment with him?* He stood and continued to watch the governor. Their eyes met.

"Caden, stay there. I want to talk to you."

He smiled weakly and nodded. *Monroe knows I deceived him about Maria. I should have just told him the truth. This job, my career, they're over.*

Monroe walked over with a serious look on his face. "These meetings are depressing." Then he smiled and shook Caden's hand. "I know you want to see your family, but I need you to do some things for me while you're down there.

"We don't know much about how the people are doing in those communities. I want you to assess the needs. Maybe we can help.

"However, there is good farm land in that area. This spring we need it planted in crops we can use to feed people there and in this area. I need you to be my liaison to local community leaders and farmers. Can you do that?"

"Yes sir."

"One more thing. As you know there is a National Guard armory in Hansen."

Caden nodded.

The governor paused as if in thought. "I told you I wanted you on as an advisor, but right now I have a more pressing problem. The commanding officer of the Hansen armory is dead. I want you to assume command."

"I'm not in the National Guard."

"You are now—Major. I need you to secure the armory and hopefully find someone local to command it. I would prefer to have you here in Olympia."

Caden took a deep breath and let it out slowly. "Yes sir, but before I go there is something I need to tell you. I…I haven't been truthful with you about Maria and Adam." As briefly as possible he explained when and how they met. When he was done he said, "So you see they are actually not my family."

"Yes, I knew."

"You knew?"

He point to Caden's finger. "No wedding ring and no mark for one. I had David do a background check on you." He shrugged. "I figured you were helping someone in your extended family or a friend. I'm glad to know the facts though. What you tell me about Maria is impressive and you did the right thing by helping her and Adam."

"I'm sorry about the deception, sir."

Monroe smiled. "Trust me in the future. Find David and he'll get you everything you'll need, and then go visit your family, find out the status of the situation in the county and then get back to Olympia by this coming Monday. We have a huge amount of work to do."

What day of the week is it? "Yes sir." Caden smiled. "I'll see you on Monday." *Whenever that is.* As he left the conference room he pulled out his phone and dialed home. Again, all he heard was a rapid busy signal.

Chapter Twelve

As Caden walked into the lobby, David walked toward the room, looking at his clip board. He talked with half a dozen people before getting to Caden.

"A secretary took Maria to this guest house." He wrote the address down and handed it, along with two keys on a ring, to Caden. "Has the Governor briefed you on what he wants?" David briefly reiterated the Governor's instructions while Caden nodded. When David was done he crossed out a line on his list. "Good. Go to this office in the Wainwright building. It's on the same floor as the Emergency Operations Center. They will get you official orders and a uniform." He handed Caden another piece of paper. "We have a staff meeting scheduled for Monday at 9:00 a.m. Governor Monroe wants a report on conditions from as many counties as possible. I'll see you then. Okay? Good." He turned.

"Oh, two things before you go. What day of the week is it?"

"Today? Monday. The meeting is next Monday."

"Yes. Just making sure." *A week at home and back here. Good.* "Also, is there a phone that I can use to call New York? I need to contact a friend in the administration."

"Try my office," He pointed, "but long distance calls are always problematic."

As Caden stepped away, David called to a person across the lobby and lined out another item on his list.

Picking up the phone, he glanced at his watch. *Nearly two in the afternoon, that would be five in New York. She'll still be at work.* After a half-hour of attempts, disconnections, phone trees and transfers he was getting worried, but finally he heard Becky's voice.

"Caden is that really you? I thought…I feared…is it really you?"

"Yes, it really is me. It is great to hear your voice. I was afraid you died in the Atlanta blast, but then three days ago I saw you on TV."

"I was afraid that you were in Atlanta when it happened. I've really missed you."

"I've missed you too," he said, but the words sounded strangely hollow. "A road block stopped me or I would have been right there looking for you. When did you get out of the city and how did you end up as the press secretary for President Durant?"

"It had been an incredible two weeks." She described being on the edge of the metro area, seeing the flash and feeling the torrent of wind buffet the van she was in. "I think I was close like you were. The remote studio was damaged. It took two days to get back on the air and almost as soon as we were, President Durant asked me to join the administration as his press secretary. How could I say, "no?"

I could have found a way. "That's a great opportunity for you, but only for a few months. Is Durant going to run for president? The election is in nine months and, the last I heard, Governor Monroe is the only candidate still alive."

"There isn't going to be an election. Parts of the country are already under martial law and by the end of the month the whole country will be. President Durant plans to cancel the elections until martial law is lifted."

"Elections are conducted by the states. The federal government can't…."

"Durant appointed new Supreme Court justices. They will approve his martial law declaration and the cancellation of the election."

"How can there be new justices if there is no senate to confirm them?"

"The senate is not in session so President Durant made nine recess appointments."

Caden was stunned into silence. Durant was acting within the letter, if not the spirit, of the Constitution.

"Caden, this is all for the good of the country. The nation doesn't need elections right now. It doesn't need a bickering congress, it needs security. America needs strong leadership and a guiding hand. Durant is that leader."

You sound like his campaign chairman.

"Come to New York as quickly as you can. Now both money and power are centered in the Big Apple. This is where the action is going to be in the coming years. Working with Durant could make both our careers. I could get you a position in the administration." She paused. "I've got to go, another meeting. I love you."

"I miss you."

"Come here quickly. We will make a great team."

He ended the call with a promise to think about it.

*   *   *

Caden looked in a mirror as he adjusted the collar of his new ACUs. *It's strange to be back in uniform.* He placed the Velcro rank insignia on his chest. *And stranger still to see the oak leaf of a major on my uniform.* Cold wind buffeted him as he left the new National Guard offices on the capitol campus. A low sun hid behind the gray buildings. Caden flipped up the collar of his uniform jacket to the cold and shifted the weight of the duffle bag on his back and then continued on toward the guest house just off the plaza. Two soldiers standing watch on the corner saluted. One said, "Good night, sir," as he passed.

Caden, deep in thought, mumbled his reply. It had been a long and perplexing day. Assume command of the armory. *What if no one is there? How do you command an armory with no soldiers?* Secure the weapons. *What if it has been looted?* Act as a liaison. *What if the farmers don't want to listen?*

The call with Becky stirred an array of emotions. He had feelings for her, but was it love? Besides beauty and education, she was career orientated and mixed well in Washington circles. Three weeks ago those last two were qualities he cultivated in himself and admired in others.

His thoughts returned to his family. *What if they are dead or gone?* He pulled out his phone and dialed home once again. The phone rang several times.

"Hello."

Caden was shocked to hear a voice and hesitated. "Ah, hello…Mom?"

The line went dead.

Did I really hear her say hello? Yes, yes I did, but was that Mom or my sister? Did the line go dead or did she hang up? He tried several more times, but never connected.

At the steps of the guest house, he slid the phone back into his pocket. The building was an old, two-story mansion with a large, covered front porch. He walked up the steps and looked back. The capitol and surrounding office buildings were in full view. Turning toward the door he fumbled with the keys. One unlocked the front door, the other had the number three on it. Caden walked up creaking stairs to the second floor. He opened the door and gently set the duffle bag down. In the dim light of a fading winter day he could see Maria curled around the baby on the bed. Standing in the doorway he paused to admire the beautiful picture before him.

She opened her eyes.

He smiled.

She blinked, then screamed.

Waving his arms he said, "Me…just me…Caden."

She sat up, held a crying Adam to her chest, and looked him up and down. "You enlisted?"

"Actually I'm an officer."

Confusion spread across her face.

"Officers don't enlist." Walking toward her he said, "I'll explain the difference later." He sat on the edge of the bed. "I'm sorry I frightened you. I'm surprised you were so deeply asleep."

"I didn't sleep well in jail."

He laughed. "No, I guess I wouldn't either." He explained that the governor called him to duty so that he could take charge and secure the armory in Hansen. Then he told her all that happened during the day, except the call to Becky.

"Are you hungry?" she asked. "This house is really a Bed and Breakfast. The owner lives in an apartment downstairs. There's food in the fridge in the kitchen."

"I'm famished." He frowned. "I haven't eaten all day."

Placing the sleeping baby in a large cushioned chair with blankets around him Maria went to the kitchen with Caden. Later in the dining room they ate, talked and laughed about everything and nothing until the moon was high in the night sky. Only when they both yawned did they return to the room.

While Caden hung up his uniform Maria said, "The bed is big and comfortable…we could…I mean you could sleep on it, in it together…well not together, separately, but to…you know what I mean, I hope… I'm going to shut up now."

Over the last two weeks they had slept in the same room, the same car, beside each other on a plane and in sleeping bags side-by-side, but this would be a new level. "Thank you, but I'll sleep on the floor. It isn't the first time I've slept on a hard surface."

She nodded.

Caden laid out blankets beside the bed, turned off the light and climbed into a sleeping bag. For several minutes he stared at the ceiling. "You still awake?"

"Yes."

"Remember I told you I lost someone in Atlanta?"

"Yes, someone you loved."

"Her name is Becky and I talked with her today."

"She's alive?"

"Well, yes, and we were, are engaged, but...." Caden sat up. In the dim light of the room he could see Maria's head turned toward him. Her eyes were open and locked on target. "It's complicated."

"Such things often are."

"No, no, you misunderstand me. I've been thinking about this all afternoon and...well... please listen."

"Okay."

"Three weeks ago I worked at the hub of power and influence in this country. My boss, Senator Stevens, was often mentioned as a future presidential candidate. That is all gone now and everything has changed, is changing. Maybe I'm changing.

"When we talked today, Becky urged me to come to New York. She said that is where the power and money are. That we'd make a great team. There was a time when the thought of being married to a woman like her was, well, exciting. I've been thinking about that and more all day."

He lay down again. "Becky may be on the power and money team," he concluded, "but I don't like the direction that team is going and it disturbs me that she is so willing, eager even, to be a part of it. I don't want to be part of that team."

After a long pause Maria asked, "Do you love her?"

"Love? I still care for her, but no I don't love her. We've moved in different directions. We're not the same people. We won't be getting married."

He waited for Maria to ask the next, more difficult question, did he love her? But, that query did not come and soon he heard the gentle rhythmic breathing of her sleep.

Chapter Thirteen

Maria sat on the porch swing with Adam, as Caden drove up to the guest house in a dark blue SUV. When he stepped from the car she said, "I wondered how we would get to Hansen."

"The guys at the motor pool told me they have several dozen abandoned cars that were towed in. Some still had keys inside." He leaned against it. "This was one of them."

"And they just gave it to you?"

"Loaned."

He picked up the bags beside Maria and they walked to the car.

"Getting a vehicle was not the problem, finding enough gas to fill the tank took me over an hour."

"Is that enough gas to get us to your home?"

"Yes and hopefully we can get more after we get there."

Caden retrieved their bags from the room and loaded them in the back of the car. Then, with Maria in the passenger seat and Adam on her lap, he drove to a parking lot near the old capitol. Several Humvees and Fuelers, a couple of APCs and a Stryker vehicle, filled the lot. "We're heading south on the interstate with this convoy."

As the line of vehicles moved out Maria asked, "Are they going to Hansen?"

"No, they're heading farther south to refugee camps outside of Longview and Vancouver. We'll have to leave before then and do the last part of the trip on our own." Caden drove over and joined the convoy near the rear.

As they rolled onto the freeway Maria clutched Adam tight in her arms. "We should get a car seat."

Caden chuckled. *I may not be married or have a kid, but I'm going to look like it.* "I'll put it on the list of things we need."

The slow progress of the convoy allowed Caden to observe much of the scene along the freeway. Boarded and burnt buildings, broken windows and yards strewn with trash were the mute reminders of the desperate exodus from Seattle and Tacoma just days ago. Humvees parked on many of the overpasses kept order on a largely empty freeway.

"I've often driven this route with my parents and when I was in college." On his right a long line of rail cars covered with graffiti came into view. "It sure looks different now."

Gradually the buildings gave way to forest. The wider shoulder and gradual slope allowed abandoned cars to be pushed off to the side. *How many wrecked and burned cars have I seen today?* As they drove by he counted a group of eight vehicles. *Have we driven past a hundred?* The convoy paused as soldiers pushed a burned truck out of the way. *More than a hundred. How many people fled down this highway after the Seattle bomb?* He recalled fleeing from Washington D.C. and then away from Atlanta. He remembered the body of Adam's mother and finding the baby. *So many people dead.*

He recognized a home in a field along the freeway and pointed it out to Maria. "An old school friend lived there." As they came close he saw the windows were broken, burn marks scared the walls and the front door hung haphazardly in the frame. Behind the home, a greenhouse stood with its door swinging in the wind.

I hope the family is okay…and my family. God, please let them be okay.

After nearly an hour the convoy rolled off the freeway and into the large parking lot of a truck stop. Children swarmed around the vehicles like bees around a hive. Adults from the tents walked toward the convoy as soldiers took up positions along it.

Fragments of plywood were scattered around the broken windows of the convenience store. Extension cords hung out the shattered windows and ran to several nearby RV's.

Along the edges of the parking lot, cars of all descriptions sat randomly. Tents lined the grassy edges of the lot.

A group of children hovered around the SUV staring in the windows. Caden gently opened the door and stepped out.

"I'm hungry." "Do you have food?" "Who are you?" "Are you in the Army?" "My Mom is sick—can you help?" "My Dad needs gas." "Where did you get gas?" "When can we go home?"

Caden had few answers. Frustrated he walked on.

A child pointed east. "Are you going up the road there?"

"Yes, I'm going to Hansen."

"There are robbers that way."

Crunching broken glass under foot, Caden walked up to the store and peered in a large broken window. Only garbage, strewn on the floor, remained.

Maria came up beside him and looked in the window. "I guess they don't have baby formula or diapers."

Caden smiled weakly. "No, I think they're out." He turned away. "I need to speak to the officer-in-charge." It didn't take long to find him talking to other soldiers hemmed in by children.

Caden gradually pushed his way through. "This isn't a camp. It's a wide spot in the road. Why are all these people here?"

"This is where they ran out of gas and," he pointed across the road to a church, "that congregation gave out food until they ran out. Many just stayed here hoping to survive until they can go home."

"If we could get them fuel could they go home?"

The officer shook his head and motioned for Caden to follow him. Between two noisy trucks he said, "Most of them are from the Seattle red zone. Their homes were either destroyed by the blast or burned in the fires afterward."

"They'll die here."

The officer nodded. "We've moved most to the southern refugee camp. These people won't go for one reason or another. Hunger will eventually change their minds." He looked east and west along the two lane country road. "Which way are you headed?"

"East to Hansen."

"One of the refugees told me bandits have blocked the road that way."

"I heard something similar. Who talked to you?"

He pointed and they walked over to a man sitting on an ice chest. Behind him was an older Ford minivan. A tarp duct taped to the top and supported by two tree limbs formed a canopy over him. It reminded Caden of the covering Maria made at Rucker.

"Henry, this is Major Westmore. He needs to get to Hansen."

Henry shook his head.

"Can you tell him about the road block?"

"We heard there were farms out that way." He pointed east. "Several of us pooled the little gas we had. We hoped to get food or maybe work for food. But, about ten miles in there is a causeway crossing a river…"

Caden nodded. "That is just a mile or so before Hansen."

"…and on the far side two dozers blocked the road. I got a glimpse of several bandits with rifles."

"How do you know they were criminals?"

"They shot at us."

"How many shots?"

"Just one that I heard, but we didn't stick around and let them improve their aim."

"So no one was hit?"

"No. We slammed it in reverse and got out of there."

Caden thanked him, started to turn away then paused. "Why are you staying here Henry? Wouldn't it be better in the refugee camp?"

"I was up north with my family." He pointed to a woman and two boys around a fire at the edge of the lot. "We were visiting friends when Washington was hit. We headed home to our farm in Oregon the next morning after Los Angles was bombed. None of us want to go to a FEMA camp. We just want to go home. If I can somehow get ten gallons of gas I'll make it." His head slumped down.

Caden had less than five gallons in his tank and no certainty of getting more.

As they walked away the officer asked, "Are you still going to Hansen?"

"Yes."

"Good luck."

Caden nodded and headed off to find Maria. It wasn't hard; she was surrounded by children. After he got her away from the kids, he told her about the roadblock. "I'd like you to stay here while I find a way into Hansen."

"No."

"Be reasonable."

"I am. I'll drive. You keep your gun ready and give me directions. Also, you might get another gun before the convoy pulls out. You know I can shoot."

Caden could find only one fault with the plan. "What about Adam?"

"Well, we are not going to leave him with strangers, so you find a way around the roadblock and we keep Adam with us."

"You're pretty logical—for a woman." He smiled and stepped away.

She thumped him on the back before he got out of range.

Minutes later he returned. "The lieutenant wished us a safe journey, but he gave me this." Caden held out a SIG P228 pistol and two 15-round magazines. Together they buckled the baby into the backseat as best they could and as the convoy pulled out of the parking lot heading south, they headed east.

The homes along the highway were damaged or burned. None appeared inhabited. As they moved away from the freeway the forest thickened and the homes thinned. About eight miles in, Caden told Maria to turn right onto a smaller road. "This will take us to a bridge that crosses the river. From there we can loop back to the highway behind the roadblock." Minutes later he said, "Slow down. Stop when you get to that bend up ahead. I'll be able to see the bridge from the other side of that hill."

Caden got out of the car and sprinted into the woods. He crested the nearby knoll and worked his way along until he had a clear view of the crossing. He strained to see as much as possible. *Wish I had binoculars.*

Logs were laid out at the far end of the span. Any approaching vehicle would need to slow to a crawl to get through the 'S' shaped barricade. Caden saw two men dressed in jeans, hunting jackets and ball caps. One sat in a sandbagged position up the side of the hill while the other stood near the far end of the log road block. Both had rifles. *This isn't set up like a bandit blockade; this is a guard post.*

"Turn around," he said upon returning to the car. "The bridge is blocked, but there is a logging road nearby I want to try."

It took ten minutes to reach the dirt road and another twenty to reach the river crossing. Where once had been a large culvert, there was now a free-flowing waterway.

Caden sighed.

"Are there any other ways to get to Hansen?"

"Yes," he looked at the fuel gauge, "but we don't have the gas to try them. Head back to the main highway. I have a hunch."

"What's your idea?"

"That these aren't bandit roadblocks, but are really guard posts."

"What kind of a hunch is that?"

He shrugged. "Perhaps a crazy one."

At the highway Maria turned right. The road sloped down into the river valley where Caden had camped, fished and played as a child. The forest was thick and reached right down to the shore of the lake less than a mile ahead. "Pull off just up there." He pointed to a wide spot in the pavement. "Wait here while I take a look."

She nodded. "Be careful."

Again he sprinted into the woods and up a hill. In a few minutes he was in a good position to observe the roadblock on the far end of the half-mile long causeway. Even more so at this distance he wished he had binoculars. But he could see that Henry had been right. Two bulldozers blocked the far end of the road. Again, they appeared to be offset to form an 'S' shaped position and he could see three men with rifles. One was clearly watching the road while the others sat near a fire.

They aren't hiding. Anyone coming down the road would see them long before they were in effective range. That is a defensive position. I'm sure of it.

Caden stood and walked down the hill toward the lake. As he stepped on the road he looked back over his shoulder to ensure that Maria couldn't see what he was about to do. *No reason to let her kill me before the bandits have a chance.* He continued onto the causeway.

Chapter Fourteen

Caden was well out on the causeway when it occurred to him that if he did get shot, Maria would almost certainly come running after him. *Great plan you came up with Caden.* But there was no turning back. One man was visible at the blockade watching him.

He stepped forward with his arms away from his body.

Hopefully they can see my uniform. Well…if they are bandits that might make things worse.

Another step forward.

Now three men watched him from behind a bulldozer.

Another step forward.

A gunshot echoed across the lake.

Still standing. Nothing hurts. He looked down. *No blood visible. All the pieces are still there.* Even though he was fine, he suspected Maria was near panic. She would come armed and dangerous. He had to calm things down quickly. "I'm Caden Westmore. My father is Trevor Westmore. We are both from Hansen. He still lives there. I'm here on orders from Governor Monroe. I just want to talk." Several moments passed. *Well, they haven't shot me—yet.*

One of the men disappeared from view.

Seconds ticked slowly by. He prayed both that Maria would not come and the men would not shoot.

He heard a car engine. *Maria?* No. The sound was from the roadblock. A pickup truck came around one of the bulldozers, then raced down the road toward him.

Caden took a deep breath, but stood still. As the truck neared he stepped to the shoulder.

Twenty feet away, the rust and red pickup stopped abruptly. A man with a 270 hunting rifle, stepped cautiously from the passenger side of vehicle. "Is that really you?"

The voice was familiar. He stared hard at the face. The hair was grayer and the forehead more wrinkled. "Mr. Michaels?"

The smile broadened. He slung the rifle onto his shoulder and stepped forward. "I haven't seen you since graduation." He hugged Caden. "You must have paid attention in my geography class, you made it back home. Last I heard you were in Washington D.C. We thought…."

"I almost did."

A car crept down the hill behind him. It was Maria. "That's my friend," he explained to Michaels.

The teacher pulled a radio from his pocket. "Glenn, it's Caden. I told you I recognized that voice. Anyway, that's his car at the far end with a friend in it, so hold your fire."

Caden waved Maria forward, and then turned back to Michaels. "So, did you guys really shoot at me?"

The driver of the pickup said, "No, not *at* you."

Michaels laughed. "Most people turn around when they see the roadblock. Those that don't, get a shot over their heads."

"That scares away most of the looters," the other man added.

Caden smiled weakly and decided, at least for now, not to ask what happened to those who didn't flee.

Maria drove up. Caden turned as she stepped from the car. Her eyes locked on him, but no hint of emotion escaped her face.

After introductions Michaels said, "I'll take the pickup and lead you back to the sheriff's office."

"I'm sure I still know my way around town. I don't need a tour."

"You may have grown up here, but you've been gone for years. Many people don't know you and a lot happened in the last few weeks. The sheriff will want to talk to you, so it's best that I go along to the office."

Caden relented and allowed Michaels to escort him.

Once back in the car Maria said, "When I heard that gunshot…."

Caden nodded.

Her voice grew stern. "You could have been killed."

"I had a hunch."

With eyes fixed on him she said, "Your hunch could have left you dead on some backwoods road and me in the middle of nowhere with a half-a-tank of gas and a baby. I know we're not married or anything, but I do…."

"I care for you too. I'm sorry. I'll be more careful."

She wiped her eyes and nodded.

After passing through the blockade they paused while one man jumped out and Michaels took over driving the pickup.

A few minutes later, as they passed a narrow two-lane country road, Caden pointed. "That's the way to the Westmore farm." His heart went down the narrow road, but he kept the car headed into town. "Hansen is three miles farther down the highway."

Moments later as they passed over a culvert where a creek ran under the road, Maria pointed at two red-headed teens, a boy and a girl, fishing along the bank.

"I've fished in that stream many times," Caden said. "There, up ahead is the Hansen city limit sign."

Maria looked around. Farm fields spread out from either side of the street to the hills in the distance. Ahead there was a motel, gas station and convenience store, but no other buildings. "City? What city?"

"Hansen isn't a city in the sense of Atlanta, but it is the county seat and," he smiled, "it has a number of multi-story buildings."

"Where?"

"Patience is a virtue. We will be downtown in less than five minutes."

"Downtown? Five minutes?" she repeated incredulously.

Caden turned at the corner. Children and adults mingled in the parking lot of the motel, but the gas station and convenience store on his right were closed. *Glass is still in the windows and they don't appear burned. No looting? That's a good sign.* After they passed a line of trees, a school came into view. Children ran about the playground.

Everything looks normal. He scanned both sides of the street. Homes on the other side of the road were intact and looked lived in. *No, something is different.* The town looked tired and run down. Piles of garbage bags lined the street in front of nice middle class homes. Some of the trash was carried on the breeze.

As they continued the houses gave way to squat gray and brown shops, stores and office buildings of two and three stories. Many of the windows were boarded up and, like Olympia, the shops were mostly closed. Caden was grateful that the looting and burning seemed to have followed the freeway and not made its way here.

As they passed a five-story building he said, "Welcome to downtown Hansen."

"Where's the sheriff's office?" Maria asked.

"Just up ahead, across from the court house." A moment later a large parking lot came into view. Caden had driven there several times before moving away. *No cars in the lot and no cars on the road.*

Michaels pulled into the lot.

Caden followed and parked beside him. Stepping from the car he asked, "Where is everyone?"

Michaels shrugged. "Most are home. There is nothing in the stores to buy so there's no work. The grocery store got its last shipment the day of the Seattle explosion. Now the shelves are bare."

"I'll get Adam," Maria said. "You guys go ahead."

As the two walked toward the sheriff's office Caden said, "So there was panic buying?"

"Yeah, there was crazy buying from the day of the D.C. blast. Some shops tried to ration supplies, but it didn't work. Gas, food and medicine were in short supply almost from the start and then quickly disappeared. After the essentials were gone people bought everything else. It was insane."

"But there was no looting?"

"Some. Outsiders mostly, but…."

He didn't press for details.

Stepping through the door Caden saw a young deputy with his chair tilted back against the wall as he read a book. Looking up, the deputy's eyes locked on Caden and he popped to attention.

Michaels stepped forward and said, "Relax Doug, it's just me and, well, look who we found. This is Caden Westmore."

"Trevor's son? Nice to meet you. Your father did a lot for this community after the D.C. attack. He got the blockade set up and organized the guards."

"Thanks. I'm sure I'll be hearing all about it soon, but right now we're here to talk to the sheriff."

Maria stepped through the door and Caden introduced her.

"Just go on in," the deputy pointed ahead.

Looking at the metal detector he said, "I have a metal belt buckle." *And a pocket knife.*

"The town has been having brown outs this morning so I've left it off. Just go in."

After being buzzed through another locked door, they reached a part of the office that he had seen only once before.

"Sheriff Hoover, this is Caden Westmore."

Hoover? Caden groaned inwardly.

"Caden?" The sheriff turned as he said the name. As their eyes met he said, "A lot of people thought you were dead. I'll bet your mother was glad to see you."

Other than the gray that speckled his short black hair and just a bit more weight, the man before him was that same person he had known as a deputy. "I haven't seen my mom yet. I came here first."

"Well, I guess I should feel honored." Without moving closer he looked Caden up and down. "I thought you got out of the army."

"I'm in the Washington National Guard actually, and I'm here on orders from Governor Monroe."

The sheriff's face grew dark. "Oh. What does he want?"

"I'm to assume command of the Hansen armory and the governor wants me to act as a liaison to county leaders and local farmers."

The sheriff walked across the room and stood before him. "Liaison? Has martial law been declared?"

Caden recalled Becky's assertion that the whole nation would soon be under martial law and simply said, "Not yet."

Hoover shook his head. "I've been here trying to protect these people for weeks while you've been who knows where.

Now you want to march into Hansen in your army suit and take command."

"I don't want any such thing."

"But, if martial law is declared in this county, you will be the senior officer here."

"That hasn't happened yet and I hope it doesn't. Look, I'm not taking command of anything but the armory. Everything else we can discuss later. Right now I want to get home and see my Mother and Father."

"What?" Hoover said in a surprised voice. "Michaels didn't you tell him?"

Chapter Fifteen

Michaels looked at his feet. "There never seemed to be a good time to tell him."

"What?" Caden asked.

"There never is a good time." Hoover sighed. "I don't know the details, but…your father is missing."

"Missing?"

"He drove up the North Road on the morning of the Seattle blast. He was going to your brother's place, but he hasn't come back."

"Peter? Sue?" Caden recalled details from the disaster map in the capitol briefing room. He was certain his brother's home was outside the blast line, but the fire and radiation zones were larger. "The Seattle blast was six days ago." Once again he tried to remember exactly where his brother lived. "Okay, we'll talk later."

Hoover nodded.

As they walked from the office Maria said, "Take the baby. I'm driving."

Caden looked her in the eye and didn't argue.

In the car, several minutes went by in silence as they backtracked their way out of town. Caden shifted in his seat. He glanced at the speedometer, sighed, and tried to will himself home. "Growing up I just wanted to get away. First college, next the military and then a job in D.C. Now all I want to do is get home. There's Hops Road. Turn."

"Okay. I remember."

Farm fields and pastures spread out in all directions with just a couple of houses visible.

"Where's your family's home?"

"You can't see it from here. Turn there ahead; see that dirt road up on the left."

She nodded and for another half mile the SUV bumped and splashed along the rutted road.

"Just beyond those trees go up the driveway. It's at the top of a small hill."

As she turned, Caden saw the white home he had grown up in. "Drive past the barn, there's a place to park between the buildings."

"It looks nice, like a traditional American farmhouse."

"It should look traditional; the original part was built by my grandfather. My father did an addition and it has been remodeled, but much of it is nearly a hundred years old."

Even as Maria pulled to a stop, Caden stepped from the car and looked toward the covered porch of the house. From behind him came the unmistakable pump of a shotgun. For the second time that day he slowly spread his arms away from his body.

Maria stepped from the car and looked toward the barn with a smile. "You must be Lisa."

"Who are you and why are you here?"

His back to his sister, Caden smiled. "Sis, is that anyway to greet your older brother." Gradually he turned and faced her.

She squealed and ran toward him, fumbling with the shotgun.

Boom!

*   *   *

Caden awoke to darkness. *What happened?* He remembered hearing his sister's voice and turning to face her. *She shot me!* His right leg throbbed. He reached down and felt the moist bandage. Slowly he rose and sat on the edge of the bed. *Robbers didn't shoot me, the guys at the blockade didn't shoot me—Lisa, my own sister, shoots me.* He looked at the bloodstained dressing around his lower leg and wiggled his toes. Muscles in his leg hurt, but the toes worked.

He looked about. On his right was the world map he had put up in high school. Pins and string still traced the route of trips across the globe he had hoped to take when he grew up. Over the years he had visited many far off lands, but now he was glad to be in his old room at home.

Gingerly he touched the back of his head as the door opened with a squeak.

Maria smiled and then called over her shoulder. "He's awake."

Before Maria could reach his bedside, Lisa burst in. "I am sooo sorry. Are you okay? I didn't know who you were and when I realized it was you ... I'm really sorry. I could have killed you."

He smiled as he looked up at the sister he had not seen since high school. "I'm really glad you failed." She was still the wavy-haired brunette he grew up with, but she was now, a grown woman.

Lisa sat beside him on the bed. "After the D.C. blast we were afraid.... I was really surprised to see you."

Maria turned on the light, pulled a chair over, and sat.

Floor boards creaked in the hallway. He looked toward the door. She had more gray hair than he remembered, but the smile from the woman coming toward him was clearly that of mom. He tried to stand, but the pain told him to sit.

His mother sat beside him on the bed and they embraced.

Wiping tears from her eyes, she said, "You being here is a bright spot in all this darkness."

Caden looked around the room with a smile. *Even if I did get shot upon arrival, it's good to be home.* "I guess I don't need to make introductions. Maria, I know you've met Lisa, but have you met my mother, Sarah?"

Maria nodded, "We've been talking while you slept."

His mother took his hand, "She's told us about your journey here, but if you're up to it," she smiled, "I'd like to hear it from you."

"The leg hurts, but I can talk." He felt the back of his head, "I've got a bit of headache. What happened there?"

Lisa blushed. "You fell against the car when I shot you."

"There's a dent in the door where your head hit it," Maria said. "The doctor thinks you have a mild concussion."

"How is my leg?" he asked.

Again Lisa blushed. "It was buckshot and most of it went in the ground. Doctor Scott thinks she got the rest out."

Caden had a thousand questions, but they were waiting to hear his story. "Okay." With a glance at Maria he said, "I'll tell you how we got here, but when I'm done you've got to answer my questions."

They agreed.

With as little emotion as possible, he described the D.C. blast and his race to leave the burning city.

His mother nodded. "The news said tens of thousands left Seattle that day. They just kept coming." She shook her head, but said no more.

"I wanted to get to Atlanta and Becky." Caden noticed the awkward glances toward Maria. "I headed through Maryland into West Virginia. I was at the Georgia border when they bombed Atlanta. I assumed Becky was dead, but she isn't."

"Where is she?" his mother asked.

"New York. She's working for President Durant." He took his mom's hand. "Things have changed between Becky and me."

"Well son, I hate to say it, but I never did think she was the right one for you."

Caden shrugged and then described the fiery wreck and finding Adam not far from his dead mother. "I took Adam with me to Fort Rucker hoping to find someone to take him." He looked around. "Where is Adam?"

"Asleep in the spare room," Lisa said.

"We got a crib out of the attic," Maria added.

His mother smiled. "It was yours when you were a baby."

Caden felt his face warm. "Okay, well, continuing on with my story. After I arrived at Rucker, I set up camp on the edge of a field near some trees. Armed robbers came during the night and threatened me and the baby. They were about to shoot Adam when Maria came out of the shadows and fired first. She killed one..."

Lisa gasped.

"...and I killed the other. That's how we met."

Maria stared at her feet.

Sarah walked over and hugged her. Looking at Caden she said, "Maria told us you met in Alabama, but she didn't mention a robbery or saving your life."

As he told of the crash landing at JBLM his mother interrupted. "You were flying into Seattle when the blast occurred?" she asked as she sat beside him.

He nodded.

"Your father was driving into the city, maybe just arriving, when it happened."

"Sherriff Hoover said he was looking for Peter. Why?"

"Finish your story, son, and then I'll tell you all I know."

"There isn't much else to say. Maria and Adam came through the crash with bruises. I was banged up a bit and spent a couple of days in the hospital, but overall I was fine. The Governor wants me to take command of the Hansen armory and act as a liaison to the community."

His mother squeezed his hand. Tears welled in her eyes. "I'm glad you're here and okay. I'm glad Maria was there for you and that you were both there for Adam. You have angels watching over you."

"Why did Dad go to Seattle? Why didn't Peter and Sue come here?"

His mother took a deep breath and let it out slowly. "On the day of the Seattle blast Peter called. I talked with him only a moment. He wanted to talk to Trevor. I'm not sure what was said, but your father grabbed his go bag and went." Tears flowed. "A couple hours later, when he would have been there…." Tears became sobs.

Lisa took up the story. "Peter called me early on the morning of the Seattle bombing. I nearly shouted into the phone….

*   *   *

"Peter!" Excited, she fumbled with her phone, almost dropped it. "I've been worried about you. I'm surprised you got through. I've been trying to call, but…."

"I'm at the station on an official line," he said in a low, but tense voice.

"Are you okay? How is Sue?"

"We're as fine as can be. I've been doing twelve on, twelve off since the D.C. blast, but…I have just a minute and I wanted to make sure my little sister is okay."

"I'm fine. The college has shut down until further notice and most of the students have left. I'm just waiting out things in the dorm. I wanted to talk to Mom and Dad about going home, but I haven't been able to reach them. I stayed with friends a few days, but they left, so I figured it was safer here in the dorm than on the roads. Have you been able to phone our parents?"

"Not yet. The phone lines are restricted for official use, but I'll keep trying. Do you have the TV on?"

"Of course. Nothing else is on. Helicopters show endless lines of cars heading away from the city in a massive horde. Everyone looking for gas and food. People being carjacked. Robberies. Murder. I've been scared to travel and afraid to stay."

"The flow of refugees has slowed to a crawl. There isn't much fuel left in the area. This might be your best time to travel. Do you have gas?"

"Yes, about ten gallons."

"Do you have a gun?"

"No, you know I don't," she took a deep breath, "but I have thought about getting one. I've heard gunshots. Not on campus, but close enough. Do you think I should buy one?"

"You can't get one now. They've all been bought or looted."

"Look Sis, I'm going to have to go any second now, but I want you to read Matthew 24:15 -18. A close friend passed it along to me just this morning. The verse spoke to me in this time of tribulation, and I hope it does the same for you."

"Okay I'll look it up."

"I love you, Sis. Read those verses and keep the news on. I've got to go."

After hanging up, Lisa looked about the room. *Where is my Bible?* She walked over and turned up the volume on the television. The now normal terrorism aftermath news continued with reports of radiation patterns from stricken cities, causality counts, rationing and announcers on the scene of FEMA camps and food distribution centers, but nothing new about the northwest.

She wasn't sure how much time had passed when her stomach grumbled. *I haven't had breakfast.* She searched the cupboard of her tiny dorm room for something to eat. *Anything will do.* On the second self she found a candy bar and her Bible. Flipping through the pages as she ate, she came to Matthew 24.

15 When ye therefore shall see the abomination of desolation, spoken of by Daniel the prophet, stand in the holy place, (whoso readeth, let him understand:)

16 Then let them which be in Judaea flee into the mountains:

17 Let him which is on the housetop not come down to take anything out of his house:

18 Neither let him which is in the field return back to take his clothes.

That's not comforting. Why did he want me to read that? Puzzled, she set her Bible aside, and leaned back in the chair to watch more news.

A TV reporter stood beside a map of the United States, "The state of California is under martial law along with the District of Columbia, Maryland, Northern Virginia and the Memphis metro area, due to terrorist attacks. In addition the cities of Baltimore, Chicago, Cleveland, Detroit…."

Wait…Peter didn't say the passage was comforting. What did he say? Something about a close friend passing it to him. And he said it spoke to him in this 'time of tribulation.' She read it again. Words jumped out at her. *… abomination of desolation…flee into the mountains… not come down to take anything… Oh God, it's a message.*

Chapter Sixteen

Lisa threw the luggage into the trunk of her small car with fear-aided ease and then slid in the driver's seat. The smell of smoke from an unseen fire drifted across the nearly empty parking lot. *Calm down. If it is another bomb Peter was warning about you don't want to get in an accident.* She turned the key and the old car sputtered to life. Taking a deep breath she shifted it into gear and headed across the campus.

Turning a corner she saw the wrought iron gates at the entrance of the campus were shut. She briefly considered ramming them like in the movies, but stopped just a few feet away. Stepping from the car she approached the gate. A thick chain and heavy lock secured it. She pulled on the chain hoping it would magically open. There was a gate at the far end of the campus, but she was certain it would also be locked. She gently bit her lip as she considered her options.

"What are you doing here?"

Lisa spun around and clamped down hard on her lip. A security guard was walking along the fence.

She rubbed her mouth. "I…I was going home, but the gate is locked."

He shook his head. "I thought everyone was gone except us."

"Us?" Lisa asked.

"Single guys on the security staff." He pointed up the hill to the oldest building on the campus. "Several of us moved in up there. Also, there's a few international students that are stuck here and a couple of professors staying in their offices, but I didn't think any others were left here." He walked up to the gate. "Are you sure you want to go off campus?"

Lisa took a deep breath and nodded.

"Where's home?"

"Hansen."

"Don't stop for anything till you get there," he said.

Returning to her car Lisa locked both doors. The guard opened one gate enough for her to exit. As she drove away from the campus onto the vacant street, she could see a cloud of smoke drifting down from the north. Turning on the radio she heard the usual litany.

"...have promised food and medical assistance. Some help is expected to arrive by air in the coming weeks, but the bulk will take several months to come by ship.

"Hospitals outside the red zones are overwhelmed, forcing the relocation of patients to facilities sometimes hundreds of miles away. In addition the massive exodus from all major cities has compounded the problem with additional injuries. All medical personal are asked to report to the nearest hospital or clinic.

"All military, National Guard and Coast Guard personnel are to report...."

Nothing new. She turned it down low.

Rounding the next corner she could see the freeway on ramp. Several cars were sitting almost blocking access. She slowed down. Something moved behind one of the vehicles. *I'm going to another on ramp.* She turned the wheel.

A shot rang out.

Hitting the gas pedal she sped to the left down a side street.

Less than a mile from the college and I've been shot at. She considered going back to the campus, but Peter's warning pushed her onward.

She roared onto the freeway at the next open ramp. A single car zipped past her as she pulled into the lane. Abandoned vehicles had been pushed to the side leaving about half of the highway clear. It looked like a post-apocalyptic movie set.

She glanced in the rearview mirror. *Soldiers on the overpass. That's why it was clear.* She smiled and hoped to see more.

Along both sides of the highway were malls and shops, but the people Lisa could see didn't seem to be shopping. Some groups appeared to be walking south. Others pushed shopping carts filled with unbagged merchandise. *Refugees and looters.*

A mile down the road she was beginning to ease off the gas pedal when she spotted another group of armed men breaking into abandoned cars. Lisa zoomed by as fast as possible but, apparently content with looting vehicles they took little note of her.

Rounding the next curve a bit too fast, she struggled to keep her car from hitting an abandon vehicle. Coming out of the bend she heard a snap like the breaking of a twig and then a high pitched whine seemed to fill the car. As it reached a crescendo she wanted to clamp her hands over her ears. Then it stopped.

Lisa glanced down. *The radio? Was that the radio?* The station it had been on was gone. Only crackle and static came from it now. She pressed search on the radio and down on the gas pedal.

Several cars sped past her.

She wanted to speed up, but was more afraid of an accident than any direct threat. Continuing south she topped several hills. Office buildings and empty parking lots gave way to houses and trees as she continued south away from Olympia. Still miles from home the more suburb setting looked familiar, but the abandon cars, burned out homes and empty neighborhoods continued the eerie surrealism. Still with no immediate threats she slowly eased off the gas.

"...back on the air using generator power."

She gasped, startled by a voice from the radio.

"Reports are coming in that a mushroom cloud is rising over southern Puget Sound or the suburbs south of Seattle. We can't see anything from our studio in Tacoma, but we are attempting to confirm it."

Lisa sped up once again.

Moments later the announcer stated, "People heading south are confirming the attack and out-of-control fires spreading away from the blast zone toward Tacoma. From our studio we can see dark clouds and heavy smoke rolling across the nearby hills. We may have to evacuate the studio."

Traffic had been light, but was now picking up as cars joined the flow south at each on ramp. *Everyone who hadn't fled the metro area just decided to leave. Thank you Peter, for giving me a head start.* Then she recalled what the announcer had said about the location of the blast, south Puget Sound or the suburbs south of Seattle, and tears rolled from her eyes for her brother Peter and his wife Sue.

She wiped her cheeks and slowed as she rolled into the county of her birth. *Two more small towns, then the exit for Hansen.* She sighed, wiped her face and then swept her eyes along the sides of the road. She wondered why the destruction was greater here than it had been in Olympia. Gas stations and convenience stores were burned and looted along with nearby homes and shops. Pillars of smoke rose from the upcoming town.

She glanced down. Her gas gauge showed just over half. If she had been coming from Seattle she would be low on fuel by this time. She imagined the desperation of a family fleeing anticipated nuclear annihilation and arriving in a small town with not enough fuel to get wherever they might be going. *I don't have any food with me and only a few gallons of gas, but I've got family nearby.*

Up ahead a motel parking lot was full of cars. Dozens of people wandered about the building and a nearby burned out gas station.

Tens of thousands drove here hoping to go on to relatives and friends beyond. How many didn't make it? Did they run out of gas and walk or did they just stay here? How would they get food? Did they die?

A few miles down the road Lisa neared the Hansen exit. She scanned the ramp and overpass for danger. She could see men, women and children along the overpass and on either side. Many watched as she approached, but none appeared to be armed. She raced up the overpass and turned left.

Immediately people held out their hands urging her to stop. Others stepped into the road almost blocking her way. She swerved to avoid one person then another and another. The crowd pressed in slowing her to a crawl. They pulled on the locked doors. The car was barely moving now. Three burly men stepped into the road thirty feet ahead. One held a crowbar.

They want my car, my gas. I might be killed or…. She knew the road ahead was straight for several hundred yards. *God help me.* She closed her eyes and rammed her foot down on the gas pedal.

The car sputtered and then roared forward.

Bang.

Thump.

Screams of terror and angry yells filled her ears.

A second later she opened her eyes. The road ahead was clear and the windshield cracked. *No, don't look! Don't look in the rearview mirror. Whatever is back there you don't want to see it.*

Lisa sped on as tears flowed. *They should have gotten out of the way. They would have stolen my car. They might have killed me.* She sobbed. *I killed someone. I'm going to jail.* More tears followed. *The guard at the college, he said, don't stop for anything.* Lisa shook her head. *No, it was a hit and run. They'll throw me in prison.* She took a deep breath and tried to stop crying, but within moments the cycle of self-recrimination and justification resumed.

Gradually the lack of people, rural setting and very familiar road gave comfort. She knew that Hansen was just a few miles ahead. *I'll talk to Dad when I get home. He'll know what to do.* With a big sigh she wiped away the last of the tears as the road descended into the river valley where the family had camped and picnicked many times. The forest was thick here and reached down to the shore of the lake only a mile ahead.

She rounded a gradual bend in the road and onto a causeway that crossed the lake. *Almost home!* Looking to the far bank she saw bulldozers parked across the road. She slowed the car to a crawl. Poles stood on either side with bodies hanging from them.

Chapter Seventeen

"What?" Caden interrupted his sister's story. "You saw bodies, hanging from poles, at the blockade?"

Lisa crossed her arms. "I told you I ran down three men and you didn't say a thing, but I say there were bodies at the blockade and you want clarification?"

Caden gestured, "Stop right there. When you hit those men you did what you had to do. I would have done the same."

His mother nodded. "That's what your father said."

"How did you get home?" Caden asked.

She relaxed her arms. "I threw the car in reverse, turned around, and headed for the logging road south of the lake."

Caden laughed. "We tried that road also. They must have pulled the culvert after you used it." He thought for a moment. "I didn't see any bodies at the blockade and I don't remember any poles." He turned to Maria. "Did you see anything?"

"No, there were no bodies, but we probably wouldn't have noticed poles."

"They were there," Lisa said.

"I never saw it, but your father told me about it," his mother added, "said it was a bad idea."

Caden shifted on the bed. "I assume Sheriff Hoover is running town security."

His mother and Lisa both nodded.

"I've never liked Hoover, but why would he hang corpses at the blockade? Has he gone crazy while I've been gone?"

"I think he's desperate," his mother said. "Nuclear bombs exploded in other parts of the country, and everyone was afraid it would happen here. People were fleeing south down every road from Seattle and Tacoma. I'm sure most were decent, but enough were willing to rob and kill…." She paused and shook her head. "Those that lived along the highway had their gas and food stolen. Cars were taken. The store and the church beside the freeway were both looted. Two deputies were murdered trying to restore order. The motel as you come into town is full of locals who lived near the interstate. They fled their homes, others were robbed and killed."

Caden recalled his trip with the military convoy. "We saw the destruction along the freeway."

"It started happening here. That's when your father went to Sheriff Hoover and proposed the blockade. He suggested the locations and using heavy equipment or logs. He even helped man the blockade, in the beginning."

Caden considered his options. Hoover had made it clear that interference was not welcome. Still, as the governor's liaison, he felt he had some responsibility to inquire about the shootings."

"What are you thinking?" Lisa asked.

I'm thinking I have no idea what to do about Sheriff Hoover. But he didn't want to say that, so he smiled and said, "I'm thinking, is there any food in this house? Is anyone else hungry?"

With help from Maria he made it down the stairs from his bedroom to the dining room. There they ate and talked about family and home for several more hours. Only when the power failed, leaving the full moon as the only light, did they go to bed.

Caden woke to crowing. He looked at the window and mumbled, "It's still dark you stupid rooster." He had grown up on this farm and knew that roosters crowed when they would, but it still annoyed him. After more crowing he knew there was no going back to sleep, so slowly he slid his legs from under the covers and sat on the edge of the bed. He turned the knob on the lamp beside him and, as light filled the room, remembered the power had been out. The clock blinked on the nightstand.

Out of habit he looked for Maria. While he never actually slept with her, for the last two weeks they had not been far apart at night. With a smile he recalled that, as the evening waned, his mother suggested Maria share the room with Adam.

Carefully he stood looking down at his bandaged leg. *Painful, but bearable.* He hobbled toward the bathroom. By the time he got downstairs, he noticed a fire in the living room woodstove. When he limped into the kitchen his mother was sitting at the table with a cup of coffee.

"You're up early," he said sitting across from her.

"You've been away from the farm too long. Someone has to feed the chickens and pig."

"I'll help."

"It's already done."

"I'll help tomorrow."

She reached back to the counter. "Your father got this after his leg operation." She set an antique, carved, wooden cane on the table. "It's been at the back of the closet for years, but I figured you might use it."

He thanked her.

Still looking at the cane she said, "I pray Trevor is all right," tears welled in her eyes, "and Peter and Susan."

"I'm sure Dad is fine, he's a survivor and Peter is a cop. He's in shape, trained and armed. Neither of them would let anything happen to Sue. Still, I should probably head up North Road and look for them."

"No," she said firmly. "Two days ago I feared you were dead and then yesterday I got you back. I can't lose you again. Your father is a survivor and so is Peter. If they are alive they will come home. If they are dead," her voice choked, "then no one should risk their life to find them."

Caden wanted to argue, but creaking stairs and floorboards announced someone coming. Maria entered wrapped in a robe and looking disheveled. "Adam's still sleeping, but...well, I thought roosters crowed at dawn."

Mother and son grinned as Maria sat at the table.

As the first rays of sunlight peeked above the eastern hills, Lisa joined the rest of the family at the breakfast table.

His mother cooked eggs and bacon and asked about Caden's plans for the day.

"I'll go talk to Hoover. I need his cooperation if I'm going to be a liaison for the governor."

Lisa rolled her eyes. "Good luck getting him to cooperate with you. He has a looong memory."

Caden shrugged. "I've got to try. Then I'll go to the armory. Also, I need to meet with the county commissioners and the emergency manager."

"Sounds exciting. Does anyone want more coffee?" Lisa stood and walked toward the pot.

Caden held up his cup, but looked at his mother. "I might be late getting back."

"Do you need me to come along and," Maria smiled, "help you get in and out of the car and up the stairs."

Caden would have welcomed her company, but the day would be boring for anyone who tagged along. "No, I think I'll just hobble along with my cane." He didn't want to leave the three most important women in his life alone on the farm, but was equally certain that they were safer together. *Maria can shoot straight and Lisa can aim a car.* He grinned at his own dark joke.

After breakfast he dressed in his uniform, complete with tattered pant leg, and limped toward the car with Maria at his side.

"Why don't you and Sheriff Hoover like each other?"

"When I was in high school his little sister, Debra, had a crush on me."

"It's got to be more than that. What happened? Did you...."

"I did nothing," he said a bit too harshly. "Well, almost nothing." With a big sigh he continued. "She was two years behind me in school and flirted with me off and on for years. On the night of my graduation there was a party at a friend's house. He let us know there would be ample beer."

"Your mom doesn't seem like the kind who would be okay with that?"

"My parents didn't know."

"Oh, this is going nowhere good."

Caden nodded. "Beer, high school grads, loud music and then Debra shows up. I'd had one too many by then, which in those days was two or three. Debra started flirting with me again and we ended up making out like only half-drunk high school kids can. At the moment Debra took off her blouse in walked the newest deputy on the force, Hoover."

Maria smiled. "You were so busted."

"He arrested everyone at the party, even his little sister, but according to him it was my fault she was there. Hoover accused me of inviting her, said I had seduced her and offered her the alcohol." Caden leaned against the car. "I had to call Dad to come get me out of jail."

"You were both young." Maria opened the car door. "You're older and wiser now and, I suspect, Hoover is also." She leaned forward and kissed him on the cheek. "Good luck and happy Valentine's Day."

The drive into town gave Caden time to think. *How come women always remember things like Valentine's Day and men never do? What should I do? Get her a card or flowers? How do you find such things at a time like this?* He shook his head and vowed to do something.

As he passed over the creek on the way into town the two red-headed teens were again along the bank, but this time with a net and what looked like a fish trap.

When he saw the Hansen city limit sign, his thoughts turned to Hoover. *He was a stern man, probably still is but, Maria is right, he is too smart to hold a grudge for over a decade.* But by the time Caden walked into the office he still didn't have a plan.

From behind his desk, Hoover looked down at the torn pant leg and bandage. "What happened?"

"Lisa accidently shot me with buckshot."

Hoover grinned. "I always liked her." He chuckled and then asked, "You going to be okay?"

"Yeah, she mostly missed." Caden looked Hoover in the eye. "Have you got a couple of minutes? We need to talk."

"Shut the door and sit down."

When the door was closed Hoover said, "What does the new military liaison need?"

Caden sighed, but decided not to respond directly. "You were elected to be the Sheriff of this county. You know the people because you've lived here since I was a kid. I can't and don't want to replace you."

He nodded.

"I want this county to be a safe place because my mother, sister, and…well other people who are important to me live here. You kept this place safe."

"Thank you. I did my best."

"There is something I wanted to ask you about. I've been told that there were bodies hanging at the blockade by the lake?"

"I don't answer to you, mister military liaison, I answer to the people of this community and…well, I kept as many of them safe as I could."

"What was done is apparently not a secret. I'm asking why. Help me understand."

"Understand?" Hoover shook his head. "How can you…." He paused and looked Caden in the eye. "You were in Washington D.C., right?"

Caden nodded.

"We saw it on TV. A lot of people were scared, but by the next morning, when L.A. was hit, people panicked. Everyone wanted out of Seattle and Tacoma as fast as possible. Many fled south toward us. While they had money the refugees bought everything and anything they thought they might need. Many took what they wanted. Stores didn't take checks, the ATM system failed, people got desperate. Along the freeway looting was widespread. When there was nothing left many of the refugees got mad. They destroyed and burned…. I've never imagined fear on that scale. The scared…the injured…the dying…. I did my best. You said I kept this place safe, but I was elected sheriff of the entire county, and over a quarter of it has been looted and burned and two of my deputies are dead."

Caden shook his head. "An army couldn't have saved the area along the freeway. I think the blockade was the right thing to do."

"That was your father's idea." Hoover remained silent for several moments and then with a sigh continued. "Two stupid kids tried to ram the North Road blockade while shooting at it with pistols. The guards returned fire, but it was the crash that killed them. I hung the bodies there as a warning to others not to be stupid and to stay away."

"What about the bodies at the other blockades?"

"There were five others. Three were looters and two were the men who killed my deputies. I shot them all."

Chapter Eighteen

Caden limped back toward his car wondering what to do now that Hoover had confirmed he killed those men. *Well, blackmail is always a possibility.* He smiled, but shook his head. *Three weeks ago I was working for Senator Stevens and enjoying the good life in D.C. and then the first bomb went off and changed my life.* He fumbled in his pocket for the car keys. *The bombs changed everyone's life. In the last two weeks I've killed one man, Maria shot another and Lisa may have run down three. Did any of us do wrong? Did Hoover do wrong?* Legally he knew the answer might be yes, but morally he found it hard to condemn the actions of Hoover or his family.

Family. He had included Maria in his thought about family. A smile spread across his face. Thinking of her that way felt good. *I need to take some time and sort out my own feelings about Maria and Becky. When, in this crazy world, will there be time to sit alone and think? Come on, you know what you feel about Maria.* He sighed deeply. *This is all so quick, so crazy.* But still he could not deny his growing feelings for Maria. *You definitely need to get Maria something for Valentine's Day.*

As he slid the key in the lock, he glanced across the street to the century old building that served as the county offices. *I still need to talk to the commissioners and head of emergency management.* Pulling out the key he headed across the street.

Ten steps led up from the sidewalk to the county offices. Caden remembered taking them two or three at a time as a child. Now, with his hurt leg, they were a formidable barrier.

Reaching the top, he found the large wooden doors locked. He considered going around the building to try each of the four entrances, but his leg pleaded for some other solution. As he stood considering his options two police cars sped past with lights flashing and sirens blaring.

Maybe Hoover can answer my questions. With a sigh he hobbled back toward the Sheriff's office. As he entered, Caden asked the deputy on guard, "Who is the emergency Manager?"

"Sheriff Hoover is the head of that office, but he left on a call a couple of minutes ago. He's also the local head of Homeland Security."

Inwardly Caden groaned, but tried not to show it. *He's head of Homeland Security too? What does the governor want me to do if Hoover is in charge of everything?*

"The Emergency Management office is at the end of the hall. The lady there handles all the day-to-day stuff."

Caden stepped in that direction.

"Oh, but the LEPC is meeting in the county office building right now."

"LEPC?"

"Local Emergency Planning Committee or something like that. The back door of the building should be open. They're meeting on the first floor, but I can't remember the room number."

By the time Caden found the location his leg felt like it was on fire. Ten people sat around a conference table as he hobbled in. "Hello, I'm Major Westmore, the new commander of the Hansen armory."

A gray haired woman said, "You're looking better this morning?"

Caden was confused.

"This is Trevor's boy," she said walking over to him "I'm Dr. Scott. I bandaged your leg last night." She shook his hand. "It is good to see you conscious, but you really should be at home in bed."

A man across the table pointed a pen at the doctor and said, "Don't lecture the man. I know you've been working 18 hour days since the Seattle blast."

Dr. Scott smiled at him then turned to Caden. "Perhaps we should both sit down."

That was a welcome suggestion. As soon as Caden sat the pain faded to a dull throb.

They took turns around the table introducing themselves to Caden. Dr. Scott was there representing the local hospital. The mayor of Hansen was next along with delegates from the fire department, civil defense, health department, city utilities, a county commissioner, a city police officer, the Emergency Manager from the sheriff's office and someone from the Salvation Army.

"We run the local food bank," the church member said.

"Do you still have food?" Caden asked.

He shook his head. "Even with rationing we ran out days ago. People are going hungry."

With that everyone looked at Caden. He was tempted, just for a moment to repeat the old Ronald Reagan line, 'I'm from the government and I'm here to help,' but decided against it. "Well, as I said I'm the new C.O. of the armory. Governor Monroe wants me to help maintain law and order in this area and assess local needs."

"Need?" The Emergency Manager said cupping her hands before her and leaning forward as if in prayer. "We have refugees from the west end of the county along the freeway. We put some up in the motel and others are at the campground. We might have a three day supply of MREs for our police and firefighters but after that…. In this county I mainly coordinated with FEMA during floods, but we can't make long distance calls and the Internet is down. I can't…."

"Okay," Caden interrupted, "I'll try and get some communication restored. Meanwhile, make me a list of what you need."

The county commissioner said, "We need everything."

With feverish intensity the civil defense coordinator took up the litany, "We've done everything we could, no one in the county plans for nuclear bombs. I've attended every meeting, done everything according to regulation but...." He shook his head. "It's not my fault."

In a much calmer voice the man from the food bank stated, "Many are already going hungry."

Another said, "The drugstore pharmacy was robbed. Three thugs tried to raid the hospital pharmacy, but...."

Annoyed, Caden interrupted, "People are hungry. The hospital must be short of medicines, but what I need is a list of critical supplies that will keep people alive."

"I'll get you a list of medical supplies," Dr. Scott said.

"In a voice barely above a whisper the Emergency Manager said, "I'll get you a list."

Caden's emotions were mixed as he left the office. If he alleviated some of the shortage it would be a big help to the community, but the need was huge and growing. He feared people would die before life returned to something reassembling normal.

He opened the door to his car. *Now, onto the armory.*

He drove east, about a mile out of town, and then turned onto a side road that led north up a large hill. The area was well wooded on the right with the left side looking down into the valley and over the town. Nice homes had been built along this part of the hill and as a young man Caden had been up here many times, but never onto the armory. As he rounded a curve near the crest a light snow fell. A few hundred yards farther and a large, gray, two-story building surrounded by a chain-link fence came into view.

As he slowed to stop at the gate a soldier stepped from the guardhouse. The guard, in ACUs, the now standard camo uniform, carried an M-4 over his shoulder. A dozen or more children played on the large grassy lawn that surrounded the main building. Despite the growing snow several adults in civilian clothing mingled among the children.

The sentry saluted and asked for identification.

Caden flashed his ID. "Who is the commanding officer and where are they?"

"Lieutenant Brooks. His office is on the second floor. I don't know the room number."

"That's fine. I'll find it." They exchanged salutes and Caden pulled into a nearby parking lot. He glanced back at the guard who was on the phone. He knew he would not have to find Brooks, the lieutenant would come to find out why a major had arrived. Using his cane, he walked as casual as possible, for a man with a limp, toward the building.

Several kids ran over to him.

"My dad is in the Army."

"What's wrong with your leg?"

"Do you have a gun?"

"When can we go home?"

Just like the kids at the refugee camps. No. He glanced at the growing number of children around him. *These kids are more…bouncy and none have asked me for food. Well, as yet anyway.*

Only as he approached did he notice the keypad beside the main door. *Do the kids know the entry code?* Before he could ask, a young second lieutenant exited, popped to attention, and saluted.

"I'm Lieutenant Brooks. How can I help you sir?"

Caden returned the salute and looked him up and down. Other than the rank insignia at the center of his chest, and the unit badge, there was little else in the way of ribbons or insignia. However, he wore a pistol on his hip.

The lieutenant stood about as tall as Caden and had close-cut blond hair. *I'm young, but this guy is a kid, probably fresh out of some college ROTC program.* "I'm Major Westmore, here to assume command. Let's go to the office."

Brooks seemed tense as he turned to open the door.

On the upper floor a small office served as headquarters for Bravo Company, the unit stationed at the armory. To his left several motivational prints hung on the wall, while the right featured recruiting posters, a picture of Governor Monroe and Adjutant General Harwich, the head of the Washington Guard, along with random thumb tacks that no one had bothered to remove. In the corner a radio played the numbing drumbeat of emergency announcements. Beside it was a SINCGARS army transceiver that was on and a shortwave radio that was turned off. Caden stopped and talked briefly with the four soldiers in the room.

The next space was a mid-sized conference room. One wall was covered in a large map of southwest Washington and on another were smaller maps of Hansen, the county and the state. A large table and chairs filled the center. In many ways both rooms were much like any of the hundreds of other military offices Caden had been in, old and in need of fresh paint, but it would serve as a decent command center.

Two open doors led to offices, but Brooks stopped, "Perhaps this would be a good place to begin the transition."

Caden handed him the written orders.

Brooks read them, came to attention and said. "What are your orders, sir?"

"I'll need a detailed report on the company's personnel and equipment status. When that is ready we can bring in the other senior personnel, but for right now I'd like a briefing from you.

"Senior personnel, well," he sighed, "that's a good place to start. Other than First Sergeant Fletcher there are no senior personnel. We're shorthanded, about half-strength at fifty-two soldiers."

Well, that's the brief on personnel. Not so good. "Why do we have children and civilians here?"

"I know it is against regulations, but many of the soldiers were worried about their families. I was the only officer here; I don't know where the commander is…."

"He's dead."

"Oh." His eyes went wide and he took a slow deep breath. "Do you know when or how, sir?"

Caden told him what he knew.

"About the civilians…well, most of our soldiers live outside Hansen, some as far away as Seattle. I authorized them to move their families here if they feared for their safety. Most chose to do so."

"Good call."

"Really?"

Caden smiled. "Really. Any soldier worried about his family isn't giving us his best." In jest he asked, "Have you broken any other regulations?"

The tension returned to Brook's face. "After the Los Angles bombing, refugees came down all the roads from Seattle." His eyes seemed to stare off in the distance for a moment. "We took a soldier, injured in a car accident, to the hospital. While we were there three armed looters attacked the pharmacy. The drugstore in town had already been robbed. I'm sure these three were addicts looking for a fix." He sighed. "They pulled guns on the staff and started shooting. I returned fire and…well…I killed all three."

Chapter Nineteen

Fifteen minutes later, as he inspected the gun vault with Brooks, Caden was still wondering how many people had died, and who really shot them. *Looters and drug addicts looking for a fix, what should they have done? Arrest them; feed them while law-abiding citizens go hungry?*

"Sixty-eight M4s and ten M9s," Brooks said with a gesture along the vault wall.

These are awful times. Hoover and Brooks have made difficult choices. How many are alive because they made those decisions? The faces of the people he had known and who were now dead lingered in his mind. *So many have died, perhaps even Dad, Peter and Susan.*

"And over here are the night vision...."

"Why are there so many empty slots?" Caden asked pointing to one row of M4 rifles.

"Two squads are deployed at the moment and one is on alert and, ah, I loaned seven to the sheriff's office." Brooks stood stiffly as if at attention. "I take full responsibility. I know there are all sorts of regulations that prohibit...."

"I assume he came and asked for them."

"Yes sir. It was when the looting began we...he...all of us really...we were trying to keep order and...."

"You've done paperwork and logged the serial numbers, of course."

"Yes sir."

Caden nodded thoughtfully. "I'm sure it was the right thing to do."

Relief flowed across the young lieutenant's face as he stood at ease.

"I'm going to need an M9. How many rounds of ammo do we have?"

Brooks handed Caden a pistol and holster. "I'd have to look up the exact numbers, but we have less than I'd like. We returned from field exercises a month ago and had not been resupplied when the terrorist attacks began."

Caden strapped on the holster as they exited the vault.

Brooks said, "I'll show you the rest of the facility. This way sir."

"My name is Caden, at least when we're alone."

"Thank you sir, my name is David."

Passing through the lobby, Caden noticed a cross carved in the stone wall and recalled that the building had been a religious school of some kind fifty or sixty years earlier. In one wing, a large room now served as a barracks. Storerooms and offices had been cleared and married soldiers assigned individual rooms. Clearly his XO had been a busy officer.

In the basement David showed him an ancient coal furnace with no coal and a modern backup generator that was low on diesel fuel.

Ammo, food and fuel. He sighed inwardly. *I need to get more of just about everything.* Fumbling in his jacket he pulled out a small notebook and wrote several notes to himself.

As they walked back toward their office, Brooks suddenly turned to his left and opened one side of a double door. "We can cut across the gym. It's shorter."

Walking into the large room, the sound of their footsteps echoed off the old hardwood floor and bounced off the wooden walls and bleachers. Large windows high above on one side provided light that cast the old gymnasium in a yellow glow.

"Assemble the men in..." Caden glanced at his watch. *Almost noon.* "one hour, 1300. We'll do the change of command and I'll speak to the soldiers at that time."

When they arrived at the office, Brooks sent two privates to make preparations for the assembly.

"Where is the first sergeant?" Caden asked, "I'd like to talk with him before the change of command."

"He's with second squad guarding the North Road Bridge over the Cowlitz River."

Caden nodded. "You mentioned we had two squads out?"

"Third squad is east of town along the highway. A few days ago we had four squads deployed guarding the north and east perimeter of the town, but things are quieter to the east."

"The north road isn't secure?"

"There is a large unofficial refugee camp just across the Cowlitz River Bridge."

"When you say large, what do you mean?"

"I'd estimate a thousand individuals."

"I can understand us not wanting another thousand mouths to feed, but why don't we let them pass through, maybe in small, manageable, groups?"

"Most of them stopped there because they were either low on gas or out of it. They can't go anywhere and now they're out of food and getting desperate. I've seen fights, riots really, and heard gunshots but, thankfully we are able to keep those problems on the other side of the river."

"How?"

"The river is running high and fast and the bridge is barricaded."

Caden nodded thinking of his father, brother and sister-in-law who were all on the wrong side of the river. *When my leg is better I'm going to need to go up that road and try to find them.* He continued to his office where he strained to concentrate on the reports and assess the readiness of his command. *Not very ready.* As he tried to come up with a plan, the lights went out.

From the next office he heard David moan. "We have been experiencing more brown outs and power failures with each passing day."

Caden nodded to no one and continued to read by the light of a window behind him, but after a couple of minutes he gave up and leaned back in the chair. Even though it was barely afternoon, he was tired, his leg ached and the dim light strained his eyes. He stood and hobbled to the window. Gray clouds covered much of the sky casting the valley and town below in shadow.

It's going to be a long hard winter no matter what the weather is like. I'm fortunate to be home…to even have a home to go to. He thought of the people he had seen walking along the highways. At that moment he wanted desperately to be with his family at the farmhouse. He realized that once again he had included Maria and even little Adam in his mental image of family.

A shiver passed through him. *The farmhouse has a fireplace and woodstove, but how many don't have that?* Again he shivered. Perhaps it was just his imagination, but it already seemed cooler in the room. He reached out and touched an ancient radiator beside the window. It was cold. *No coal for the boiler.*

Brooks stepped into the office holding two cups of coffee and handed one to Caden. "We might as well drink it while it is still hot."

"What causes the power to go out more each day?"

Brooks shrugged.

"Why doesn't the backup generator come on when the main power goes out?"

"We're so short of fuel I'm only using it at night."

Caden nodded. *All I need is more food, fuel, ammo and soldiers, and this command will be ready for anything.* He grinned and Brooks gave him a quizzical look, but he ignored it and sipped his coffee.

David did the same and then said, "I hope we can get people back home and get the economy moving. If we don't and the power fails for a long period of time...well, just imagine, heat, communication, refrigeration, cooking, it's all electric."

"If we don't find or grow a lot more food in the next month or two most of us won't need to worry about electricity."

Static crackled over the radio and Caden glanced that direction and then at the still dark lights.

David smiled at his confusion. "The radio has battery backup."

They both returned to their coffee.

Forty minutes later Caden stood in a darkened hallway still considering what to say. As he did he stared at the backs of those assembled in the gym. About forty soldiers stood in formation waiting for him to enter. Behind them were about ten civilians, mostly women, and about as many children. A podium stood at the far end with Brooks to the right of it.

He took a deep breath and marched into the room.

"Company, attention," Brooks announced.

"At ease," Caden responded. As he walked up to the podium he still had only a vague idea of what he wanted to say. *Give them a sense of purpose, a mission and direction.*

After reading his orders aloud, Caden scanned the faces of the assembled soldiers. Taking a deep breath he proceeded. "I was in Washington D.C. on that terrible day. I know the horror and the pain of loss that many of you have experienced.

"I traveled with Governor Monroe back to Washington State. From the moment I met him he has been striving to solve problems brought on by the terrorist attacks. He is working hard to get people home and the economy up and running. Food and fuel are being distributed. Power is being…will be restored.

"We are going to be a part of that process. The road ahead will not be easy, but each of us has a role in the restoration of this nation."

The lights blinked, came on for a moment then died. Caden sighed and continued. "Our orders are to assist local authorities in maintaining law and order and help provide aid. Together with Sherriff Hoover we are going to secure Hansen, the farms around it and outlying communities. The army already has secured the freeway. It is open to travel, both to the north and south. We are going to clear the state highway from Hansen to the on ramp so that the town can be supplied." He looked up at the darkened ceiling, "The lights will come back on. The day will come when you can go home."

Looking out at those before him, Caden could see emotions ranging from hopefulness to despair.

"Finally, Lieutenant Brooks has done an outstanding job. I concur with his decision to move families into the armory. We are going to keep our loved ones safe while we do our job."

A murmur of approval swept the gym.

That seems like a good note to end this on. Caden stepped away from the podium and said, "Lieutenant Brooks, dismiss the men." Walking quickly through the ranks of soldiers he exited the gym.

From the hallway he heard, "Company attention. Dismissed."

Back at the office Caden sat staring out the window. He could barely detect the position of the sun through the gray clouds that cast the world in shadow. He felt the cold now on his nose and ears. A few snowflakes flitted through the air outside.

"Excuse me sir."

It was Brooks' voice. Still looking out the window Caden said, "Yes?"

"I just wanted to say that I liked what you said, and not just the comment about me. I think it helped."

He smiled and turned to face Brooks. "Thanks. I hope it did."

The radio crackled and then a frightened, hurried voice was heard. "Company HQ this is second squad." From the small speaker the sound of gunfire and metal scraping metal seemed to fill the room. "We're under fire."

Chapter Twenty

One of the privates in the office grabbed the mic. "Roger Second Squad, we read that you're taking fire." He looked to Brooks expectantly.

Brooks turned to Caden. "Fourth squad is the duty rapid response unit."

"Deploy them."

While the private relayed word that help was coming, Brooks grabbed the mic for the building intercom then slammed it down apparently remembering the power was out. Pointing to a PFC he said, "Find Corporal Sanchez and have his team reinforce second squad."

Helmet in hand, Brooks headed for the door.

"XO," Caden said, "I'm coming with you." Brooks started to protest, but he insisted. "I need to see the situation."

He nodded and left at a jog. Caden hobbled along behind cursing his throbbing leg and ankle. As they hustled out the building two Humvees sped out the gate.

"Here," Brooks called, "We'll go in my truck." He pointed to a red Ford pickup.

Jogging toward it Caden said, "I didn't figure you for a pickup kind of guy."

"It was abandoned and I thought it would be useful."

Sliding in Caden noticed a shotgun behind the seat.

Brooks turned the key and the trucked lurched forward, shot out the gate, and down the hill. Then turning right he sped toward the fight.

Caden had rarely driven out this way, but he knew they were only a minute or two from the bridge. "Isn't there a power plant a few miles up the North Road?"

"Yes, beyond the refugee camp, but it was closed last year. It's a coal-fired plant and couldn't meet the new environmental regulations."

"That's right and the mine is next to it."

"The coal from that old pit is high in sulfur so they closed it down about five years ago. These last few years they brought coal in from out of state."

Caden thought for a moment. "I wonder if we could get the plant back up and running?"

"We could try. That might solve our power problems."

"That's what I'm thinking. And is the city hydroelectric dam functioning?"

"Just barely. We drive out with a couple of workers every other day to check on it."

He could hear shots now. Brooks pulled off on a simple dirt lane. Fifty yards up he stopped beside a green tent.

Strapping the helmet to his head and staying low, Brooks moved forward. "We can see the bridge from over there." He reached the position first and, picking up binoculars, he said, "Those civilians are either desperate or drunk."

Caden hobbled up to the sandbagged and camouflaged observation post a moment later. Borrowing the binoculars he looked down at the fire fight. It was clear what happened. Some of the refugees got a dump truck, sped it across the bridge and slammed it into the bulldozer the soldiers used to barricade the road. Apparently they hoped to smash through the blockade, but the dozer won. The front of the truck was crumpled and twisted. The bulldozer had been moved a foot or two or perhaps the soldiers had parked it at a slight angle, either way, it still blocked the bridge.

The windshield of the truck had been shattered. Looking through binoculars, Caden saw several bullet holes in the remaining glass. The body of the driver was slumped against the door. About half-a-dozen refugees with rifles were behind the dump truck firing on the soldiers. Caden shook his head. *We're engaged in a fire fight with our own people.*

Hundreds of refugees remained on the far side of the river, huddled behind cars and trees, trying not to get shot. "We've got good firing angles on the shooters, better cover and more men." *The guys on the bridge aren't going to break through the barricade; they're going to get themselves killed.* Caden said, "I need to talk to the First Sergeant."

Brooks led the way down the dirt lane to the main road. Staying low and following the gully he led Caden toward the fight. Bullets flew past them hitting the embankment and trees a few feet above where they stood in the ditch.

Caden leaned to the left to get a better view of the soldiers ahead.

Brooks turned. Their eyes met for a moment, and then he slammed to the ground at Caden's feet.

"Brooks...David, are you okay?" Caden dragged the lieutenant to the lowest point of the ditch then dropped beside him as blood flowed down his face. Caden struggled to get the helmet off the wounded man, afraid of what he might see. Finally tossing it aside he looked for the wound, but all he could see was blood. He struggled to wipe away the flow with his hand and sleeve. *Where is the wound?* "David can you hear me?"

His eyes popped open. "What happened?"

"You've been hit. Stay still while I find the wound."

"Shot...in the head?" He reached up to the wound and then pulled back with a moan as he gazed at his bloody fingertips.

"Stay still." Caden moved closer. He pulled a gauze bandage from his ACUs and gently wiped some more. "Oh."

"What do you see?"

"You know head wounds bleed a lot, right?"

"Yes."

"Well, you have a two inch cut in your scalp. It just sliced the skin, but otherwise it looks okay." He took a clean bandage from David's ACUs, and placing it on his head, said, "Hold this right here." He took a roll of gauze and wrapped it around his head and tied it. "All the blood makes it look like some horrid wound, but you'll live."

Caden picked up the discarded helmet and examined the bloodstained gash along one side. Handing it to David he grinned, "It has character now. Are you able to walk?"

Brooks nodded.

Staying lower than earlier, they moved toward the barricade with Caden in the lead. The First Sergeant fired from a prone position as the two crawled up. Tapping the soldier on the back Caden said, "Hold your fire."

The First Sergeant looked at him and then Brooks. "You okay sir?"

"Yes, just a cut. Major Westmore is the new commanding officer. Do as he says."

"Hold your fire," the First Sergeant yelled. "Hold your fire."

Within a few seconds the soldiers ceased firing.

"Have any of the soldiers been wounded?" Caden asked.

The First Sergeant smiled at Brooks, "Just the lieutenant."

It was a long half-minute before the civilians stopped firing.

When there was silence on the bridge Caden called out. "Your position is hopeless. Retreat off the bridge and you will not be harmed."

A voice called out. "How do we know we can trust you?"

"You're just going to have to."

Another deeper voice said, "We've got women and children over here, but no food. There hasn't been any for days."

Caden rubbed his forehead in despair.

"We have pregnant women and sick children here. We're all starving. What have we got to lose?" the deep voice declared.

Caden turned to Brooks, "Get a medic and a deuce and a half down here...and fifty MREs." Then he shouted, "Don't shoot I want to talk."

Both Brooks and the First Sergeant started to object, but Caden shook his head. Eyes fixed forward he rose slowly, spread his hands apart, and stepped over a line of sandbags. "My name is Major...ah, Caden. You, with the deep voice, what's your name?"

"Neil...Neil Young."

"Please, come forward and talk to me."

Seconds later, a big bull of a man with a scraggly beard stepped from behind the dump truck.

Caden held out his hand as the big man neared. "Hi Neil. I arrived here yesterday to find out what is needed and try to organize help."

The big guy looked at his torn and bandaged leg and then at his bloody hands and sleeve. "I guess it's been a rough couple of days." He shook Caden's hand. "What did you want to say?"

"Conditions are desperate everywhere, but if there is a way to help I'd like to try. How many pregnant women are in your camp?"

"About twenty and maybe twice that many really sick kids. The doc says its dysentery and typhoid."

"You have a doctor? That's good to know." Caden sighed. "I'm trying to get food, fuel and even steady electricity, but I can't promise much. If nothing changes in a week, maybe two, the town will be out of food."

"We're a week or two ahead of you. When you run out of food, we'll already be dying of starvation and disease."

"Here is what I can do right now. If someone needs to be hospitalized, we'll do it. I'll get a medic down here to work with your doctor. I'll get a tent and supplies so we can set up a rudimentary field hospital. We'll transport the seriously ill to the Hansen hospital. I've ordered food to be brought here, not much, but I will try to get more. That is the best I can do."

Neil's eyes grew tired. "I believe you, but I'm not sure everyone will." He sighed. "I'll get the doctor, the pregnant women and the sickest kids to the bridge."

The two men shook hands again and parted.

Caden told the First Sergeant to have the medic work with the camp doctor, get the sickest to the hospital and distribute the fifty MREs to those who needed it most.

As the two walked back toward the pickup Brooks held out his keys. "I think you should drive."

The lieutenant's complexion was pale, in stark contrast to the dried blood that still covered part of his face.

Caden took the keys. "Yeah, let's get back to the armory and get some coffee."

Looking off in the distance Brooks said, "I noticed the combat badge on your uniform. Were you in Afghanistan?"

"Yeah. Two tours."

"Was it bad? Did you...."

Caden stopped.

"Sorry, I shouldn't have asked."

"No. It's okay, David." He sighed deeply. "I was in combat multiple times on both tours and yes, I've killed people."

"Does it get easier? Do you forget their faces?"

"Combat is never easy, but yes, I think it gets easier." He slowly shook his head. "About the other thing…I've never forgotten the faces of those I've killed or my friends who have been killed."

Brooks took a deep breath. "Thanks. I thought it was just me."

Caden opened the truck door and then paused. "You know, Churchill once said, 'There's nothing quite as exhilarating as being shot at and missed.' Maybe you should look at it that way. You're alive and that is a good thing."

"Today isn't the problem."

"Oh? The looters at the hospital?"

Brooks nodded.

So it was you that killed them. "Let's get that coffee."

The generator was running by the time they got back to the armory. Brooks opted for a long shower before getting coffee. When he returned to the office his complexion had improved. Except for the bandage on his head, he looked like a typical young soldier.

Taking the last sip of his coffee Caden said, "I want one of us here at night."

"I've been living at the armory since the Atlanta bombing."

"Well then I guess you need a night off?"

"I'm fine. I'll stay. I think I need an early night anyway."

Caden wrote down his phone number and then added his address and a simple map to his house and handed it to Brooks. "If anything happens, call me or come get me. Otherwise I'll see you in the morning."

With the electricity still off, and the sun setting early that time of year, the roads were dark and lonely. As he drove down the main street he shared the road with a single sheriff's car. Candlelight shining in the window and the smell of wood fires greeted him as he passed by homes on his way out of town. Snow flitted in the air. It would have been pretty, almost Christmas like, if he didn't know the tragedy, hunger and cold that caused it.

Candles and lanterns shone through the windows, casting the living room and kitchen in a soft, yellow glow as he stepped from the car in front of his family home. Waving his arm he announced, "It's me, Caden." *Don't need any more shooting tonight.*

Maria stepped out the door with a wide smile.

Caden sighed. *Totally forgot about Valentine's Day.*

As he limped into the light her smile changed to fright. "Are you okay? Where are you hurt?"

"Oh," he said looking at his bloody sleeves. "I'm okay. It's someone else's." He came up the steps and hugged her. "It's good to be home."

Lisa came out onto the porch. "Are you…."

"I'm fine. Let me sit down and I'll tell you all about it."

An hour later he had told everyone the story of his day and had a dinner of stewed chicken, corn and potatoes. The food was good, but each mouthful brought back images of the desperate people north of town. *I hope we can find a solution fast for them.*

In the living room, he sat in his father's recliner and felt the cares of the time drain out of him.

Sitting next to him with Adam, Maria said, "We traded a young rooster and a couple of hens for some rabbits."

"Dad had some cages, but no rabbits, so we traded for a buck and two does." His sister added. "Now, in a couple of months we'll have another source of meat."

"That's great. If everyone bartered like that, there would be a lot less hunger than there is.

Light hit the living room curtains casting the room in a colorful glow. Lisa stood, grabbed her shotgun, and peeked out the window. "Someone is coming up the driveway."

Maria blew out the lantern as his mother smothered the two candles.

Caden came up behind his sister and recognized the red Ford pickup. "He's a good guy sis, don't shoot him."

She elbowed her brother. "I'm never going to hear the end of that am I?"

"Nooo," Caden said with a big grin, "My grandchildren are going to know all about the day my baby sister shot me."

Brooks stepped out of the car as the whole Westmore clan filed onto the porch.

At the bottom step the lieutenant came to attention and saluted.

Caden returned the salute, "Is there a problem XO?"

"Hopefully not sir. We received a phone call about 30 minutes ago. The Adjutant General has ordered all commanders back to Olympia for a meeting at 0900 tomorrow." He handed Caden a sheet of paper with handwritten details.

After reading it over he asked, "Did they say what it was about?"

"No, but on the radio coming here I heard that President Durant has activated the California National Guard to assist Chinese advisors."

A bewildered look spread across Maria's face. "Chinese?"

Chapter Twenty-One

Caden rubbed his chin. "What are the Chinese advising us about?"

"The radio said they want to ensure the fair distribution of their food aid."

"Why do we need their help to ensure fairness?" Lisa asked.

"We don't," Maria replied.

They're not worried that we will misuse the food aid. I thought they were covering something up with their own involvement when they disarmed the North Koreans. This is just another step in their worldwide chess game—a game I think we might lose. "I guess I'll let you know when I get home tomorrow.

Lisa looked at Brooks, "You said that all Guard units were activated. What does that mean?"

Caden answered. "It means we are no longer subject to state authority. We're under federal government command." *And I'm liking this less the more I think about it.* "But the only thing I know for sure is that I'm to attend a meeting tomorrow, so let's not get too worked up." *There will be plenty of time to get upset tomorrow.* "So XO, why did you drive down here? The phones are working—I think."

"They are," he said heading back to the car, "but I thought you might need this." He set two, five-gallon gas cans, on the ground. Then he handed Caden a neatly folded uniform, "And you might need this since I got blood on your ACUs,"

"So that was your blood?" Lisa asked. "He told us what happened. That was you? Are you okay?"

He gently touched the side of his head "Ah…yes, yes and yes ma'am. The medic sewed me up."

Lisa invited him inside, but he declined. "I better get back to the armory. I'll have four soldiers and a Humvee here at 0730 to accompany you."

Thinking the Humvee was excessive he started to object, but then reconsidered. *If I'm not well protected Maria might insist on riding shotgun and I don't want that. The safest place for her is right here on the farm.* "Have the soldiers bring four MREs with them in the morning. Thanks."

As Brooks drove away and the family filed back into the house, Lisa turned to him. "So, what's his first name?"

"David. Why?"

She smiled. "He looks good in a uniform."

*   *   *

The soft glow of the oncoming sunrise heralded a new day as a Humvee pulled up in front of the farmhouse. One young soldier in a flak jacket and carrying an M4 climbed out.

In his new ACUs Caden stepped out on the porch carrying a briefcase that belonged to his father. In it was the list of needed supplies from the emergency manager and a map of the area. He hoped to get everything his community needed, but knew that was highly unlikely. He turned to his mother, and hugged her. "When my leg is better I'm going up the North Road and look for Dad, Susan and Peter."

"Your father is a resourceful man. He'll come back to me. I hope with Peter and Susan, but we can talk about it later."

Dad is a resourceful man and if he is alive he will find a way back, but people are killing each other out there for food, drugs and gas.

"Okay Mom, we'll talk about it later." He hugged his sister and Maria.

Maria pulled him back tight. "Be back tonight."

He smiled, hugged her again. "That's my plan."

The soldier climbed into the SUV with Caden and following the Humvee they headed toward the freeway.

At the causeway barricade they stopped and Caden told the guards that he would be back that evening, hopefully with other trucks. Then the Humvee and car crossed over into the ten mile no-man's-land between the blockade and the freeway.

As they approached the freeway overpass, Caden noticed several burned-out cars that were not there a couple of days before in the otherwise deserted church parking lot. Across the street, in the convenience store parking lot, were a dozen vehicles, but only one was familiar. Turning to the soldier beside him he said, "I'm going to pull off here for just a moment. Tell the guys in the Humvee."

Using his radio, the soldier informed the others.

The few people in the lot were all male. Caden saw desperate eyes follow him across the lot.

The Humvee circled back as Caden stopped beside a worn Ford minivan with a tarp duct taped to the top and supported by tree limbs. Turning to the soldier with him he said, "Tell everyone to keep watch." He stepped out as a thin man with a graying beard came around from behind the van. "Hello Henry. I've got something for you." He handed him a five gallon gas can. "I know it is not enough to get you to your farm in Oregon, but it's all I can spare."

Henry's eyes widened. "Thank you. It might be enough. If it's not we'll walk the rest of the way. Thanks." He called to his wife and boys. "We better be quick. Most of the people here are criminals or crazy. The only reason they leave us alone is that we're armed and don't have anything."

Caden glanced over his shoulder. Four soldiers stood behind the SUV and Humvee with their weapons pointed at several, dirty, wild-eyed men as they cautiously approached. "Yeah they look desperate enough to do something stupid."

"Hey, you got more gas?" One man called out.

One boy tore the tarp from the car as Henry poured the fuel into his tank. Caden handed the four MREs to the wife. With tears in her eyes she thanked him as the family climbed into the minivan.

Another man, holding a pistol, yelled, "Hey, you got more food?"

"Henry's auto sputtered, shook and then started. He did a 'thumbs up,' to the soldiers.

Caden called to the soldiers, "Let's move out fast." The soldiers jumped in and all the vehicles quickly drove out of the lot.

The SUV and Humvee pulled onto the freeway heading north and, in his rearview mirror, Caden caught a glimpse of Henry and his family heading south. *God, I hope they make it home.*

*   *   *

The meeting was held in the same conference room as the one he attended just days before. When he walked in all the seats were taken at the table. Caden recognized Governor Monroe, his chief of staff David Weston and, from his picture at the armory, Adjutant General Harwich of the Washington National Guard, but not anyone else.

Clusters of people stood along the walls, including one group of military officers. Caden was tempted to walk over to them, but the way was blocked by other groups.

Chairs were brought in and Caden finally got one along the wall.

After about five minutes the governor stood. "Thank you all for coming. The president is about to address the nation. The speech will be carried by the national media, but we were planning a meeting for Monday so, I felt it best we watch it together and have the meeting right afterwards. If we have to make plans based on the President's address we can do so right then."

With that someone turned on a large television on the wall. An announcer was just concluding his comments and then President Durant appeared on screen.

"My fellow Americans," he began and for several minutes engaged in the normal political platitudes. "While we hunt down those who aided the terrorists we will also restore this great nation. To speed the process of restoration I am taking the following actions today."

This was the part he wanted to hear. Caden leaned forward.

"As acting President of the United States I have already imposed martial law on several states and regions. I am now extending that to all fifty states and territories. The Posse Comitatus Act is suspended…"

The military can now arrest civilians. Is that legal?

"…and I am suspending the writ of habeas corpus."

And the military doesn't need to charge someone with a crime when arresting them and citizens don't get a day in court.

"Contrary to reports in the media I am not activating all Guard and reserve units. While I have considered it, many state governors wish to retain more direct control of their Guard soldiers so, at this time, only select companies in Maryland, Virginia, Georgia and California have been called up."

Good! I don't work for President Durant—yet anyway.

"However, all military commands are ordered to cooperate with our allies to maintain order and distribute aid. This relief will soon be arriving from a number of countries. In the east I have asked our NATO allies to take the lead in relief efforts. China will manage aid in the west.

Murmurs of disapproval swept the room. "We got the short straw on that one," a man to the left of Caden muttered.

"And finally, until we have put these terrorist attacks behind us and our economy is back on its feet I am postponing presidential elections."

A collective gasp swept the room.

The president doesn't have the right or power to postpone the election. Caden struggled to hear Durant over the debate that now flooded the auditorium.

"We should not, we must not…liberty must temporarily bow…greater good…security…food…back on the job…We will rise from…Thank you and God Bless America." The screen went dark.

Immediately people on both sides and across the table asked Governor Monroe, "Are you going to drop out of the race?"

Monroe sat silent for a moment as if taking it all in. Then he slowly shook his head. "No. While I believe…I know, that President Durant does not have the authority to postpone the election, he remains the lawful president at least until the next inauguration. Until that time I will cooperate with him in every way that I can, within the Constitution. However, I intend to remain a candidate and speak out on issues where I believe the President is wrong, such as his attempt to postpone the upcoming election and allow Chinese troops into the country."

The Governor then called for reports from advisors, cabinet officials, FEMA and area Guard commanders. While Monroe was the hub of discussion, a variety of smaller groups formed around the room. David Weston seemed in constant motion bringing people to the Governor, or getting some fact or figure for him.

As the Governor spoke with various advisors, Caden overheard long discussions about flu and other illnesses. He checked his list. *No request for flu vaccine.* Briefly he considered adding it, but the list was already long. *Why add things no one asked for?*

It was well over an hour before the Governor met with Adjutant General Lowell. They spoke briefly before David Weston called over one of the Guard commanders. Finally, the Chief of Staff called Caden to meet with the Governor and General Lowell.

The General introduced himself and then asked about troop levels and supplies.

"I have 53 soldiers, which is just over half strength. That number is adequate for the moment. However, I need to be resupplied with ammo." He handed the general a list.

Caden then laid a map of the Hansen area on the table and described his plan. "We'll secure the state highway out to the interstate and the North Road toward Tacoma. Also there is a coal power plant here," he pointed, "I want to try and get it back up and running, but as we expand our area of control I'll be stretching my manpower and thinning my positions."

Monroe traced his finger along the North Road. "Opening this route would help move supplies and people. Also we could use the power from the coal generator. The eastern half of the state is good, but on this side of the mountains we don't have enough electricity because of damaged or destroyed transmission lines. Can you absorb the people from the refugee camp into your community?"

"No, we're critically short of food and other necessities." He handed the governor his list. "But if I had enough gasoline and some food I think I'd be able to get most them to the FEMA camp here," he pointed on the map, "or home if they still have one."

Monroe nodded. "Everyone has been handing me long lists like you have, but I'll ask Weston to speak with FEMA and gather what they can.

The sun dipped low in the winter sky as Caden's SUV pulled onto the freeway behind the Humvee and leading three supply trucks and a fuel tanker. The vehicles were full to the point that some ammo and medicine was stacked in the back of his SUV, still the convoy had less than half the supplies he requested. Caden told the young soldier with him to drive and he sat in the passenger seat with an M4 leaning between his legs. He was exhausted, but all he had done today was listen and talk. He struggled to stay awake while formulating a plan to use his limited supplies to clear the refugee camp and feed the town. *It will be good to get home tonight.*

Bang!

Caden jerked his head about. *What? A blown tire?*

The driver cursed loudly.

The car skidded to a stop slamming Caden into the belt.

Throwing the car into reverse the driver weaved the car backward.

Muzzles flashed.

Caden rolled the window down and returned fire.

The Humvee pull back to the curve, stopped across both lanes, and the soldiers jumped out and returned fire.

Glancing quickly to his side he realized they were at the off ramp to Hansen. "Pull in there," he ordered. The other three trucks followed them into the empty parking lot. Everyone was out of their vehicle in a second.

Caden tossed the M4 to the young soldier and pulled his pistol from the holster. "You guys," he said pointing to the men from the trucks, "stay here and guard the supplies." With the soldier from his car he moved forward into the forest. "Radio the others and tell them we are on the right flank in the woods."

The young man nodded and reported in with the others at the Humvee.

Minutes later Caden was just off to the side of the makeshift roadblock. "Have the men hold their fire."

When the shooting stopped, Caden crawled up to the barricade. There was blood, but no bandits.

Turning to the man with him he said, "Tell everyone we've secured the blockade. Have them clear it from the road and secure the perimeter. Also tell them I'm heading back that way. I don't want to get shot."

Caden jogged along the highway to the lot. Throwing up the back hatch of the car, he pulled ammo boxes toward him grabbed several magazines and reloaded others. Out of the corner of his eye he glimpsed two of his soldiers escorting a civilian. "Are you guys okay?" he asked without turning.

"Yes sir. The shooters appear to have run off. The only one we captured is this old guy."

Caden turned and locked eyes on a grey-haired man that, weeks earlier, would have been dismissed as a bum.

The old man's eyes widened. "Son?"

"Dad?"

Chapter Twenty-Two

The face was gaunt, the beard scraggly. Disheveled grey hair topped his head and he wore a heavy tan jacket that needed a wash. But under the dirty hair and grime Caden could see the face of his father, Trevor Westmore.

The older man stepped forward and embraced his son. "I've been worried about you ever since that first horrible day."

Caden hugged his father. "I was worried about you too, Dad."

"I thought…I, well…you're alive, thank God."

Stepping back from his father, Caden asked, "What are you doing here? I expected you to be somewhere along the North Road. You didn't shoot at us did you?"

"No! Well, not exactly. I was up on the hill there," he said pointing, "watching the guys at the blockade from behind. I had only been there a few minutes when I heard the sound of trucks coming. I was certain they would ambush whoever came down the road. When the lead Humvee rounded the bend I knew I had to act and fired my shotgun. At that range I was sure it wouldn't hurt anyone, but that you would hear it and probably see the muzzle flash. By-the-way, when did you go back in the Army?"

"I'll tell you all about it later, but right now I need more answers, like did you find Peter and Susan?"

Suddenly his father looked much older. "I never found Peter, but I did find Sue. She is in a backroom of the church," he said with a nod toward the building across the street. "I left her there while I checked out the blockade."

"Come on. Let's get her. We need to get moving before the bandits decide to come back." Caden ordered the men to finish clearing the barricade then regroup in the convenience store parking lot. "Keep an eye out for shooters and be ready to move when we come out of the church."

His father retrieved a pump shotgun from the soldier beside him and pulled a flashlight from his pocket. Caden followed as his dad led across the street and through the church parking lot. As they went his father asked questions. "How's your mom? Have you seen Lisa? Has there been any more looting?"

Caden did his best to answer the questions. Near the convoy there had been sufficient light, but as they approached the church darkness closed in. He turned on his own flashlight. "Do you think Peter was too close when they detonated the bomb?"

"I hate to think about what might have happened to him. Susan and I were almost too close to the blast. I can't see how your brother would have survived. I saw the flash and then both of us heard and felt it before seeing the mushroom cloud rise over a line of trees to the north. My old truck was the only auto that was still running. It amazed me how many people were in the area. As we sped away from the growing mushroom cloud, everyone ran in a panic toward my truck."

The front doors to the church had been broken open. Caden pulled his pistol from the holster as he crossed the threshold. Automatically he flipped a light switch inside, but nothing happened. By flashlight the two men proceeded. Trash and debris were scattered on the floor of the lobby.

"This way," his father whispered as he moved to the left.

Looking at the empty water bottles, beer cans and food wrappers that littered the way, Caden asked in a low voice, "Are you sure no one is in here?"

"I checked earlier. We were going to spend the night here and then push on to Hansen in the morning."

"If it's deserted why are we whispering?"

His father chuckled. "I don't know. By-the-way, Sue is armed with a pistol."

As they passed a lavatory the smell of human waste hung heavy in the air.

Reaching the middle of the hall his father stopped. "Susan it's me. I'm with Caden."

There was no answer. Slowly he opened the door.

Susan stood just inside. Her hair was a mess and she was wearing a heavy old army coat, but Caden was focused on the pistol she was only slowly lowering to her side. With her free hand she put one finger to her lips and said in a barely audible whisper. "There are other people in the building."

The two men stepped in the dark room. Caden stayed near the door and watched the hall.

"How did I miss them earlier?" his dad wondered out loud.

"They came in after all the shooting," she said. "They ran down this hall, but I don't know where they are now."

"They must have circled back," Caden said. "They probably left supplies or something else important here."

"You don't have a radio on you do you?" his father asked.

"No." Caden thought for a moment then said, "I'll lead the way out. Whoever is in here is either avoiding us or hoping to trap us. Either way, I don't want to encounter them, but if we do I'll shoot. That should bring the soldiers."

"Why not just shoot now and alert them?" Trevor asked.

"I don't want to pull them away from the convoy unless it is necessary. We have three trucks full of food, ammo and medicine and a fueler out there." He took one more look down the hall then said, "You two stay low."

"That's a little hard to do right now," Sue said.

Caden wondered what she meant, but he pushed it from his mind and focused on the immediate task of getting out of the building.

His father picked up a bulging army backpack and slid it on. Caden turned to the hall, looked both ways, then carefully stepped from the room. With Susan in the middle the three moved silently toward the lobby.

Arriving at the end of the hallway, Caden leaned slowly forward leading with his pistol.

A shot rang out splintering the wood just above his arm, but not hitting him. He dropped and fired two shots at a figure silhouetted by light from the convoy.

A man screamed in pain.

Another shot hit the wall near Caden.

His father stepped to the corner and fired his shotgun.

Caden heard running and then a muffled shot. He waited several seconds and then cautiously looked around the corner. Two headlights now illuminated much of the lobby. Caden used his flashlight to fill in the dark areas and discovered a body on the floor near the entrance.

Suddenly the headlights blinked out.

Caden ducked back into the hall and then cautiously peeked around the corner.

Two soldiers burst into the lobby sweeping their rifles back and forth.

Moving back behind the wall, Caden called to them and, only after they acknowledged him, did he step out.

"We heard shots," one soldier said. "A man ran out with a gun. We shot him and came looking for you."

"You did well. Check that end of the church. Dad, keep watch back down the hall."

"You killed him," a woman screamed as she ran in the lobby from the sanctuary. The screamer was followed by a second woman and two small children.

The crying and cursing woman collapsed in sobs on the body by the door. A young boy stood beside her with tears streaming down his face.

Caden kept watch while the soldiers checked the rest of building. The woman continued to cry while cradling the body in her arms. The other woman sat on the floor with the children. Their faces looked gaunt and miserable.

After several minutes the two soldiers returned. "We found one body on a pew in the sanctuary. I suspect he was the one wounded at the barricade. The rest of the building is empty."

Caden nodded. "We need to get the supplies to town. Let's get moving." Approaching the two women he said, "You can come with us, but…."

"Look at all you've got, trucks that I bet are full of food, but we're starving. See him," she said as she yanked the arm of the boy beside her, "my boy hasn't eaten in days."

While the women continued to loudly curse and shout, a soldier pulled back the sleeve of one of the shooters. "These are gang tattoos."

"How do you know?" Caden asked.

"I'm a police officer in Seattle, or I was…."

"You were lucky," another soldier said.

"Yeah, I guess. Well, anyway, I've seen these tattoos before. I suspect there are warrants out for the males. If they went to a FEMA camp they would have been identified and arrested."

Caden turned and stared at the women. He had planned to deliver them to the sheriff, just in case, but if this soldier was right they might not come willingly.

During his reflection the woman continued to yell and curse. *In the last two weeks I've had too many guns pointed in my direction and too many angry people in my face.* "Shut up woman and…."

"No! I deserve to eat. And you know what? You deserve to die!" She yanked a pink pistol from inside her coat.

Shots rang out.

Caden wasn't sure, but it seemed like everyone, the two soldiers, his dad and Sue all fired at nearly the same moment. The impact of the shots spun the gang woman around and now she lay across the body of the man she had loved.

Kneeling beside her, Caden checked for a pulse, but found none. He saw multiple gun and buckshot wounds, but not much blood. *She was dead before she hit the ground.* Standing, he looked around the lobby. "Where's the boy?"

"He ran off," the other gang woman said. "He's good at that."

I've got to get the supplies secured in the armory. I don't have time to hunt for a kid that doesn't want to be found. Turning to the woman Caden said, "You've committed no crime that I know of. You're free to go, but I suggest you come with us."

She shook her head. "They'll take away my kid."

Exhaustion swept over him like a wave. Caden shook his head slowly then turned to his men. "Move out ASAP." Turning to his father and Sue, he said in a softer tone, "Let's go home." He marched from the church. *Death has become common, too common.* Clear of the carnage he paused, looked back and then turned to his men. "Move the bodies outside, and cover them with something." It wasn't enough, but it was all he could do. "Get their weapons and put them in the back of the SUV."

Minutes later, Caden walked past a young soldier washing his bloody hands with a bottle of water. "You drive," Caden ordered and sat in the passenger seat. His father and Sue climbed in behind him. As the convoy pulled away from the church, thoughts of the firefight mixed with joy at finding his father and Susan. All of this was tempered by the uncertainty about Peter. Caden felt drained and knew that he was coming down from a combat-induced adrenaline high.

As a teen, he had wanted nothing more than to get away from the small town of his birth. College, ROTC, the army, and a job in D.C. all seemed to set up the small town boy for a career in the big league of Washington politics. Now he could think of nothing better than all of his family being reunited in Hansen.

Turning to his father he asked, "Why didn't you travel back the way you went, along the North Road?"

"At first I did, but after the blast it became a big parking lot. Nobody was moving except for some guys on motor cycles. Someone tried to steal a bike and got shot and that led to more fighting and shooting. I got off that road when I could and headed toward the freeway, but even on the back roads the going was slow. It took us the rest of the day and most of the night to get to the outskirts of Olympia.

"It was late at night...early in the morning really, when we reached the Nisqually River outside of Yelm. Troops had set up a check point at the bridge to keep people from going north toward the red zone...."

"People were trying to get in?" Then Caden recalled the night of the Washington D.C. blast and how some people headed into the city.

His father nodded. "I had set out for Tacoma earlier that day and would have gone even after the blast. Anyway, at the check point, troops had set up a field hospital. Sue was feeling nauseous and I was concerned because we had been close to the blast."

"Were you exposed? Are you sick?" Caden asked.

"No I'm fine, not ill."

Satisfied that there was no immediate problem, Caden said to his father, "What happened? Why did it take so long to get this far?"

"When we stopped at the med station, I got out a gas can and filled the tank. Later, when we came out, the truck started and then died. Someone had punctured the gas tank and drained it."

"I'm surprised you couldn't fix a puncture hole."

"I could patch it, but where would I get more gas? By that time you couldn't buy any, so we walked."

They continued talking until they reached the Hansen blockade. Caden and his driver got out of the car and walked up to the guards. "We have three trucks of supplies and a fueler," Caden said.

"You got food in those trucks?" one of the men on the barricade asked.

"We sure do," the driver replied.

Caden had his men pass out one MRE for each guard on duty. Everyone seemed happy.

When the last truck was safe behind the barricade Caden told the senior man, "I'm going to take my family home. Go to the armory and unload the Ammo, communications gear and the first truck of MREs. We'll distribute the remainder to the town and refugee camp in the morning after I arrive."

"Yes sir," the soldier replied and soon the convoy was moving along the road.

Ten minutes later Caden's SUV rumbled up the long dirt driveway to the farmhouse. Maria and Lisa stepped out on the porch as he slowed to a stop. Trevor stepped from the car first.

"Mom," Lisa yelled, "come here you've got to see this." Then she leapt from the porch into her father's arms.

Walking out the front door his mother stifled a scream and nearly fell down the steps as she joined Lisa in hugging Trevor. Then Sue emerged from the car and the excitement spread.

Caden walked over to Maria and hugged her then stood with his arm resting on her shoulder while the three others got reacquainted and came to terms with the fact that Peter was not with them.

After several minutes of hugs and tears, Trevor explained to his wife and daughter how he had no chance to find Peter before the nuclear bomb went off.

His mother comforted Sue and the two consoled one another about Peter. Finally his mother looked down and gently touched Sue's belly. "Is the baby all right?"

"The baby is fine, but I'm exhausted."

"Baby?" Caden asked.

"I'm pregnant," Sue replied.

Chapter Twenty-Three

They talked long into the night, swapping stories of their journeys and of Peter. Caden again told how he found Adam at the wreck along the highway where his mother died, that thieves later threatened them and Maria came to their rescue. His father told of driving up North Road and arriving at Peter and Sue's home.

"He found me in the corner of the bedroom with a pistol," Sue said. "Peter told me Trevor was coming, but it was a good thing he called out to me. I was really scared because everyone was leaving, and there were sirens, reports of looting and the sound of gunshots."

"We were barely out of the house when we saw the mushroom cloud," his dad added.

"My head was bouncing off an airplane fuselage at that moment," Caden said.

"Did you leave a dent in it," Lisa asked.

With a smile he replied, "Should I tell Dad how you shot me?"

Lisa threw a cushion at him.

"You shot him?" his dad asked Lisa.

His mother and Maria laughed as Trevor looked from face to face for an answer.

Caden couldn't recall what time he went to bed, but when the old wind-up alarm clock rang to life he moaned and slapped at it. Sitting up he hoped for an easy day.

He followed the smell of coffee to the kitchen, and found Maria warming a baby bottle on one side of a camp stove.

"You want breakfast? I think I can do eggs and pancakes on this thing."

"Black coffee would be great."

After two cups he felt alive enough to eat. "Eggs might be good."

"Coming up." She cracked an egg on the edge of the green camp stove. "You look awful,"

"Thanks. I'm just tired," he said with a yawn. Hopefully today will go smoothly." After eating he stood, stretched and headed back to the bedroom to put on his uniform.

Maria was waiting at the foot of the stairs with a bag as he came down. "I made you lunch."

He smiled. They kissed and he headed off to the armory wondering how he could feel so married, but not be. He was still smiling as he reached the main road. He expected that there would be no other cars during his short commute however, he gradually became aware of an unusual number of people. Some were talking, others walking, but all of them seemed to point or stare at him. *Don't get paranoid. They're curious because you're driving a car and in uniform.*

Nearing the city limits he passed clusters of people going in his direction. *Where are they were all headed so early in the morning?* A police car sped by with sirens blazing and turned up the hill toward the armory. Ahead another crowd walked briskly up the same road. He pressed down on the accelerator.

What's going on? He glanced at thirty to forty people on both sides of the road. Some ran up the hill. *Why are they all headed toward the armory?* He was tempted to stop and ask, but their faces were gaunt, desperate and fearful. *Get there and then assess the situation.* As the chain link fence came into view, so did fifty or sixty people clustered around the gate.

As he neared, he was forced to slow down to avoid hitting several individuals in the street. Soldiers at the gate, guns at the ready, ordered the crowd back. Most of them moved to the side of the road, but some of the men waited until the last possible moment.

As he passed through the crowd a man yelled, "Are you going to share the food? We're hungry too."

"We're all hungry. How come you get to eat?"

"My children are…."

Something banged on the car and the voices rumbled into a chaotic chorus of despair.

Caden breathed a sigh of relief as he passed through the gate. He quickly parked, exited the car and slammed the door behind him. Marching across the parking lot he saw Lieutenant Brooks and Sheriff Hoover coming toward him. Caden changed direction and the three converged in the middle of the parking lot. As Caden neared his XO he glared. "Why didn't you call me?"

"I did sir, but you had already left," Brooks said. "Then I called the Sheriff."

"I just got here a minute ago myself," Hoover added.

"Okay," Caden said taking a deep breath. "How did they all find out about the food?"

"What I've been able to figure out sir is that when the convoy went through the blockade someone told the guards about the MREs and gave them some."

Caden shook his head in frustration. Apparently the guards had told family and friends, and word of the supplies had spread quickly through town. "I didn't think we needed to keep it secret. I thought everyone would be happy we had food."

Hoover chuckled. "They're glad you have it because now they know where they can get it."

"I plan on sharing a lot of the supply. That's why I got as much as I could."

"I was sure that was your idea." Hoover gestured toward the fence, "They're not sure, but they *are* hungry."

Caden frowned in worry. "We need to distribute the food this morning. I want to do it in an orderly manner and I don't want to issue it from the armory. Are the supplies secured?"

Brooks looked at the growing crowd. "Yes. For now. The ammo, gear, and meds you ordered to be unloaded have been locked up with our supplies. The MREs are in the mess. The rest of the food and fuel is still on the trucks in the depot."

"Where do you want to distribute the food from?" Hoover asked.

"I'm going to let the LEPC decide that, but they need to make a quick decision."

"LEPC?" Brooks asked.

Caden tried to remember. "Local…Emergency, ah, Planning…Council."

"Committee, I think?" Hoover grinned. "I'm supposed to be a member of that. I've been so busy trying to maintain law and order I haven't attended any meetings, but I know the members. I'll make a few calls."

Caden nodded and then said, "Make sure your deputies and their families get fed and bring your patrol cars up here later and we'll fill their tanks."

When the sheriff stepped away, Caden turned to Brooks. "I want you and Hoover to handle security for the food distribution in Hansen. I have another job I need to take care of."

An hour later two trucks rolled out of the armory. One headed for the high school with Sheriff Hoover and several deputies escorting. The other truck proceeded to the Salvation Army church on the opposite side of town with Lieutenant Brooks and a squad of soldiers accompanying. Hoover used a bullhorn to tell the crowd where the food distribution would take place.

After the last of the hungry throng headed down the hill, four other vehicles departed. A supply truck and a fueler led by a Humvee, and followed by a dark blue SUV, made their way to the blockade on North Road. The small convoy parked on the hill overlooking the camp. Caden stepped from the car and proceeded down the hill toward the blockade. He was pleased to see the large green tent of the field hospital at the edge of the refugee camp and seeing soldiers and civilians walk back and forth across the bridge, he breathed a sigh of relief. The barricade was still in place, but clearly tensions had eased since his last visit.

As he reached the bottom of the path the squad leader came up and saluted. "Can I help you with something, sir?"

"Yes, sergeant, I'd like to speak with the leaders of the refugee camp."

"Yes, sir. Come with me. The area around the med tent has become a meeting place. They should be near there or we can ask the doctor."

With the squad leader, Caden proceeded to the bulldozer and sandbag barricade. There the sergeant ordered two more soldiers to follow them as they continued across the bridge to the field hospital.

Beyond the medical tent was a sea of cars and people. Smoke rose into the gray February sky from several fires. He recalled that this was a park, complete with a ball field. Just above the people, cars and campers he could see the top of the backstop. The grass that should have covered the area had been trampled into the cold earth until all that remained was brown dirt and mud. Those around him moved with a listlessness that reminded him of old zombie movies. The scene was complete with dirty gray clothes and blank expressions, but he knew that it was not some life sucking disease; hunger was killing these people. He scanned the crowd once again looking for a familiar face, then turned toward the tent.

Neil Young, the big man he had meet on the bridge two days earlier, stood before him. "Well Caden, have you come to see how we are doing?"

"Actually, I'm looking for you."

Caden considered the crowd of desperate faces that encircled them. *If I mention the word food here there could be a riot.* "Is there any kind of formal leadership of this camp?"

"Kind of informal, but yes, me and one other."

"I'd like to meet with both of you back on the other side of the barricade as soon as possible."

A murmuring crowd gathered as Caden and his soldiers headed back onto the bridge and toward the barricade. When he crossed over the sandbags Caden looked back at a growing crowd around the med tent. A couple of minutes later the mob surged forward behind Neil.

This could get ugly--fast.

The soldiers on either side of him fidgeted with their weapons.

About halfway across the bridge, Neil stopped. "Everyone please listen. I have no idea what the army wants to talk with us about, but if you continue toward the barricade someone could get shot. Please wait here and I promise I'll tell you what is going on."

Caden sighed with relief as Neil and a woman continued toward the barrier alone.

Once on the other side of the blockade, Neil introduced Theresa and asked, "What did you need to talk about?"

"I've got a truck full of food and another with gasoline up on the hill."

Their expressions brightened immediately.

"I'm going to use the food and fuel to clear this camp."

Theresa frowned. "Who are you to decide how food gets distributed?"

Caden ignored the question. "If you stay in this camp you will die. The town cannot support any more refugees and there is only enough food in the truck for a day. Eat the food and use the gas to get to a better place, either back home or to the FEMA camp."

"How do we know the FEMA camp will be better?" she asked.

Caden glanced over the barricade. The crowd moved forward like a slow motion mob. "I'm told that food is tightly rationed at the camp, but there is food. You're starving to death here."

Theresa and Neil nodded. "How do you propose to do this distribution?" he asked.

The entire squad now stood behind the sandbags with rifles ready.

After more discussion the three of them shook hands and climbed onto the treads of the dozer. Caden held up his hand, signaling for quiet. "We will distribute food and fuel from the north end of the camp." There was an audible gasp at the mention of food and word was quickly, and loudly, relayed to those out of earshot. For many seconds Caden could not continue because of the crowd noise. Again he signaled for quiet. "We will provide one meal per person and five gallons of gas for each car with the stipulation that you leave this place. You can return home or go to the FEMA camp south of Longview."

It was dark before Caden returned to the armory and plopped exhausted into his office chair. He rubbed his throbbing leg as he thought of the hundreds of people who left the area, and those who remained. A few stayed because their cars wouldn't start, others remained because of sick family members either in the town hospital or the field station.

The doctor remained behind to treat them and Neil helped fix cars. *I'll keep the blockade in place, but we can use the road now and check out the old coal power plant.* Resting his head in his hands he continued to think about all that had transpired when there was a knock at the door. "Come."

Brooks stepped in holding two cups of coffee. He handed a cup to Caden and sat down. "It's been a long day, but I think a good one. All the food that we took into town was distributed and, I think, eaten on the spot."

Caden took a long slow drink. "Yeah, that's what happened at the refugee camp too. North Road should be clear by tomorrow. Send a squad out to the coal power plant and start looking for people who can operate it. Offer the civilians food, medicine, protection, whatever it takes to get the plant running."

"Do we have enough food and medicine to be spreading it around?"

"No, but I'll work on that. You just get the plant running, if it's possible."

"I'll send the men out in the morning."

The next evening as the sun bent low over the hills west of Hansen, Caden sat at his desk. Dark shadows spread across the room and instinctively he turned the knob of the lamp on his desk. He was surprised by the glow of the lamp. *We have power! Good.* For a moment he wondered if the men out at the coal plant had it running. Brooks had led a squad out at first light and later in the day brought out several civilians who had worked in the plant, but it was too early for them to have it up and running. He scribbled a reminder to get a progress report on Monday.

He picked up the next paper that required his attention. *I had hoped for a slow day yesterday and received it today.* He grinned. *The tedium of paperwork is a nice change.*

There was a knock at the door. "Come," he called, still reading.

"You're late for supper."

Startled at the sound of Maria's voice, he looked up and grinned at the sight of her leaning against the doorframe holding a basket. "What have you got there?"

"Let's see," she said and pulled out a bottle. "Blackberry wine, made right here in town."

"Nice."

"I've also got bread, butter, cheese and crackers. Now all I need is someone to help me eat them."

"I think I can assist you with that." Caden stood and moved toward Maria, but as he did he could see the staff in the outer office. "Let's find somewhere private." As they stepped into the hallway, Brooks and Lisa approached. "Let me guess," Caden whispered to Maria. "This was Lisa's idea."

"She might have mentioned it, but I didn't object."

"Lieutenant Brooks," Caden said as they passed, "I'm going to have dinner with this lovely young lady. Keep an eye on things for the next hour or so."

"Yes, sir."

Ten minutes later Caden and Maria found an uninhabited storeroom and borrowed an old wooden table and two mismatched chairs from the barracks for their dinner.

The last rays of the sun cast long shadows across the brown crates and green ammo boxes that took up much of the room. Caden started to turn on a light, but then noticed a candle left by the door of the room. "We haven't had much time alone or much time to talk." He lit the candle and set it in the middle of the table.

She pulled two wine glasses from the basket. "That is why I thought it would be a good idea to come here."

"I hope you have a cork screw."

She handed it to him and he opened the bottle while she buttered the bread.

"I didn't think there was food left in any store in town. Where did you buy all of this?" Caden asked.

"We didn't buy it. The stores are empty. Your father traded two guns, some ammo and a bottle of scotch for a cow and calf."

"He's been busy today, but I asked how you got the wine, cheese, bread—everything."

"Lisa and I traded a gallon of milk and two dozen eggs for the wine and cheese. We made the bread and your mom still had crackers."

"Where are you doing all this trading?"

"You know that park in front of the Hansen library?"

"Sure," he said pouring the wine.

"Well, people gather there to barter things. Everyone went today, except Sue, she's still pretty tired, and we traded for things we need and," she lifted the wine, "a few things we just wanted."

Caden noticed a small handwritten label that read, "Please return the bottle when done." He pointed it out to Maria.

"Yeah, the family that makes the wine said they aren't sure they can get more bottles, so they're asking people to return them. They're going to work out some sort of a discount if you do."

He smiled as she took a sip of wine and stared into her eyes, marveling at how well and quickly she fit into the family and community that he was only now rediscovering. *Maybe we can hold civilization together until things get better.* He reached out and touched her hand. "Maybe you and I…."

A soldier burst into the room. "Sir, Lieutenant Brooks sent me to find you." The man took a deep breath. He thought…you should know…President Durant…he's placed the state under martial law…and…activated the Guard units."

Chapter Twenty-Four

Caden had little motivation to get out of bed, other than maybe to shoot the rooster. The first rays of morning sun pushed back against the darkness of his bedroom, but he closed his eyes, rolled onto his side and pulled up the blanket. Why not get a few more hours of sleep? No crisis called for his attention this Saturday morning—then he heard the scream.

In an instant he was at the only window of his room. It looked out over the main field of the farm, but he could see little in pre-dawn twilight. He was certain the cry came from outside. *Probably from the barn.*

He threw on his clothes, grabbed his SIG pistol and hurried downstairs.

His mother stood in the living room, "Trevor and Maria are outside. I think it was Lisa."

Sue came down the stairs as he ran out the front door. Immediately he spotted his father at the front of the barn and Maria, with a rifle, off to the side. His dad signaled for him to go to the back.

Once there, Caden threw open the rear door, looked left and right and then hurried in. The interior was so dark, he saw almost nothing. Immediately he took cover behind a stack of hay bales to his right and waited an agonizingly long time for his eyes to adjust. The first thing he saw was Maria silhouetted in the open door of a horse stall. With a wave of the arm he signaled her to move and she ducked into the shadows.

Next he saw Lisa. A young man stood behind her. One hand clutched her jacket, the other arm was wrapped around Lisa's neck like a sleeper hold and so the knife was to the side of her throat. By the position of the knife Caden could tell the assailant was not a trained killer. Beyond those two, near the front of the barn, his father stood in a shooting stance.

Caden tried to maneuver for a clear shoot, but the guy kept turning, using Lisa as a human shield.

"All I want is food! Get me food and I'll leave!"

"Put the knife down and we'll get you food," Trevor said.

"No! I'm not stupid. Get me food or I cut her throat."

"You cut her throat and I'll kill you," Caden replied.

"I'm hungry. All I want is food. The last meal I had was a lousy MRE two days ago. Believe me I'll kill her." The man pointed at Trevor with the knife. "You, old man, get me…."

With no knife against her neck, Lisa kicked back hard against the man's leg and dropped like dead weight.

Trevor fired a single shot.

The man fell backwards and hit the floor with a thud.

Father and daughter ran to each other and embraced. Lisa, cried, "I just wanted to get the eggs and milk for breakfast." Leaning into her father, between sobs, she continued. "I didn't think…didn't bring my gun…he came out of the dark…grabbed me so quickly…I didn't see him."

Caden checked for vital signs and, looking to his father, shook his head.

"It's all right," he said to Lisa. "If he had just come to the door and asked…maybe…."

Back in the house Caden called and talked briefly to Hoover.

A couple of hours later a single deputy came to the farm. "Do you know his name?" he asked while writing notes in a pad.

"No," Caden responded.

The officer asked a few more questions as he continued to write. "There have been attacks on other farms, the food bank...any place where there might be food. People are desperate." There was no mention of any further investigation. The sun was high in the sky before a van from the sheriff's department came and took the body to the morgue.

Caden stared as the vehicle rumbled away. *Death in America has become common...inconsequential.* It was not the fact of death that caused him pause; it was the brutality of casual killing. He had seen that in Iraq and Afghanistan, but not in America. Perhaps it had always been there in the poorer, gang-infested, neighborhoods, but he had not seen it until recently and now it came to the barn beside his home and threatened to take his sister. What next, a gunfight in the house? It was a solemn day at the Westmore farm.

The next morning as everyone sat around the breakfast table Lisa asked, "Can we go to church?"

"That's a good idea," their mother said.

"And the swap meet," Maria suggested, "It looks like a nice day to go out."

"I'll pack the extra eggs and milk in a cooler," Lisa added.

"We can't all go," his dad said, shaking his head. "Someone needs to stay here on guard until things return to normal."

Caden wasn't interested in church. He wanted to say he would stay and guard the farm, but he had a mouth full of pancake.

"I'll guard this week and go with you next week," Trevor said.

Sue put her hands on her belly. "I should stay home too. I'm still tired from all the walking we did to get here." She turned to Maria. "But I will take care of Adam for you." Maria started to speak, but Sue insisted it was the least she could do.

Caden saw that Maria, Lisa, and his mother really wanted to go. He swallowed his mouthful of pancake and said, "Okay then, let's make a day of it."

After breakfast Caden returned to his room to dress for church. He was glad that he had just dumped clothes into his duffle bag, including several nice shirts and ties had been stuffed inside, even a suit. He wondered if his mother had ironed the clothes because they didn't have the wrinkles he remembered. *Did I hang the clothes in the closet? Did I even unpack when I got here?* He couldn't recall.

He put on a pair of slacks, a pastel blue shirt and royal blue tie. As he reached for the suit jacket he stopped. *No place to conceal a pistol.* In the closet he found a heavy jacket, put it on and then slid the SIG into the inside pocket. *From now on I go everywhere armed.*

The events of yesterday morning again intruded on his thoughts. *The guy could have slit Lisa's throat and stolen whatever he could find. We wouldn't have known until later. We do need to keep a guard here. Maybe we should stay in pairs. No, that would be difficult. If we could keep in better contact.... Where are those two GMRS transceivers I bought in West Virginia?* As he continued to dress, he looked around the room, but didn't find the radios.

Everyone walked out on the front porch as they got ready to leave. The sky was clear blue and for a February day it was mild. *Could the radios be in the car?* He walked over and checked under the driver's seat.

Maria came up beside him. "What are you looking for?"

"Those GMRS radios." He continued to look while talking. "Remember, we used them in Alabama?"

"I remember. They're in the back of the car."

Walking toward the rear of the vehicle he asked, "Are you sure?"

"Yes."

He opened the rear and immediately saw the three pistols, including the pink Ruger, taken after the gunfight at the church. He had forgotten about them. *They'll be good for trade or additional security.* He paused as the killing in the church lobby flashed through his mind. *The woman was killed. Sure it was self-defense, but it should be investigated. Aren't these guns evidence? Should I turn them over to Hoover?* He smiled grimly. *Didn't Hoover shoot some looters? Was there any inquiry of that? No one seems to want any bother about the barn shooting.* He was certain there would be none about the church shooting, but still it seemed wrong to keep the weapons. In the end, he decided to hold on to them until he could talk with Hoover. He picked up two pistols, leaving the pink one alone. It was senseless, but that gun gave him a bad feeling, he didn't want it in the house.

Caden was about to tell Maria she was wrong about the radios when he spotted them in the corner partially under the seat. Clutching them and the pistols he walked over to his father. "These transceivers will be good for keeping in touch around the farm. We can trade the weapons for things we need, but keep them until I clear it with the sheriff."

Soon he was driving the three ladies to the church just outside of Hansen, where he had been baptized as a teen. As he passed over the creek on the main road he looked for the red-haired kids who often fished there, but was disappointed.

He had good memories of friends, cookouts and ballgames while in the youth group, but it had been ten years since he set foot in the building. He struggled to recall the last time he had been in any church other than for a wedding. It wasn't that he was an atheist or even an agnostic, but in his hell-bent pursuit of a career he had little time for God. However, if it made the women in his life happy, he was willing to go and even smile.

The church, a large, white, wood-frame building that dominated the top of a hill, was just ahead. They followed a horse-drawn wagon full of people into the parking lot. There were a dozen cars parked in front, but as the church bell tolled most people came by foot. At the edges of the parking lot three horses were tied to trees. The wagon pulled up close to the front door. Kids jumped from the back as a couple of adults disembarked more slowly, then the man led the horse and wagon to a tree in a grassy lot beside the building.

As they entered the sanctuary, Caden's thoughts were far away, recalling a hayride with the youth group as a teenager. The morning sun, shining through a large stained glass window, warmed his face and brought his attention to the present. The congregation stood and sang a hymn acapella. He looked back at a corner where he once sat with young friends and recalled summer camp and the Boy Scout troop that the church sponsored. He took in a deep breath as if trying to suck in the atmosphere so full of light and life that it washed away the darkness of the previous weeks.

His mother selected a pew near the middle of the sanctuary and the rest of the family followed. Caden stood silently, holding Maria's hand. He didn't know the words of the song they were singing, but he liked the sound.

A couple of hymns later, a middle aged man walked to the front as the congregation sat.

"Good morning everyone. For any new people, I'm Jim, an elder here at Hansen Community Church. Before we get started there are just a few announcements." He paused to look at his notes. "Dave, the owner of the farm supply store, donated a greenhouse to the church. We're going to use the large area behind the building for growing vegetables this spring. We need help assembling it and to put up a security fence. If you can assist, sign up at the desk just outside the sanctuary. Also, if you know where we can get more greenhouses, let us know."

Good idea. Caden recalled seeing one along the freeway behind the burned-out home of a friend. *There are probably more. We need to find a way to use things that no one claims.*

Jim continued his announcements, "...and if the power stays off, like it has this weekend, the Doran's will need help at their dairy and are willing to pay in milk, butter and cheese. Several farmers have told us that, if gas stays in short supply, they will need help with spring planting and probably harvest. They are willing to pay in food. That sign-up list is also out at the desk."

Caden continued to think about greenhouses and other equipment the community might be able to find and gather. Suddenly he became aware of a different voice. An older man now stood at the front of the congregation.

"...will never forget those terrible events of less than a month ago. Many of us have lost family. Most of us know someone who died. The nuclear fires have tested the nation and our community. The aftermath of those terrible days continues to test us and they will be with us for years to come, but like Shadrach, Meshach, and Abednego of old, our nation has been through many fires and we have come out of it with our faith intact.

"God did not bring this wickedness down on us; He is not the author of evil. What we have seen is evil, in all its forms, working against the will and the plan of God.

"Much that was good has been burned away and lost, but like metal forged in flame, what is left behind is stronger than before that dark day. Now, as it says in Revelation, we need to, 'wake up, and strengthen what remains.' Our work isn't done and the path will not be an easy one, but we need to take on this yoke and move forward. We have a community to rebuild and a nation to restore."

Caden nodded inwardly. He had never put it into words, but strengthening what remained seemed an appropriate description of what he had been trying to do since he returned home. He stood with others as the music played and in that moment it seemed the struggle to save Hansen was a burden they all shared equally, but more than that, it was as if his own personal burdens were shared by everyone in the congregation. His mother would call what he felt the Holy Spirit. Caden wasn't sure, but it felt good to be there. The next time he had the chance he would come willingly.

The sun was just past its zenith as Caden, Maria, Lisa and his mother, stepped from the car near the barter market. Lisa retrieved the cooler with the milk and eggs the family would use for trading and together they walked toward the bustling swap meet.

The library was surrounded by tables and stalls. The mixture of these with colorful tarps, smoke, music and lots of people gave the park a third-world bazaar look. As they neared, he saw Sheriff Hoover talking with two deputies off to one side of the square. "I've got to talk to Hoover. I'll catch up with you," Caden said to the ladies. As he approached, the deputies departed into the market.

After exchanging greetings, Caden got right to the point. "I have three pistols my men and I took from a shooting at the church by the freeway. Do you need them for an investigation?"

Hoover sighed and his face seemed instantly older. "Do you know how many murders we averaged in this county before this year?"

Caden shook his head.

"Four. Last year was a bad year, we had five. One was a double killing. Do you know how many have been killed in the county in the two months of this year?"

Again he shook his head.

"Neither do I. But it's been hundreds, maybe a thousand, including two of my deputies." He stopped, breathed deeply and let it out slowly. "The Highway Patrol hasn't been to Hansen since that first attack on Washington D.C. I haven't been able to contact the state crime lab since the Seattle blast.

"You've been trying to do the right thing since you got here and I appreciate that. I can't hold the threads of civilization together alone. I trust that you did what you needed to do." He paused and gave Caden a whimsical grin. "And besides, now that martial law has been declared, you're in charge. What are your orders?"

It was Caden's turn to sigh as he recalled the breathless announcement of martial law on Friday. "I haven't received any orders since the declaration. We've been working well together. I don't want to change that relationship if I don't have to."

"I'm glad to hear you say that."

Before anyone could speak Hoover's radio crackled. "415 in progress, corner of Birch and Main, the Salvation Army church. Request backup."

"What's a 415?"

Hoover shook his head and his eyes narrowed. "A disturbance. Probably people think there's still food at the church."

Caden asked if he needed help.

"No, you go on to the marketplace." He looked up at the clear blue sky. "Enjoy the day. I've got to go." The sheriff walked briskly to a patrol car and was off with sirens blaring.

Just inside the bazaar was a large bulletin board where community announcements had once been posted. Now the board was cluttered with "will trade for" signs. One in particular caught his eye. "NEED INSULIN. Tell me what you need." It was followed by an address and phone number. Caden shook his head. *Who would trade away insulin?*

Next he came upon a man seated in a lawn chair with a rifle across his lap. On the blanket before him were a 12-gauge shotgun and two small-caliber rifles. Beside him sat a cardboard box with eight Labrador Retriever puppies bouncing around inside or hanging on the edges. On the front of the box, in bold black letters, was written, "Future Guard Dogs." Caden laughed out loud.

The man smiled, "I'm thinking they will come in handy in the days ahead."

"I think you're right," he replied and walked on. Past that on his left, a woman had chickens in a large cage. A goat was tied up beside her. A deputy stood talking with a woman at another stall. On the table between them were dozens of jars of honey and honeycomb. The deputy and Caden exchanged nods as he walked by. Farther down, he noticed a couple selling trout and other fish that he couldn't name. The woman caught his eye, she had long, wavy, red hair.

On a nearby table were packages of dried meat. The sign hanging below read, "Deer, Elk and Beef Jerky for Trade." At the next stall was an old man reloading and selling ammunition. The sign beside him listed calibers and read, "Will Trade for Brass." Several guns were on display behind the counter.

"What does he mean, 'Will Trade for Brass?' Does he want scrap metal?"

Caden turned and smiled at Maria a step behind him. "Sort of. In this case he wants used bullet cartridges. He can reload them and make new ammo."

Maria watched as he made one.

"Where's Mom and Lisa?"

"Trading for food we need."

Caden stood beside Maria and together they watched as a few more cartridges were reloaded. He hadn't seen any paper money during his walk through the market. He noticed a few silver coins passed in trade, but the de facto currencies were guns, ammunition and food. With those anyone could barter for anything in the market.

They walked together for a minute along the stalls when suddenly Maria tapped him on the arm and pointed, "We need a car seat."

Caden followed her gesture to a stall that looked like a yard sale. There amongst the clothes, pots, pans and toasters was a car seat. "For Adam?" Caden shook his head. "No, duct tape will do."

Maria hit him on the arm. She took several steps closer. "She has cloth diapers. We need those too."

"I got cloth diapers back at Fort Rucker."

"You got four."

"What?" he smiled. "That's not enough?"

Exasperation spread across her face. "No!"

Caden breathed out slowly. "Okay, do we have anything left to trade for it?"

"Probably not, the eggs and milk will have been exchanged for other food by now."

Caden recalled the pink Ruger and retrieved it from under the seat of the car. He didn't show the pistol when asking what the woman wanted most in trade for the baby seat.

"I need food for me and my kids."

He headed toward the booth where the old man reloaded cartridges. Caden wasn't concerned about ammo for his SIG, he could get that at the armory, but Maria had only a few rounds for her pistol. "I need .38 ammo and whatever else you will trade for this Ruger." He laid the pink pistol on the table. Minutes later he walked away with 100 rounds of .38 and 550 rounds of .22.

Caden gave the .38 ammo to Maria. "This is for your gun. Now come with me."

"How is this getting us diapers and a car seat?"

"You'll see." Caden went back to the first stall he had visited. "Pick a puppy."

"Why do we need a puppy?" Maria asked. "It's another mouth to feed."

Caden pointed to the Future Guard Dogs sign. "If we had one, Lisa might not have been attacked and that guy might not have been shot."

After a moment she nodded. "And this gets us a car seat?"

"Well, no this doesn't, but be patient, and pick one."

She pointed to a cream colored pup that was crawling on top of the others as if to get attention.

Caden traded 50 rounds of .22 ammo for the little dog and wondered if he overpaid.

Maria held it in her arms. "Well how are you…" she glanced at the belly, "little girl?"

The dog licked her face.

Next he stopped at the fishmonger. He smiled at the young girl helping at the stall. It was the same red-haired teen he had seen fishing at the creek the last few days. "Are the fish fresh?" he asked with a whimsical grin.

"Oh yes," the girl replied, "my brother and I caught them this morning before church."

He swapped 150 rounds for two large Rainbow Trout fillets.

At another stall he exchanged 20 rounds for two cans of mixed vegetables.

When Caden laid the food on the table the woman was eager to barter.

Walking away with the seat, he assessed the trades. *I got rid of the Ruger and now have a car seat and more diapers for Adam, 100 rounds of .38 ammo for Maria and I still have 330 rounds of .22 ammo. I think I did okay.*

Maria, still cuddling the puppy, leaned over and kissed Caden on the cheek. "Thanks."

The deal just got better! "You're welcome," he said with a smile. "I don't want to carry this seat all over the market. Let's head back to the car. Maybe Mom and…." Seeing a man in camo uniform, he slowed and stopped. It was Lieutenant Brooks smiling and talking with Lisa as they, along with his mother, strolled in their direction. *It's been a great day, I hope there isn't a problem.*

As they neared, Brooks saluted. "Good afternoon sir; your father said you might be here. We've received word that a presidential delegation has arrived in Olympia and all Guard commanders are to report there on Monday for a briefing and orders."

Chapter Twenty-Five

The first thing Caden noticed, as his five-vehicle-convoy approached Olympia, was that the freeway had been cleared of abandoned cars. Then he noticed the traffic. There wasn't much for what should have been the morning rush hour, but there was some. About half-a-dozen cars, all with passengers, were in the southbound lane. As he scanned the roadway, two military fuelers passed him heading north.

But, there were many broken windows, wrecks and debris still visible from the highway and despite the cool February weather, the grass was long and unkempt.

Farther along he saw the old school bus with the wild paint job race south. He grinned as the smell of french-fries reached him and he recalled the vegetable oil fuel.

He also noticed lights in some homes and businesses. Even though power was out in Hansen, it was on in Olympia. As they pulled off the freeway, he hoped Brooks would be able to get the old coal power plant back online and restore reliable electricity to their small town.

Caden's SUV, followed by two supply trucks and a fueler, rolled toward the capitol complex. He pulled into one of the many available parking spots and the Humvee and trucks continued on to the supply depot to get what they could.

As soon as he stepped into the capitol, aides informed him that a press conference with the presidential delegation and Chinese officials was in progress.

"Was I supposed to be at it?" Caden looked at his watch. It was only minutes after eight in the morning.

The aide caught his glance. "The new Secretary of Homeland Security wanted to start early. Evidently there is a lot to be done."

At the back, where Caden entered the room, many were standing. Slowly he moved along the wall looking for a good view. Most of the room was filled with chairs that were occupied with reporters, Guard and regular military officers and, judging by blazers and badges, FEMA, DHS and other state and federal officials.

Becky's voice caught his attention and he looked to the platform at the far end of the room. In surprise, his heart skipped a beat. There at the lectern was Becky, his fiancée. Impulsively he stood behind a tall reporter and was immediately disappointed in himself. He would need to talk with her, and put an end to their relationship, but right then he didn't want to exchange smiles and possibly a discreet wave of the hand. With a sigh, he stepped out from behind the reporter and turned his attention to what Becky was saying.

"...efforts of FEMA and the entire Department of Homeland Security, there are still approximately 30 million displaced citizens. Estimates of those killed range from four to six million with an equal number of injured. That is why this country has recalled its military forces from Europe and Asia."

As Caden listened he noticed a Chinese army general standing on the podium along with Carol Hatch. He had attended several meetings with Carol as an Under Secretary of Homeland Security, but he now assumed she was the new Secretary of DHS. He watched with growing unease as Carol and the Chinese general spoke to each other in whispers. Becky, never at a loss for words, continued to speak.

"While we believe that all the perpetrators of these terrorist attacks have been caught or killed, we are going to need long-term assistance to recover. Much of the aid has been promised by the government of China."

When Becky paused a reporter across the room quickly spoke up. "General Lau, is it true that tens of thousands of Chinese troops are already in San Francisco and Oakland?"

The General stepped forward with a smile. "A few hundred soldiers are working in those ports to expedite food and medical distribution—not tens of thousands."

"General, some are saying the treaty just signed by President Durant and your government formalizes repayment procedures for U.S. debt to China and that the Chinese soldiers are here as part of that treaty. Is your government attempting to ensure that America repays its debt?"

"China and the U.S. have signed a treaty of mutual friendship—that is so. Regarding the repayment of debt by your government I can only say that I am here merely to manage food and medical assistance."

Another reporter jumped up. "But Chinese soldiers are not just in San Francisco and Oakland. I've seen some at the port of Tacoma and I've read reports of them at Long Beach and Eureka."

Thousands of troops…all the Pacific ports. It sounds more like an invasion than a relief effort.

The general smiled. "Some soldiers are here with me and have inspected the port of Tacoma. They are at those other ports under the terms of the treaty of friendship. For the duration of the emergency they will ensure the aid is quickly and fairly distributed."

"Chinese currency is showing up in those ports," Another reporter said. "Why is that?"

"Our soldiers are paid in yuan. Some of it would naturally leak into the surrounding community."

"Are Americans being paid in yuan?"

"Despite the fact that your dollar has ceased to function as a currency we are not paying American workers in yuan. Currently we are paying American laborers with vouchers for food and fuel."

A reporter in the front row stood. "When do you believe that the current crisis will end and your soldiers will be able to return home?"

The General sighed. "We are here as peacekeepers, to distribute aid and assist with stabilization—that is all. Our troops will be here only for as long as needed to implement the newly signed treaty. I am a military man. Our departure is a political decision."

Becky raced to the microphone. "Thank you. That is all the time we have for questions." Everyone on the platform turned and walked briskly through a side door.

Caden left the briefing room as quickly as possible, but didn't see Becky in the packed hallway. Heading toward the Adjutant General's office, he saw David Weston. The two men moved from the traffic into an alcove along the hall.

"What do you think of this friendship treaty?" Weston asked.

"I think Durant is panicking and making some bad decisions." He shook his head. "Having hundreds, maybe thousands, of foreign troops in the country doesn't set well with me either, even if they are doing relief work. We can do that and," he said with a frown, "I don't believe they will march back on the boats when this emergency is over. Does Governor Monroe? By-the-way, where is he?"

"The governor does not support the treaty, and believed that his presence would be interpreted by many as approval for it, so he chose not to attend the press conference."

"All you heard is the spin President Durant and the Chinese government want everyone to hear. General Lau is a politician as well as a soldier. I'm sure he's been told to deliver the talking points and he will do it well, but my sources are telling me it's not the whole story."

Caden gave him a questioning look. "Are you saying that Durant is part of some Sino-American deception? I don't like him, but why would he do that?"

"Perhaps I can find out. The ceremonial transfer of authority for the port of Tacoma is tomorrow morning." He made a discreet nod in the direction of another Chinese officer. "But I'm to meet with Major Cheng this afternoon and finalize the letter of understanding. He has a reputation of being a hot-tempered, no-nonsense soldier." He wrote down an address and handed it to Caden. "Meet me there, okay?"

Again he looked at Weston quizzically. "What are you planning?"

"I haven't worked out the details yet but," Weston gave him a mischievous grin. "I've got some questions I want to ask the Major."

Caden had never been down to the port, nor had either of the two soldiers he brought along, so it took them a few minutes to find the building where the meeting was being held. As they drove up the Chinese delegation was just outside the gate. There was an American guard at the entrance, but two uniformed Chinese soldiers flanked him. *A bit premature isn't it Major?* As Caden stepped from the vehicle he patted his holster. He wondered if he should have issued side arms to his fellow soldiers. *No, don't be silly. David is a politician. He fights with words not guns. What could happen?*

Caden and Cheng exchanged salutes as he approached.

"Where is Mr. Weston?" the Chinese officer asked.

"He is coming by another vehicle and should be here momentarily." *I hope.*

Seconds later a silver limousine pulled up and backed into a parking spot near the group. David Weston stepped out from the front passenger side carrying a black briefcase.

Caden looked on questioningly. *Why is David riding around in a limo and who rides around in the front of one?*

Weston walked briskly toward the Major. After shaking hands David said, "I have the draft letter of understanding with me here," he patted the briefcase with his free hand, "but before we begin there are a few things I don't understand. Why does President Durant want to give companies controlled by the Chinese military authority over our western ports?"

The Major appeared surprised. "You make it sound so menacing,"

"Well isn't it?" Weston asked "Would you allow us to control ports in your country?"

He tilted his head back as if looking down his nose at Weston. "The situation does not warrant your country controlling our ports."

"Why does our situation warrant your control of them?"

Major Cheng looked tired, "I do not answer to you. Come. Let us complete the business at hand."

"Is it the price we have to pay for the food assistance? If we want to eat do we have to give up our ports and our resources?"

The Major's eyes flared with anger and for several moments he stared at Weston. "You Americans owe my country nearly one and a half trillion dollars and now you ask us for billions more in aid to feed your peasants." He glanced left and right. "How will you repay us for this kindness? President Durant has already advised creditors that the United States cannot make the next interest payment when it is due. Your currency is worthless; your people are in panic, your factories sit idle, you have no exports.

"Despite your situation, the Chinese government has graciously agreed to provide hundreds of tons of food and medicine on credit. However, the Chinese people do expect to be repaid."

Weston smiled sarcastically, "You said our economy is ruined, if it is, how do you expect to get paid?"

"Why do you ask me this, you have heard the answer. Your President Durant understands the situation better than you. He has signed a new Most Favored Nation trade agreement with the People's Republic and a second treaty granting China the right to manage your Pacific ports for the next ninety-nine years while your western states provide needed raw materials to Chinese industry."

"What! Ninety-nine years! Why should America agree to that?"

"As I have previously said, President Durant has already agreed to the terms and, if I may be so blunt, if you refuse you will starve."

"No treaty is binding until it is approved by the Senate."

"Such legal niceties are no longer practical. The Chinese government has found working with President Durant more advantageous than awaiting some future restored government. Obey your President or forsake our most gracious offer of assistance."

Caden shook his head. "America is stronger than you think. I know we can get the country back to work and feed ourselves, without sacrificing liberty or our natural resources to you."

"The matter has already been agreed upon. As the treaty declares, Chinese troops will soon manage security for western mines, oil fields and Pacific ports. Surely, you would not want to violate the laws of your country."

Weston stepped close to Cheng. "Yes, I think I do want to violate that treaty."

The two Chinese guards ran toward the general.

"And when the American people hear about this treaty many of them are going to want to shove it back where it came from."

"You are a fool." With a shake of his head he said, "But you are not my concern. President Durant must deal with American agitators."

"I'm no fool…"

"You and Governor Monroe should be arrested."

"…I am a patriot." With the last word Weston planted his finger in the Major's chest.

At that moment the first Chinese soldier arrived at the side of the major and slammed the butt of his AK-47 across Weston's nose.

Caden jumped forward to catch his friend, but Weston fell to the pavement with a loud thud. Blood covered much of his face.

The second soldier reached the group and raised his rifle to strike another blow.

Caden pulled out his pistol and shouted, "No!"

Major Cheng's hand was already out to stop the second strike.

With gun still drawn, Caden stepped over his unconscious friend. "We'll take David and leave."

Cheng nodded and moved back.

He lifted Weston with the help of the two American soldiers. The injured man moaned as they moved him. Only then did Caden notice the microphone under David's jacket. A wire ran down to what looked like a cellphone on his belt.

The limo that Weston arrived in sped off.

What is going on here?

*   *   *

David Weston's swollen eyes blinked, opened and slowly seemed to come into focus. "Where am I?" His voice had a nasal quality.

Caden decided not to tell him that much of the left side of his face was black, blue and purple. "Olympia General Hospital." He smiled. "Did you have a nice rest?"

"How long was I out?"

"Just over a day." Caden pulled out his phone. "The governor was here earlier. He said to notify him when you woke up. He wants to personally thank you for getting Major Cheng to admit to the details of the treaty and then he wants to strangle you for pulling such a dangerous stunt."

"What happened?"

"You don't remember?"

"Most of it I do, just not why I'm here with...." He felt the bandages on his head. "I remember arriving at the port in the limo and...." He looked confused. "What happened?"

Caden had replayed the incident so many times in his head it was easy for him to retell it to David. "...so, the soldier smashed you in the face with the butt of his rifle, broke your nose, and you hit the pavement so hard you have a concussion. But what I don't understand is why you chose to hide a news cameraman and reporter in a limo?"

"I couldn't roll up in a news van. If Major Cheng had any idea he was being filmed he would have done his best to talk like a diplomat. I wanted him to speak frankly about the treaty and what he thought, so I needed an unmarked vehicle with plenty of space and tinted windows. When you think of ample space and tinted windows, what vehicle comes to your mind?"

Caden laughed.

"Did they get the video on the local news?"

"They sure did. Durant won't let the networks touch it and has tried to keep it off the Internet, but the Olympia media was using it within the hour. Reporters and others friendly to Monroe's campaign have passed it along. I know it has been seen in much of the west and perhaps the entire nation.

"Oh, and despite Durant's best efforts, the clip of Major Cheng saying Governor Monroe should be arrested went viral about the same time President Durant's order to do it was reported by the media. The timing made it look like Durant is a puppet of the Chinese military."

"He's ordered Monroe to be arrested?"

Caden nodded. "The governor is the voice of the opposition."

Weston looked down at his hands and sighed. "Durant is no puppet, but he is an arrogant fool and he is in over his head."

"I always believed he was a self-centered egotist, who enjoyed power, but it doesn't matter what we think, the press, at least those outlets not under Durant's control, are showing your video over and over again. The silence of the New York networks on the issue just plays into the public doubts about Durant. You getting your nose broken by the butt of a Chinese rifle made it all the more dramatic."

Weston moaned. "I didn't plan on that. I just wanted the treaty stopped."

"Well, I think you accomplished that. As of this morning, Senator Cole of Montana has spoken against the treaty and five states have appointed new senators and instructed them to reject the treaty. Those states have also adopted resolutions to hold elections in November. Another six states are discussing appointing new senators and holding fall elections."

"Good."

Caden sighed deeply. "But Durant's not backing down. His arrest order for the governor still stands. He's even threatening to arrest the new senators and he still says there will be no election. I don't know what's going to happen if he doesn't back down."

"War...that's what will happen...civil war."

Chapter Twenty-Six

"Governor Monroe will be arrested soon." Becky pointed her finger at Caden's nose. "You need to be smart or you'll be in the next cell." She threw up her arms and in an exasperated voice asked, "How could you point a pistol at a Chinese official?"

"I pulled it to stop the soldier, not Major Cheng. My friend, David Weston, had just been hit and...."

"They're here to help us! And how could you be a part of that awful video?" In a mock male voice she repeated some of what he said, 'America is stronger than you think.'"

"I believe that, and the rest of what I said about not sacrificing liberty or our natural resources to China."

Becky laughed sarcastically. "Do you really think America is strong now? Millions are dead, injured or homeless."

"People are returning. Look around, homes and businesses are...."

"Yeah, they're going back in Olympia, Boise, and similar hick towns, but there was rioting in New York just last week and other large cities like Boston and Chicago are war zones. Gangs rule entire districts, looting is rampant...troops are still working their way through Baltimore to Fort Meade. Don't you see? We're on our knees and unless we get massive aid quickly millions will starve. We need help, not you brandishing a gun or Weston planting his finger in the chest of a Chinese official. You do realize they are the largest economy now?"

"China is using this tragedy to establish a sphere of influence on our west coast. Do you realize it's a ninety-nine year treaty?"

"Do the math. How long will it take to pay back a trillion dollars?"

Caden shook his head. "Even so, will the Chinese troops just march back on the boats when the treaty expires?"

"Who knows, but whether they leave or not isn't going to be my problem, or yours."

"So you don't care if they stay after this crisis is over?"

"I didn't say that."

He shook his head. "I can't agree to the treaty and just leave it for my children or grandchildren to deal with the consequences."

She placed her hands on her hips. "Right now you don't have any children and I'm beginning to think that you may never have any—at least not with me."

Caden drew a deep breath and let it out slowly. "No you and I never will. We moved in different directions and I don't see a future for us. It's not your fault, this month has changed me…probably changed everyone."

Becky stared at him for several moments then spoke with slow deliberation. "You are a different man, that's for sure, but you're the one without a future. Change your allegiances or you'll end up in jail." She turned and marched from the room.

Caden walked slowly from the office. He had done the right thing, but wasn't pleased with how it went. What he wanted to do was talk with Maria. The phones were available only for local calls during the day. He had tried last night, but didn't connect. He longed to be back there, to hear Maria's voice. Even the sound of Adam crying would be welcome right now. Becky was wrong, he did have a son and he was pretty sure there would be more children, but not with her.

He looked out a nearby window. The shadows that stretched across the plaza said he was late. A quick check of his watch confirmed it. He shook his head and hurried down the hall. By now the emergency session of the legislature had begun.

As he passed the grand staircase of the capitol he saw half-a-dozen Guardsman with M4s in the lobby. Evidently expecting trouble, their attention was focused on the entryway. Beyond them, just outside, he saw Becky through the glass doors as she hurried down the steps.

Caden continued to the House chamber gallery. Two state patrol officers stood watch at the entrance. *No one would be foolish enough to try and arrest Governor Monroe here.* He opened the door and stepped in.

The gallery was full of reporters, officials and apparently average citizens. Caden found a seat at the back. Ten or more people on the chamber floor were attempting to speak. After several moments the Speaker pounded his gavel.

Governor Monroe raised his arm, asking for silence. When the room was somewhat quiet he began. "By getting the video, David, my chief of staff, has accomplished what I have been trying to do. He showed the people that President Durant is moving the nation in the wrong direction. Durant has sacrificed freedom for security and sovereignty for food.

"However, just pointing that out is not enough. We need to show the country the right direction—that we can have both security and freedom. While it may be hard, we can recover with our sovereignty intact.

"We can restart the economy here in the Northwest and across the nation with just short term aid and no foreign troops. However, if we can't do that, then I will end my campaign and, if Durant still wants it, I'll surrender for arrest."

The gallery and chamber floor erupted in shouts of "No," and "Never."

Monroe scanned the crowd. "Thank you, but the fact remains that either my vision for the future is right, and America follows me, or it is wrong and I must face the consequences."

A delegate asked to speak and was recognized. "President Durant wants to arrest our governor because he is the voice, the personification, of the opposition, but it is not because he opposes Durant, that I support Governor Monroe. I back him because he believes in the founding principles of our nation."

Another representative jumped to his feet. "Yes. Exactly. This is about what kind of nation we are going to be." He turned and looked at Monroe. "This isn't just about you Governor, but only you can be the voice of it."

Caden had studied Locke, Jefferson, Tocqueville and others while in college, but the role of government had always remained a philosophical question, something discussed late in the evening over drinks with friends. This was not such a casual discussion. This was a turning point, a precursor to civil war. Some would go down the winning road; others would, as Reagan once said, 'end up on the ash heap of history.'

Even with the delegates from metro Seattle dead, injured or scattered, the debate was contentious and went on for hours, but before it was gaveled to a close, two-thirds of the legislature backed Governor Monroe. Washington State would appoint new senators to congress, hold elections as scheduled in November and the state would not endorse the Sino-American Treaty of Friendship or the new Most Favored Nation trade agreement.

Caden buttoned his coat as he stepped into the cold night air. The multitude of delegates and observers streamed past him out of the building. He sympathized with those who had just pledged their lives, fortunes, and sacred honor. *But I need to talk with everyone at home before...before what? Before I get myself arrested or perhaps killed fighting the mightiest army on the planet.* Glancing at his watch, he shook his head. *It's late...early really...I'll get some sleep and head home in the morning.* He walked down the steps of the capitol and proceeded across the plaza toward a hotel that was serving as officer's quarters. He was in that no-man's land of darkness between the lights of the capitol and the hotel when he heard footsteps behind him.

"Major Westmore, we need to talk."

Caden turned and, as they approached, could discern the faces of General Collins, the JBLM base commander who ordered Maria's release and then kicked both of them off the base and Adjutant General Harwich of the Washington Guard. He both cringed and saluted. *What now?*

They were all going to the hotel, but talked little until they were inside. There, in General Harwich's room, they talked for several hours.

After leaving the two generals he lay on the bed thinking about the events of the day. Sleep came grudgingly.

On the drive back to Hansen he yawned repeatedly, but not out of boredom. The uneventful trip allowed too much time for weighty thoughts. Memories of combat came to mind. *Destruction, blood and death…could all of that be coming here?* He prayed that Durant would change course, allow elections, and a new congress.

The sun had not yet peeked above the trees as Caden pulled up the long driveway to home. Sue sat under a light on the porch with a shotgun across her lap. With the windows rolled up and the bouncing of the car on the dirt driveway, he couldn't hear her announce his arrival, but he could see it. His mother and father came out on the porch and Maria stepped from the barn carrying what, at first, looked like a rake or shovel.

Stopping the car, Caden hesitantly stepped out. Maria was running toward him with a smile on her face, but with a pitchfork in her hand. Only as she neared did she drop it and throw her arms around him.

They held each other tight.

"I was…we were worried."

He nodded. "I missed you. I tried to call, but couldn't get through."

"What kept you away?" she finally asked.

"There's a lot going on."

As they turned to walk back to the house Maria retrieved the pitchfork.

Gesturing toward it, Caden asked, "What's up with that?"

"When I go to collect eggs the rooster has been getting aggressive. The two of us are going to have a little chat."

Caden laughed. "Talk to him later. I need to speak with everyone."

*   *   *

Trevor rubbed his unshaven face. "You really think war is coming?"

"I hope not, but if President Durant won't allow elections, or accept the new congress then, I think, war is likely."

"Everything you've told us this morning…the Chinese carving out a sphere of influence on the west coast, Durant controlling the media and trying to arrest dissenters…." Trevor shook his head. "I've been frustrated with the way this country has been going for years, but…well, what can we do about it?"

"That's the thing I need everyone to understand." One at a time, Caden looked at each member of his family. "Hansen is a small town, out of the way. I can't imagine that anything will happen here, but it could, and I've been ordered to make contingency plans and increase readiness."

Maria looked concerned. "What does that mean?"

"Get the armory ready to fight."

"No," his mother said resolutely.

"People are going hungry," Sue said. "Medicine is in short supply. Why are we talking about war?"

"Because," Caden replied, "the events that caused the suffering also put Durant in power."

Trevor leaned forward resting his chin in his hand. "We don't choose the time, only how we react to it."

"We're all Americans," Lisa said. "Will the guys at the armory fight their countrymen?

"I don't know. We did once before, during the Civil War, but I've been trying to figure out a way to explain it to the soldiers."

There was silence for a moment.

"Who are the rebels?" Maria asked.

Caden shrugged. "I guess we are."

Maria shook her head. "One side is struggling to preserve or restore the nation and one side is breaking it apart. Which side are you on?"

"I want to preserve America."

All the family nodded in agreement.

*   *   *

Caden sat across the table from Lt. Brooks and First Sergeant Fletcher. "…and so I believe I must take a stand and do my part to change the direction of this country. Durant says he is the president because of the constitution, but ignores entire articles of it. We are a republic, but he has not allowed a new congress or elections and he is stifling the press.

"Some will call it treason," Caden said with a sigh, "but I am a patriot and I need your help to strengthen what remains of this nation and restore and preserve what we have lost."

Brooks shifted in the seat. "The convoy came back earlier this week with more food and the cannery donated a couple thousand cans of vegetables that they couldn't ship, but town's people are still hungry and I'm not sure starving people will support a war."

Caden nodded. "We should be getting more food from Canada, Australia, New Zealand and," he shrugged, "maybe even China, but unfortunately Durant chose the time, we can only respond. Either tyranny or war is coming. Both ways the civilians will get hurt."

There was silence for several moments then Brooks spoke again. "We took an oath to obey the orders of the President."

"Yes," Caden said, "but the first line of that oath is that we will support and defend the Constitution of the United States."

Again there was silence.

Fletcher took a deep breath and let it out slowly. "You will need to explain this to the men."

"Yes," Caden said, "As soon as we are done."

Fletcher and Brooks exchanged nods and then together stood to attention.

Lt. Brooks looked Caden in the eye. "What are your orders, sir?"

Chapter Twenty-Seven

From the far end of the table, Brooks leaned over the large paper map of the county held in place by coffee cups, staplers and a hole punch. "Do you really think they will come through Hansen when they try to arrest Governor Monroe?"

Fletcher rubbed his chin.

Looking at the other two, Caden said, "I think Durant will try federal marshals or FBI first, but if that doesn't work he'll try with military backup."

"That doesn't mean they'll come through here," Brooks said shaking his head.

"That's right, Hansen is an out of the way hick town and so far that has been our salvation. Let's hope it continues but..." Caden traced the route of the highway along the map, "there are only a few mountain passes and Hansen is on the highway to one of them."

Brooks and Fletcher nodded.

Walking over to the state map on the wall, Caden pointed to the joint base north of Olympia. "If I were planning the attack for Durant, I'd want to ensure this huge Army base is with me or eliminated as a threat. Then I'd head south from there to arrest Monroe and control the capital."

"So, you think the people here are safe?" Brooks asked. "They won't be attacked?"

"I think it's unlikely Durant's forces will come this way, but we need to be ready." Caden looked at the clock on the wall. *Why do all my meetings end so late?* He moved the cups and office equipment off the map. Glancing at Brooks he asked, "Before I head home is there anything I should be updated on?"

"Well…power in the town is up and stable. One generator at the coal power plant is operating. Unfortunately we had to cannibalize the second generator to get it running. However with the one operating generator and the hydroelectric dam, we have enough power for the town and surrounding community."

Lifting his cup, Caden took a big gulp of lukewarm coffee. Despite the taste, he smiled. "I'm glad to hear that."

"We've added more soldiers," Fletcher said.

Caden raised an eyebrow.

"Our muster is now sixty-three. A few are stragglers just now getting here. Others were on leave and can't get back to their regular units so they came here, and two guys enlisted before the attacks, but hadn't yet reported, so they asked if they could report with us."

"Thank you both for that good news." *If war doesn't come, we might just make it through this crisis.* He rolled up the map and secured it with a rubber band. "Start drilling the men on the rifle range early tomorrow and make a list of necessary supplies. I need to talk to the sheriff, so I'll be in late."

The next morning as the smell of breakfast drifted upstairs, Caden stumbled down dressed in his uniform. The world was still dark, but a light was on in the kitchen. The radio on the window sill, told of relief supplies from Canada being distributed in Hansen.

Sitting on the far side of the table feeding Adam, Maria looked his uniform up and down. "You do know it's Saturday, right?"

"The military isn't really a Monday through Friday job." He sat across from her. "I've got to talk to the sheriff."

She frowned. "At least call and make sure he's there before you go."

Pouring coffee he nodded. "Good idea."

The man who answered the non-emergency line assured him Hoover was in. "Do you want to hold?"

"No, I'll talk to him in person. Just tell him I'm coming." After a quick breakfast he went straight to the sheriff's office, but once inside was told Hoover went to the hospital. Caden was startled. "I just called. They said he was here. Is he okay?"

"Hoover's fine. It's his Mom." The deputy shook his head. "She's not doing well."

He hurried out of the building. *This is not a great time to be adding worries. Is there a good time?* As he slid into the driver's seat, Caden knew he had to warn the sheriff that war was possible.

Driving toward the facility he pondered the name, *Hansen General*. A month ago he lived in metro Washington D.C., home of giant world-class hospitals such as *Walter Reed* and *Georgetown University*. Since a high school skiing accident, he had not been to the old brick building that served as the community medical facility. He had no idea how many beds were in the place, but he was certain he could count them on his fingers.

A few blocks down he turned the corner and was immediately confused by several modern buildings. *A drugstore, a clinic, a medical professional building…where is the….* Then he saw another structure partially hidden behind the others and a line of cedar trees. Ahead a sign read, 'hospital parking.' He pulled into a surprisingly full lot.

A tent village existed along one edge of the parking area. Campers, RVs and cars filled about half of it. Inside a group of people huddled around the front desk where a harried worker tried to answer questions. A deputy stood to one side.

"Where's Sheriff Hoover?" Caden asked.

"I saw him come in a little bit ago." The deputy pointed right. "He went that way, but I'm not sure where."

Caden walked in that direction and was soon lost in a maze of pastel blue passageways. The rooms were filled and nurses hurriedly wove around cots that dotted the halls. He would need more than fingers and toes to count the beds. Ahead he saw a familiar face and called out. "Dr. Scott!"

"Hello. How are your injuries?" The doctor asked as she approached. "I meant to get back over and see you but," she glanced around the ward, "it's been hectic."

"I can see you're busy. The leg is fine." *Itches once in a while, but if I say that you might want to examine it.*

"And your head? Any double vision…headaches."

"No. I'm fine," He looked at the beds scattered about the hall. "Were this many people from the area hurt?"

"Many are locals who were injured during the panic and looting along the freeway and in town before the blockade. Some have chronic illnesses like diabetes and HIV. They can't get medicine now, so they come here. Others drove away from Seattle looking for medical care and found this place. We're overwhelmed, but we try and help."

A nurse called to her.

"I've got to go."

"Oh, before you do. I need to find Sheriff Hoover. Do you know…."

She pointed. "Down this hallway and take the first left. Ask at the nurse's station."

As soon as he turned the corner, Caden saw the sheriff's tan uniform at the end of the hall. As he approached he saw Hoover staring through a large window into a room. Inside a gray-haired woman lay in a bed surrounded by people. "They told me you were here to see your mother. Is she okay?"

Hoover glanced in Caden's direction, shook his head, then returned his gaze to the room. "She had a heart attack the day of the Seattle blast and has barely hung on since. Some people have lost the will to live. I'm afraid she is one of them. Half of those in the senior home are dead from shock, stroke, heart attack, neglect or…." He shrugged.

"Your mom isn't that old and she has family." He gestured toward those in the room and was suddenly embarrassed. Hoover knew his relatives, but Caden wasn't sure who these people were. "They're family—right?"

"Yeah," he pointed, "Dad, my uncle Jim, Aunt Carrie and," he gestured toward a woman coming down the hall, "you remember my sister."

Caden turned. "Debra?" It had been ten years since he had last seen her, but instead of the slender high school girl he remembered, a much heavier woman stood before him. But the surprise came from more than that. There was too much makeup, too much jewelry, and *way too much* cheap perfume.

"Well, hello," she said and popped her gum. "I heard you were back in town."

Caden smiled. "Hello, it's nice to see you again." He glanced at the sheriff and knew there would never be a way to express it, but he was now, and would forever be, grateful that Hoover had arrested them that night at the graduation party before anything happened.

Small talk ensued for a minute then Caden said to the sheriff, "I need to discuss something with you. Together they moved to a corner next to a storage closet.

"There is no easy way to say this so here it is, I think civil war is coming to America."

Hoover blinked and stared off into the distance for several moments. "Does this have to do with the Chinese and that treaty? I heard about that on the radio."

"Yes, and the fight might come to Hansen."

The sheriff banged his fist on the wall, and cursed. "Aren't there enough problems?"

"We don't want this fight. Durant is the one forcing it."

"Tell me Mr. Military, what is going to happen here if your war breaks out?"

"It's not my war. Hansen might be fine—I don't know, but I've been ordered to stop any units loyal to Durant."

Hoover shook his head. "And just how do you plan on doing that?"

A nurse hurried by.

"I can't provide details here. Come up to the armory this afternoon and I'll explain what I can."

*   *   *

Three vehicles pulled to a stop in front of a small diner on a quiet Olympia street. Stepping from the middle vehicle Caden thought about home. *Considering that a war might be coming, be grateful that I had a few hours off.* That was what he had told Maria when, right after church, he had left for the armory and then straight on to Olympia, but the look on her face was not one of gratefulness.

"I'm surprised there are any restaurants open in Olympia," General Collins said.

"Aren't there any around the joint base?" Governor Monroe asked.

"One, but you pay a first-rate price for a third-rate meal and I have no idea where they get their food."

A guard hurried from the lead jeep and opened the door as the trailing vehicle parked behind.

Stepping in, the Governor said, "This will be a decent meal for a five-star price. The family that runs this place purchases their food from local farms. They're still able to do that, but they tell me that the cost is steep and rising."

Caden noticed David Weston seated at a long table near the rear of the diner. He still had a bandage across his nose and bruises under his eyes, but thanks to the video and two area TV stations getting back on the air, he was now a local celebrity.

Three men sat across from David. When they turned, he recognized the state treasurer, secretary of state and the chief of the state patrol. After everyone shook hands, Governor Monroe sat next to Weston. Generals Collins and Harwich sat across from each other with Caden at the end of the table between them.

The restaurant was empty except for a man in a business suit sitting in the corner. His hair was dark with silver sprinkled throughout. Caden thought he might be part of the protection for the governor, but within moments of their arrival, he paid his bill and departed.

The waiter was soon at their table.

"Do you have coffee?" Weston asked.

"No, sorry, we ran out a few days ago."

Recalling that he had some with breakfast Saturday, Caden wondered how much his dad had stashed away.

The waiter put on a big smile. Tonight we have chicken roasted with Herbs de Provence, garlic, onions and olive oil…."

Chicken or nothing. Well, it sounds like they tried to do something nice with it.

"…and we have new potatoes steamed with mint."

Good.

"For vegetables," he said in an excited voice, "we have corn or broccoli."

Caden recalled how President Bush had banned broccoli from the White House. He had similar feelings. *Corn it is. I'll bet it's canned.* He was amused that despite the limited options it took longer for orders to be decided. He knew he was one of the lucky ones. Early on he had been able to buy enough food, water and gas. Now he lived on a farm surrounded by other farms. Selection might be limited, but he and his family would eat.

While the discussion continued, two of the soldiers came in and sat at a table near the door. One had a pistol and the other an M4. Caden assumed the other two were with the jeeps outside. He patted his holster. No one expected trouble tonight, but caution was prudent.

When the waiter had everyone's order, Governor Monroe pointed to the soldiers by the door. "Get them whatever they would like."

For the next hour, over a simple meal of chicken, corn and potatoes at a nondescript diner they discussed the likelihood of war and the future of the country.

As long as the discussion had been on policy and relief efforts Caden was engaged, but the subject had turned to the economy. He pushed his plate back as his eyes drifted to the soldiers by the door and their quiet discussion. The artwork on the walls and thoughts of home danced through Caden's mind.

Weston's phone chimed and he quickly pulled it from a pocket.

"That phone is official business," Governor Monroe said to those around the table. Then in a hushed voice he added, "I think he keeps it on even when he showers."

Everyone laughed.

"Huh?" Weston said slipping the phone back in his pocket.

"I'll explain later," the governor said. "What was the call?"

He shrugged. "The screen said it was the Emergency Operations Center, but the call dropped before I heard anyone."

"I'll go by the EOC when we're done," General Harwich said.

Dropped calls were too common to be of concern.

The governor nodded. "We're nearly done."

The treasurer continued a discussion of currency issues.

Caden continued his contemplation of restaurant artwork until a familiar engine sound focused his attention. His eyes locked on the street. The two soldiers by the door stopped talking as a Stryker vehicle lumbered past. Caden turned to General Collins. "Was that from your base?"

The general's eyes narrowed. "It must be." He stood and walked toward the door.

Chapter Twenty-Eight

Caden watched General Collins march from the diner and go left, in the direction the Stryker had gone. Caden followed him, but hesitated just outside the door.

The glow from streetlights and a few windows cast long sinister shadows as Collins walked along the middle of the empty road toward the vehicle parked at the corner. The gunner had the M2 machine gun pointed at the diner.

Instincts that had served Caden well in combat now roared again to life. He looked back up the street and, as he expected, another Stryker was parked at that corner. A squad of soldiers and two civilians stood nearby.

One of the guards from inside the restaurant joined Caden on the sidewalk. "What's going on?"

Caden whispered, "Find a way out the back and get everyone to safety." *Where ever that might be.* He stepped inside with the soldier and, looking at the group of civilians said, "Everyone needs to go—*now.*" He felt like a mouse sniffing cheese at the edge of a trap. *Any second now this thing will spring on me.* But he needed to assist the general and give the governor and others more time to get away. He sighed, tapped his holster, and joined General Collins down the street.

Looking up at the young soldier behind the M2 in the turret, the general demanded, "On whose authority are you here?"

"I don't know sir."

"Then get me someone who does—now!"

A young lieutenant stepped out. "Sir, we were ordered to provide protection for the U.S. Marshals."

"Lieutenant that is not what I asked. I can see what your orders are; I want to know who gave them to you."

Footsteps clicked on the pavement behind him. He turned.

"U.S. Marshals." The man held up his badge.

It was the restaurant customer with salt and pepper hair. He was followed by another man in a business suit.

"I'm Deputy Marshal Reid, this is Deputy Marshal Smith."

Caden grinned inwardly. *Why didn't I see it before? Reid looks like one of the Men in Black. Actually both of them look like movie federal agents.*

Reid continued. "At our request Colonel Shaw ordered them to assist us with the arrest of Governor Daniel Monroe. Both of you need to leave the area immediately."

The General turned from the Marshal back to the lieutenant. "Stand down and return to JBLM."

"Yes sir." The young officer took two steps backward toward the Stryker.

Reid demanded, "He is not going anywhere until we have...."

Two shots rang.

Everyone flinched.

The Marshals and Caden went for their guns.

Caden was quickest. As he moved the pistol slightly to cover the two marshals he was certain the shots came from behind the diner. *The others must have left the diner and ran into trouble.* "Actually, I think it is time for the General and me to leave."

Soldiers ran down the street.

Collins nodded. "A change of plans lieutenant, the Major and I will be joining you, but we aren't going back to base." He, Caden, and the befuddled young lieutenant, hurried up the ramp into the Stryker as more lights came on up and down the street.

The lieutenant climbed into the driver's seat.

"Go to the parking area behind the diner," Collins ordered.

Caden and the General sat on opposite benches in the cramped rear of the vehicle. More shots rang out.

A bullet ricocheted off the vehicle with a loud ping as they bumped over the curb and into the lot.

Looking back the lieutenant said, "Several civilians are pinned down behind a dumpster."

That must be the governor and the others.

"Pull up beside it and open the back," Collins commanded the lieutenant, and then turned to Caden. "If those are our people get them in here."

Caden jumped out as the two federal marshals rounded the corner and shot at him. He leapt behind a car. The turret gunner provided cover fire, pinning the marshals down. There was no time to think about the wisdom of shooting at federal agents or why army units were now involved. Caden was functioning on well-honed combat instincts. He returned fire.

"Get in the vehicle now!" The god-like voice of General Collins commanded over the Stryker loudspeaker.

Both the turret gunner and Caden provided cover as several civilians ran up the ramp. *The treasurer, secretary of state…there goes the highway patrol chief…and Governor Monroe. The soldiers, Weston, are they already inside?* He squinted into the dark as the last three came into view. Weston and a soldier carried the other man into the vehicle.

Caden ran in as the ramp lifted. With a roar from the engine the vehicle headed off.

The wounded comrade lay in the middle of the small compartment. His trouser leg was torn and blood soaked. Someone used a belt as a tourniquet.

Caden felt for a pulse, but found none. Only as he looked up did he see the governor staring at the floor in bloody clothes. He held a pistol by three shaky fingers.

"Governor, are you all right?"

He looked up. The color was gone from his face. His eyes unseeing.

The other soldier covered his fallen friend. "We couldn't stop the bleeding." With a tilt of the head toward Monroe, the soldier added. "He tried to help...pulled off his belt and wrapped it around the leg. Then he grabbed the pistol and shot one of the civilians shooting at us. I saw the guy drop."

I've seen this before. "Governor, you're in shock. Give me the pistol."

The Governor looked down and gripped the pistol tight.

General Collins directed the lieutenant to the Emergency Operations Center.

The state treasurer puked on the floor.

As the smell of blood and vomit filled the cramped compartment Caden reached across to the Governor. "Give the pistol to me, please." He touched Monroe's hand. It was cool and clammy. "Just let it go. I'll take it." Gently Caden plied the pistol from the governor's hand.

Setting the weapon on his lap, Caden leaned back and sighed. *It's going to be a long night.*

For nearly a minute the drone of the engine increased and then became a steady whine.

Looking up to the turret gunner, General Collins asked, "You see anyone following us, soldier?"

"No sir."

"Keep watch," the general said, "This isn't over."

"How do you do it, Caden?"

Caden opened his eyes at the sound of Weston's voice. "Huh?" He blinked and then focused on the governor's Chief of Staff sitting across from him.

Weston repeated the question. "There's a body on the floor between us. We've all been shot at. I feel scared and sick. How do you stay calm?"

Caden's mind raced back to his first days in Iraq. "I wasn't calm the first time…or the second. I was scared…still get scared, but eventually combat becomes…." Unable to find the right words he shrugged, leaned back and closed his eyes.

A minute later the lieutenant said, "State patrol vehicles and officers in SWAT gear up ahead."

The turret gunner yelled, "They're aiming at us. What should I…."

"Get down here!" Collins ordered. "Don't get yourself shot." He slapped the driver's shoulder. "Stop."

The two generals and the patrol chief exited the back with their hands up. When they were recognized the vehicle was allowed to proceed to the Emergency Operations Center.

General Harwich ordered the EOC duty officer to report.

The officer glanced at Governor Monroe's bloodstained suit then turned back to Harwich. "Sir we tried to contact you and the Governor, but phone lines are down. Soldiers from an unknown unit took control of the switching center about 40 minutes ago. The state patrol reports at least two Stryker vehicles and perhaps a squad of soldiers engaged in street fighting near the waterfront." He circled the location on the map with his finger.

General Collins grunted. "Yeah, we can confirm that. Do you have a situation report from JBLM?"

Pointing to the communications center he said, "Colonel Johnston informed us via the radio that elements of several units have mutinied and he is engaging them."

"I'll need to use your radio," Collins said and started to walk away.

Governor Monroe touched his arm. He still looked pale, but seemed to have regained his composure. "The next twenty-four hours will determine the future of this country." Eyes focused on Collins, he said, "I need you to secure the joint base. If Durant's forces seize the control of those units, the airfield and equipment, they'll head this way in force and we won't be able to stop them. Can you keep control of JBLM?"

"Yes Governor, I can." He hurried to the communications area.

"Looking at General Harwich he said, "Durant has loyal units in Oregon." He pointed to the freeway heading north from there to the city. "How can we protect this route?"

"Most of Durant's support is in the Portland-Salem area. I'll take the 81st Brigade and 96th Troop Command and secure the border by controlling the bridges."

"I want you here advising me. Put someone else in charge of the southern defense."

Harwich looked truly disappointed. "Perhaps Major Westmore could command those units?"

Caden's jaw dropped. "Ahhh…"

"No," Monroe said. He traced his finger along the highway through Hansen. "I'm worried about this route."

"It's a small mountain highway," Harwich said. "Trucks would have to go slow and the road is easy to block. I wouldn't use it to attack Olympia."

"Still it worries me." He looked Caden in the eye. "You know this area. If they come that way, stop them."

"Yes sir, I will."

Chapter Twenty-Nine

Caden wanted to immediately head back to Hansen, but he needed to alert the armory so he joined General Collins at the EOC communications center.

The general talked over a secure radio link to the joint base. "Hold the airfield and the freeway. I'm convinced that is what they want. I'm going to deal with a couple of units here and then go to JBLM."

It took only a minute for Caden to contact someone at the armory using a SINCGARS radio. He didn't have a secure link so all he said was, "Tell the XO to implement the Hansen route contingency plan. I'm leaving for there right now." He cringed, thinking he had said more than he should over an unsecure radio, but there was no taking it back. "Out."

Within minutes Caden raced down a nearly empty freeway. Once he left Olympia, trees lined much of the now deserted highway. *Six lanes of emptiness.* It was times like this, sealed in a car, surrounded by darkness, that doubts pressed in on him. *In just a few hours I could be fighting units of the most powerful military in the world. What are my chances of living through this day?*

Becky had asked him to join her on Durant's team. She believed they would have been a powerful, and well-off, couple. Visions of state dinners, meetings with world leaders and living large in D.C. with Becky at his side, filled his head.

Those thoughts were gradually replaced by images of Hansen, the farm and family. *Family.* His thoughts turned to Maria and Adam. *It may not be official, but they are family just the same.* Even though he tried to put the small town of his youth behind him, the values of that place had become a part of him. He could never abandon it, or Maria and Adam. *There must be a way to protect my family, my home and my country.*

The speedometer inched toward ninety. He slowed only as he went up the ramp to Hansen. On the far side of the overpass, soldiers stood guard behind sandbags. Two-by-fours had been fashioned into a checkpoint gate. Several military vehicles were parked in the convenience store lot and, for the first time since he had been back, lights illuminated the church. He came to a stop at the gate.

The soldier immediately recognized him and saluted. "Welcome home, sir. I hear we might be fighting soon."

"Pray we don't," Caden replied. "What's going on at the church?"

"Cleaning and repairs, sir," the soldier said as they raised the gate.

Restoration and destruction, serenity and conflict, how often have I seen them side-by-side? He drove on into the night. The blockade at the far end of the causeway was gone and the bulldozers moved up the hill. Farther along the highway he saw a faint light flickered in the darkness and wondered if it came from the Westmore farm. He turned down the narrow road and to the family home.

The barn door hung open, swaying gently in night breeze. A weak light came from inside. His father stepped out, followed by the puppy.

Caden noticed a holster on his father's hip. Stepping from the car he said, "I had planned to go straight to the armory, but saw the light on."

"Well, I'm glad to see you, but I guess I should have shut the door. I forgot how far you can see a light out here at night."

Caden nodded and together they walked back to the barn. "What are you working on?"

"The old Deere tractor. The carburetor is gummed up." He shook his head. "I think it's the new ethanol gas." Picking up a wrench, he returned to his work.

"Dad, I think there may be fighting around Hansen in the morning." Caden felt like a child telling his father he had done something wrong.

Trevor sighed, dropped the tool on the bench and sat on a bale of hay looking at his son. "I knew this day would come. I hoped it wouldn't reach our town, but I knew the conflict was coming."

"Really?" He told his father the events at the restaurant and what Governor Monroe had asked him to do. "I shouldn't have even stopped here. I need to get to the armory. "

The older man hugged his son. "Go on. Do your duty. We'll be fine." Tears welled in his eyes. "Now go. You've got a lot to do."

"Tell Maria and Mom...everyone, I love them."

"You'll see Maria soon."

He smiled at his dad's vote of confidence and left before his own tears came.

Every light seemed to be on at the armory. Again he was stopped at the gate, but quickly allowed to pass. Several trucks idled as soldiers climbed on. Walking across the parking lot he noticed a familiar face. "Lisa?" She stood at a table passing out coffee and MRE's to soldiers loading onto the trucks.

"Hi brother, would you like some coffee?"

"No. What are you doing here?"

"Helping out."

"I see that, I mean...."

She laughed. "I know what you mean." Still handing out coffee she said, "David was at our house eating dinner when the armory called. I drove him back and stayed to help. Maria is here too." She pointed.

"Maria?"

She carried a box of MREs and at the sound of her name their eyes met. She smiled, put down the box and raced into his arms.

He didn't know what to say so he just held her for a moment. "I'm glad to see you, but you need to go somewhere safe."

"Where would that be?"

He had no answer.

"When you leave with the soldiers, Lisa and I will go back to the farm."

He nodded and then as if by mutual agreement, they kissed. The warmth of her lips enveloped him and he knew as long as she was with him, he would be happy. Stepping back, his eyes lingered on her. "I've got to go."

"I know."

Caden hurried into the armory and found the XO, First Sergeant Fletcher and the squad leaders in the small office area. "What's our status?"

"Three of our soldiers are in position at the pass east of town," Brooks said. "However, fog is limiting visibility. Hopefully it will lift in time. We're in radio contact and...."

Caden shook his head. "When we're done here, send one man down the far side of the pass. They can relay any contacts to the scouts at the summit."

"Yes sir. The squad leaders have done the pre-combat inspection. Will the MOPP level be zero?"

Chemical, biological warfare? I sure hope there's none. "Yes, zero."

"Then the men will be ready to go in thirty minutes."

"Good." Caden glanced at his watch, it was just after midnight. "If they're coming this way we should know before dawn." He left to pack his combat gear. When he returned Brooks, a sergeant and a corporal were in the office.

"We're ready to move out." Brooks said, "These two will be staying here to relay situation reports to...."

The radio crackled. "Base this is Recon 1. Forward position reports 18 vehicles, jeeps, Humvees and deuce and a half trucks moving west toward the pass." The transmission paused. "Forward position reports they are under fire."

Caden took the mic and said, "Recon 1, the convoy may be listening in on your transmissions. Proceed to position 2 immediately. Over."

"Roger Base. Out."

We've lost the pass without a shot. That was our best chance to stop them. He relayed the report to the operations center and advised JBLM would need to secure the North Road. Then he turned to Brooks. "Deploy the troops to the fallback position."

"The causeway? But...."

"We've discussed this. Do you have a better plan?"

Brooks shook his head.

"Then deploy the men along the west bank of the causeway. If Durant's forces push it they could be here in a little over an hour." He picked up the phone and dialed 911. "This is Major Westmore, inform Sheriff Hoover that in just over an hour a large military convoy will move through town. I recommend everyone stay inside and allow them to pass through." Moments later Caden's phone rang.

"Well, Mr. Military."

"Hello Sheriff."

"I thought you were going to head them off at the pass. What happened?"

"It doesn't matter. We won't fight them in the town. Just let them pass through. That's all I can say. I've got to go." He turned to Brooks. "Everyone leaves the armory. Move out."

It took well over an hour for the convoy to reach recon position 2 at the east edge of town. The two remaining scouts fell back to position 3, a jumble of blackberry bushes along a stream near the turn off to the Westmore farm. Hours later the scouts still reported no contact.

In the pre-dawn darkness Caden looked through his binoculars from position 3. He could barely see a group of Humvees on the west edge of Hansen. The damp and cold made him shiver. "They've been there for hours. Why haven't they made a move?"

The question had been rhetorical, but one of the privates beside him shrugged.

As they continued to watch the convoy the red-haired boy and girl Caden had seen so often in the area strolled across the field to the stream carrying fish traps.

Caden froze.

The teens moved along the bank for a while, and then put their traps in the water just twenty yards from the recon position. The two sat idly nearby looking in the direction of the trucks. *Go home kids.* But there was no way to communicate the message without exposing his position.

Caden pulled out his radio. "CW returning to unit." Looking at the scouts he whispered, "Keep watch on the convoy. When they move out, alert us." Crouching, he headed back around the corner and then on to his jeep. As he climbed in the vehicle he felt the vibration of his phone. "Hello?"

"Hey, you know who this is."

"Yes." He recognized Hoover's voice.

"I'm guessing things aren't going according to your plan. Most of the convoy is parked at the city limit."

Thank you for calling and telling me what I already know. "I thought they would just drive straight through town. I'm not sure why they stopped."

"The commander asked me if there was another way around the lake. He even looked at my maps. I think they know you're waiting for them and they're looking for another route."

"There isn't another way," Caden said flatly. "Is there?"

"Nope. Not unless these guys are amphibious or they want to build a bridge."

"Good, but we shouldn't talk. They could be monitoring your phone."

"Actually they're working to take down the phone system. Good luck, Mr. Military."

Caden parked his jeep well up the hill from the lake and walked down toward the shore. His unit was dug in along the tree line on both sides of the road. Several yards up the highway two huge Douglas firs had been cut down blocking it and several more trees were notched and primed with C4.

Walking among the sixty soldiers under his command, Caden confirmed that they were well concealed and then climbed into his foxhole and waited. He placed a few more sandbags along the edge and moved the biggest rocks he could find to the front. *My orders were to stop Durant's forces from getting through to Olympia and, at the moment, I've done that.* He looked up at the still dark sky, anxious for dawn.

With a crackle the radio came to life. "Forces deployed west of Hansen this is the U.S. Army convoy commander. I'm coming forward under a white flag in a single Humvee with a driver. I want to talk. I propose we meet on the causeway. Do you copy?"

The voice sounded oddly familiar.

Brooks raced along the tree line to Caden's position. "It's not safe, don't do it."

"Being here isn't safe. Meeting him is no worse and buys us more time. If I have to, I'd rather fight them in daylight." Into the radio he said, "Copy. I'll meet you there." To a nearby private he said, "You're my driver."

As Caden and the soldier walked up the slope, Recon 3 reported a single Humvee moving along the highway.

The driver rummaged through the first-aid kit, setting the green bandages aside and retrieved some long white gauze. He then tied it like a streamer to the antenna at the rear of the jeep. Together they headed slowly down to the edge of the lake. The other vehicle was already on the far side. The drivers moved deliberately along the road toward each other.

Roughly in the middle they stopped and the convoy commander walked to the front of the Humvee. Caden stepped around the front of the jeep. As they neared, he recognized the man he had first met at a blockade on the Georgia border, the officer who had helped him from the pit of despair and convinced Maria to get on the plane when they all flew to Washington state. "Hello, Lieutenant Turner. How are you doing?"

"Actually its Captain now." The man looked at him carefully. "Caden? I thought you were a civilian."

"So did I," he grinned. "Well, congratulations on the promotion, but I can't say that I'm happy to see you here." Caden wanted to draw out the conversation so he said, "I thought they sent you to Korea."

"It never happened. The Defense Department is pulling troops out of there and Japan."

"Are you still able to get letters from your wife?"

"Yeah," he smiled, "the post office is functioning." Then the humor drained from his face. "I have orders from the Commander-in-chief to assist with the arrest of Governor Monroe...."

"I no longer recognize the orders of President Durant."

"I don't want to fight you, but if you block the convoy, I will. It will be bloody for both of us."

Caden nodded.

Turner looked frustrated. "A lot of good men will die today."

"I know that. Don't attack. Durant wasn't elected and what he is doing is unconstitutional and violates everything that...."

Turner threw up his hand. "That's treason and I won't hear it. I'm going back to my convoy and you should return to your rebels."

"We're not rebels..."

Turner already had his back to Caden and walked away.

Reluctantly, Caden climbed into his jeep and the two men parted company.

Back in his foxhole a few minutes later, Recon 3 came over the radio, "Vehicles are moving forward with troops along the side of the road. We've got to move."

In the distance came the sound of gunfire. Recon 3 fell silent.

Through the light of early dawn, Caden saw five Humvees pull up and stop on the opposite shore. Turner's troops hurried into positions as gunfire from both shores commenced. *The rest of the convoy must be behind the trees.*

Pings and thuds sounded on both sides as he lowered his profile behind the rocks and dirt at the edge of the foxhole. A tree limb fell in front of him and a bullet ricocheted off a nearby rock. Gunfire became a continuous roar.

They're expending a lot of ammo. Do they think we will return fire and run out first? Just in case he turned to a nearby soldier. "Unless you have a good shot, hold your fire. Pass it along."

Turner can't get by us this way. It's three hundred yards across the lake. We could shoot back and forth all day to no great effect and, apparently, he doesn't have mortars.

Gradually the soldiers from the armory slowed their pace, but the troops on the far side continued and roared the engines of the Humvees.

The sun was still behind the trees, but daylight now illuminated the battlefield. Caden spotted a soldier running along the tree line of the far shore. He fired and missed. The man raced for cover.

"…come in. Please Caden, come in."

Was that Maria's voice on the radio? "Maria? Is that you?"

"They shot two of your men near the farm. After they left I went to help them but they're dead."

"Get away from there!"

"I will but I've got to tell you—the convoy is heading down the road by the farm. I think they're going to the logging road where the men removed the culvert."

All this shooting and noise—it's a diversion. "Roger, thanks. Now, get away from there."

His mind raced. Caden ran to Brooks. "Keep fifth squad here and hold this position. I'm taking the rest of the soldiers to the logging road."

Caden was leaving only ten men to guard the causeway. Turner had been outmaneuvering him all morning. If Caden was wrong this time and Turner attacked across the causeway his men would be overwhelmed, but decisive action was required.

Two deuce and a half trucks carried all of Caden's soldiers down the bumpy logging road. They stopped about a half-mile from the river. Caden heard a bulldozer nearby. With point men in the lead, he deployed the squads perpendicular to the narrow dirt road.

Progress through the forest was slow. The bush, knolls and trees provided many places for an opponent to set an ambush. With each yard forward the bulldozer roared louder and Caden's apprehension grew greater. Each twig that snapped under his feet sounded to him like a thunderclap.

A gunshot.

The men dropped to the ground.

Rapid fire.

The guardsmen shot blindly into the forest.

"Cease fire! Cease fire," Caden yelled. He listened. The steady roar continued, but it came from hundreds of yards in front of them. *They're not shooting at us, but if Turner's men didn't hear our shots, this is our chance to get close.* Then together they moved out.

By the sound of the dozer and gunfire, Caden knew he was only a few hundred yards away so, with the First Sergeant and a few other men, he crawled ahead. Seeing two soldiers about thirty feet ahead, they stopped.

Caden signaled he would shoot the one on the left, Fletcher should get the other.

That accomplished they quickly moved on to the ridge line above the river. Peeking out from there they could see the main body of the convoy. Turner had about 100 soldiers firing as they moved up the slope from cover to cover toward the opposite ridge. Near the top was a dump truck at an angle across the road blocking any retreat of the convoy.

They don't know we're here. Caden had no idea who his allies were, but he was thankful for the help.

The bulldozer worked to narrow the river where the culvert had been. Logs had been cut and brought down to the shore. One already spanned the opening where the culvert had been. Caden wasn't sure if the plan was to make a temporary dam or a bridge. In either case it wasn't complete and he was there to stop it.

Turning to Fletcher, Caden said, "Get the men and deploy them along the ridge. Tell them not to fire until I do." Then he waited anxious minutes as the men came up and positioned themselves along the edge.

Finally Fletcher gave him the thumbs up.

Caden took careful aim at the dozer driver. He pulled the trigger and the man dropped.

All the guardsmen opened fire.

Many of Turner's soldiers fell. The others scurried for cover.

The sound of gunfire rose to a constant thunder.

Bullets pinged on both sides as dirt flew up in Caden's face.

A man to his right rolled down the slope and lay motionless.

Bark and tree limbs fell like rain.

It was clear to Caden that he held the superior position and Turner's losses were much greater. After a few more minutes he shouted, "Cease fire."

The crescendo of fire peaked and faded into silence.

"Your position is hopeless," Caden shouted, "Throw down your weapons and you will not be harmed."

There seemed to be confusion from the convoy, and then a female voice shouted, "We surrender."

"Pile your weapons in the road and line up along the shore." As the soldiers of the convoy stacked their arms, Caden, had the medic check the wounded and, with the rest of his men, crossed to the other side of the river. "First Sergeant, secure their weapons and search them." Looking at the soldiers he had just been fighting he asked, "Where is your commanding officer?

In a shaky voice a young woman said, "I guess that's me."

"Where's Captain Turner?"

"We don't know, sir."

Pointing to her he said, "Come with me." Together they checked the wounded and the dead.

Caden found Turner half-submerged in the river. He pulled him from the icy waters and collapsed alongside him. Cold fingers checked for a pulse, but the gaping wound to the neck told him the sad news. Gently he closed the eyes and cradled the body in his lap. *You said a lot of good men would die today. I knew it would be true, but I swear I never thought one of them would be you. I'm sorry.*

He didn't know how long he sat there, mourning the death of his friend. Hearing movement behind him he rested the head on the shore, stood and saluted a fallen comrade.

Turning, he saw Maria with tears in her eyes. All Caden could say was, "How? When?"

"I came in the dump truck. We wanted to help."

Caden looked beyond her. His father, Hoover, Neil Young and several deputies in SWAT gear along with other civilians stood with his men. He hugged Maria tight as sadness rent his soul.

Epilogue

Holding a silver platter, Caden eased down the hall trying to avoid the squeak of floorboards. He turned the doorknob and slowly crept across Maria's room. On the tray was a cup of coffee, a ring and a note that read, "With all my love, Caden."

She stirred, but didn't awaken.

Pleased, he set the plate on the nightstand and followed the scent of breakfast downstairs. Stepping into the kitchen his mother held up an egg. "The hens laid seven this morning. Breakfast will be ready in a couple of minutes."

He smiled and headed toward the sound of the television.

In the living room his father switched quickly between news programs.

Caden sat beside him.

Local reporters dubbed the actions of earlier in the week as the Battle of Olympia and spoke of little else. The victory at JBLM was the big news; the skirmish at Hansen was just a minor footnote. The New York networks, under the control of Durant, talked of a battle with insurgents and terrorists and the need for greater security.

Caden shook his head. *An awful bloody struggle has just begun.*

He stood and walked to an old roll-top desk in the corner of the room. Finding pen and paper he sat and stared blankly out the window. *What could I write? What could I say that would bring some meaning or comfort?* He sighed and with sudden determination wrote the first words that came to mind. "Mrs. Turner, I knew your husband, he was a good and honorable man."

Glossary

ACU   Army Combat Uniform.

AK-47   The AK-47 is a selective-fire military rifle, developed in the USSR, but also used by the People's Republic of China. In chapter 25, a Chinese soldier hits David Weston in the face with an AK-47.

CID   United States Army Criminal Investigation Command (USACIDC, usually abbreviated as just CID) investigates serious violations of military law within the United States Army.

EOC   An Emergency Operations Center is a central command and control facility responsible for carrying out the principles of emergency preparedness and emergency management, or disaster management functions.

Fueler   An army fuel truck.

GMRS   The General Mobile Radio Service (GMRS) is an FM UHF radio service designed for short-distance two-way communication similar to Citizens Band (CB) radios, but requiring an FCC license.

Humvee   High Mobility Multipurpose Wheeled Vehicle (HMMWV), commonly known as the Humvee, is a four-wheel drive military vehicle.

JBLM   Joint Base Lewis-McChord (JBLM) is a large military installation located nine miles south-southwest of Tacoma in Washington state.

LEPC   Local Emergency Planning Committees (LEPC) are quasi-governmental bodies, generally at the county or municipal level that do emergency planning.

M11   United States military designation for the SIG P228 pistol. See SIG P228.

M2   The M2 is a Browning .50 caliber machine gun.

M4   The M4 is a common U.S. military magazine-fed, selective fire, rifle with a telescoping stock.

M9   The M9 is a semiautomatic, 9mm, pistol in common use by the United States military.

M35   A military truck in the 2½ ton weight class, often referred to as a "deuce and a half."

MOPP Level MOPP is an acronym for "Mission Oriented Protective Posture" and as used in the book it refers to the level of protective gear used by military personnel in a chemical, biological, radiological, or nuclear combat situation. MOPP Level zero means gear will be carried, but not worn.

MRE   Meals, Ready-to-Eat (MRE) are self-contained, individual military field rations.

MURS   Multi-Use Radio Service (MURS) is an unlicensed two-way radio service similar to Citizens Band (CB).

Recon   Military slang for reconnaissance.

ROTC   The Reserve Officers' Training Corps (ROTC) is a college program for training commissioned officers.

SIG P228   A compact pistol in use with many law enforcement agencies and the military where it is designated as the M11. Caden is given a M11, 9mm .40 S&W, in Chapter 13 along with two 15 round magazines. Caden refers to the M11 by the SIG name.

SINCGARS   Single Channel Ground and Airborne Radio System (SINCGARS) is a combat radio currently used by United States which handles voice and data communications.

Also by the Author

A Time to Endure   The exciting saga of Major Caden Westmore continues in this, the second book of the *Strengthen What Remains* series. In the first book, *Through Many Fires*, terrorists use nuclear bombs to destroy six American cities. Now, the nation's economy teeters on the verge of collapse. The dollar plunges, inflation runs rampant, and the next civil war threatens to decimate the wounded country. In the face of tyranny, panic, and growing hunger, Caden struggles to keep his family and town together. But how can he save his community when the nation is collapsing around it?

A Time to Endure will be released on December 12, 2014.

*   *   *

Titan Encounter   Justin Garrett starts one morning as a respected businessman and ends the day a fugitive wanted by every power in the known universe. Fleeing with his 'sister' Mara and Naomi, a mysterious woman from Earth Empire, their only hope of refuge is with the Titans, genetically enhanced soldiers who rebelled, and murdered millions in the Titanomachy War. Hunted, even as they hunt for the Titans, the three companions slowly uncover the truth that will change the future and rewrite history.

*   *   *

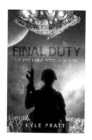

Final Duty – The Alien War Anthology   Twenty years after the death of her father during the Battle of Altair, Lieutenant Amy Palmer returns to the system as an officer aboard the reconnaissance ship Mirage. Almost immediately disaster strikes and Amy, along with the crew of the Mirage, must face the possibility of performing their final duties. Final Duty is a military science fiction anthology that includes a novella and two short stories set in the same genre and universe.

If you like what you read

I am an independent writer and so I don't have an advertising budget. If you have read one of my books and found it entertaining, please tell your friends. Also, books that have reviews sell more than those that do not so, if you liked the story, please consider writing a review on Amazon. If you don't like the story tell me why at kyle@kylepratt.me.

Made in the USA
San Bernardino, CA
05 March 2015